Oystercatcher Girl

Gabrielle Barnby

TP

ThunderPoint Publishing Ltd.

First Published in Great Britain in 2017 by
ThunderPoint Publishing Limited
Summit House
4-5 Mitchell Street
Edinburgh
Scotland EH6 7BD

Cover image, *Oystercatchers* by John Thompson, Yellowbird Gallery, Birsay, Orkney, www.yellowbirdgallery.org

ISBN: 978-1-910946-15-2 (Paperback)
ISBN: 978-1-910946-17-6 (eBook)

www.thunderpoint.scot

Dedication

For mum and dad.

like an insect's prize. A guitar begins to play with
t. The gentle reverberations spread into the high-
g. The spaces between the notes stretch longer and
ie always took a moment to find a comfortable
for his guitar; it was like an embrace.
or music was one thing he and Tessa had in
en though she barely practised, she was often
or solo parts. When she was fourteen she stopped
ike that, to infuriate her father. It was the kind of
uld do.
e altar as it was for the annual school concert. I was
d row with Ronald. Robbie shared a stand with
as first desk for violin. His face was calm as he
smile was about to break open on his lips. At the
was long, and now and then he had to flick it away
of the head.
clown, Ronald prodded Tessa in the back with his
pieces and she had grinned back at him. When
d back he caught my eye.
o was that? Ten years? Fifteen years?
notes fade.
arers pause and adjust. The reflection in the polish
l tinted as they move, distorted arches and pillars
e box's surface.
enna are the first to follow.
ined by Robbie's mother and sister, then by Tessa's

begins to play. A handful of bars of introduction
ng starts, strong and brave. Among the singers are
eagues from Flotta and fire-crews from mainland
re are sopranos from the festival chorus and
e in between.
les a hymn book in front of me. Neither of us sing.
glued to Tessa.
g really well,' Lindsay whispers, 'both of them.
be impossible. Wouldn't it be impossible?'
ible to follow the words of the hymn but I open
mouth in time with the music. When Tessa is close
raises her hand. She does a small wave and smiles.

3

Acknowledgements

The blustery shores of Orkney and the warmth of the people I have come to know have been a great source of inspiration while writing and editing this book. I'm grateful to everyone who welcomed a stumbling story maker into their lives.

My particular thanks go to Tracy and Barry Leslie, who despite their cultural and linguistic differences were generous sounding boards for the passages of dialect contained in the book. The excellent Orkney Dictionary by Margaret Flaws and Gregor Lamb (www.orkneydictionary.com) also proved a most helpful resource. There is variation in nearly every aspect of orcadian dialect usage by age, gender, area and context. My aim has been to share some of this colourful language while keeping the text accessible for all.

The Stromness Writing Group continues to provide enduring support and friendship. My writing has also been guided by comments from Syliva Hayes. Fiona Fleming, Babette Stevenson, Shaun Gardiner, Joanna Buick and Bill Ferguson - thank you for your patience.

I'm grateful to David Hall for answering questions on police procedure and to Carolyn Sheehan for showing me the recompression chamber in Stromness. I have benefited from information from The Orkney Book of Birds by Tim Dean and Tracy Hall as well as on-line documents from the Orkney Research Centre for Archaeology.

I'm indebted to John Thompson for the front cover image, something I long had in mind. It is a great pleasure to see the book in such beautiful wrappings.

Finally, thank you to my husband, my children and my wider family, for all their encouragement and their distractions, both of which I love and need.

Chapter 1

In the fleshy light of St Magnus Cathedral the smooth coffin lid appears white. Within this giant refuge from the wind nothing else catches my attention, not the shards of colour in the high round window, not the flames dancing on the candle sticks.

Heads lean and bob, but I keep focus, seeking the coffin like searching for a face in a crowd. Here and there, fingers rise and touch against lips or press the underside of noses. The silence is solitary; everyone in their own empty cathedral.

In the very front row there is what looks like a gap, but it's just a head lower than the others where a little girl sits. Jenna is wearing a dark green dress with a white collar. Seeing her brings a swell of grief, tender, sharp and clean.

The minister stands; like a box of puppets the congregation copies.

'Thank you for coming here today to celebrate Robert's life. And thank you for your heartfelt and moving tributes. They are testament to his good character and generous spirit.'

She looks down briefly at her notes, adjusting her glasses before resuming.

'Together let us pray that everyone who grieves will be consoled. Just as everyone who dies will find eternal rest. We pray for Robert's parents, for his sister and brother. We ask that they are comforted in this time of sorrow. We pray for Robert's daughter Jenna, we know that she will remember his kind attentiveness as a father. We pray for Robert's wife Tessa…'

Tessa is next to Jenna, her narrow shoulders held rigid. Her pale neck stands out starkly against the black collar of her jacket.

'…that she will find strength in her grief, that her friends and family will keep Robert's memory alive with her…'

The tissue clasped between my fingers will not compact any further. The words of prayer begin to lose meaning.

Tessa can't be buying any of this I think, but then I see her shoulders begin to quiver. A small heat-haze wobble, a less keen observer might not notice. There's a tight pain across my larynx,

weakness rises up throug[h] cope when I can barely st[?] anyone meant to cope?

My best friend.

Someone nearby is sobb[ing] being a wholly suitable pla[ce] the noise is embarrassing. [?] away the marching drops, [?] away from this moment, th[?]

From outside, there [?] oystercatchers coming up [?] old shore used to be.

Do the birds somehow [?] have claimed from them?

Six men file into positio[n] Robbie's brother James, h[?] were in the line waiting t[?] cathedral. In the shadows [?] taken on some feature tha[t] bones, fine lips, muscular [?]

On the other side is Bria[n] Neil. Neil's gaze never rises[?] he looks ten years older sin[ce]

Tessa's younger cousin[?] something about the way [?] to a pub table than a funer[al] were to carry the coffin.

Does Robbie have to be [?]

Stacks of bones are ent[?] around me, bones and rel[?] once hung to dry in the cat[hedral] in the high passageways [?] rooftops.

I want to shout somethin[g] is screwed shut.

I'd rather Robbie stay[ed] overlooking Scapa Flow, th[?] from war and peace. Robb[?]

The coffin moves, craw[?]

door, held u[?] a lone vocal[?] vaulted ceili[ng] longer. Rob[?] resting plac[e]

A talent [?] common. [?] singled out [?] playing, just [?] thing she w[?]

I picture t[?] in the seco[nd] Tessa who [?] played, like [?] time his hair [?] with a shake[?]

Always the [?] bow betwee[n] Robbie look[?]

How long a[?]

The guitar [?]

The pall-b[earers] becomes co[?] drag along t[?]

Tessa and [?]

They are j[?] parents.

The organ[?] then the sin[ging] Robbie's co[?] Orkney. Th[?] everything e[?]

Lindsay sh[?]

My gaze is [?]

'She's doi[ng] God, it mus[t]

It's impos[sible] and close m[y] to us Lindsa[y]

Acknowledgements

The blustery shores of Orkney and the warmth of the people I have come to know have been a great source of inspiration while writing and editing this book. I'm grateful to everyone who welcomed a stumbling story maker into their lives.

My particular thanks go to Tracy and Barry Leslie, who despite their cultural and linguistic differences were generous sounding boards for the passages of dialect contained in the book. The excellent Orkney Dictionary by Margaret Flaws and Gregor Lamb (www.orkneydictionary.com) also proved a most helpful resource. There is variation in nearly every aspect of orcadian dialect usage by age, gender, area and context. My aim has been to share some of this colourful language while keeping the text accessible for all.

The Stromness Writing Group continues to provide enduring support and friendship. My writing has also been guided by comments from Syliva Hayes. Fiona Fleming, Babette Stevenson, Shaun Gardiner, Joanna Buick and Bill Ferguson - thank you for your patience.

I'm grateful to David Hall for answering questions on police procedure and to Carolyn Sheehan for showing me the recompression chamber in Stromness. I have benefited from information from *The Orkney Book of Birds* by Tim Dean and Tracy Hall as well as on-line documents from the Orkney Research Centre for Archaeology.

I'm indebted to John Thompson for the front cover image, something I long had in mind. It is a great pleasure to see the book in such beautiful wrappings.

Finally, thank you to my husband, my children and my wider family, for all their encouragement and their distractions, both of which I love and need.

Chapter 1

In the fleshy light of St Magnus Cathedral the smooth coffin lid appears white. Within this giant refuge from the wind nothing else catches my attention, not the shards of colour in the high round window, not the flames dancing on the candle sticks.

Heads lean and bob, but I keep focus, seeking the coffin like searching for a face in a crowd. Here and there, fingers rise and touch against lips or press the underside of noses. The silence is solitary; everyone in their own empty cathedral.

In the very front row there is what looks like a gap, but it's just a head lower than the others where a little girl sits. Jenna is wearing a dark green dress with a white collar. Seeing her brings a swell of grief, tender, sharp and clean.

The minister stands; like a box of puppets the congregation copies.

'Thank you for coming here today to celebrate Robert's life. And thank you for your heartfelt and moving tributes. They are testament to his good character and generous spirit.'

She looks down briefly at her notes, adjusting her glasses before resuming.

'Together let us pray that everyone who grieves will be consoled. Just as everyone who dies will find eternal rest. We pray for Robert's parents, for his sister and brother. We ask that they are comforted in this time of sorrow. We pray for Robert's daughter Jenna, we know that she will remember his kind attentiveness as a father. We pray for Robert's wife Tessa…'

Tessa is next to Jenna, her narrow shoulders held rigid. Her pale neck stands out starkly against the black collar of her jacket.

'…that she will find strength in her grief, that her friends and family will keep Robert's memory alive with her…'

The tissue clasped between my fingers will not compact any further. The words of prayer begin to lose meaning.

Tessa can't be buying any of this I think, but then I see her shoulders begin to quiver. A small heat-haze wobble, a less keen observer might not notice. There's a tight pain across my larynx, weakness rises up through my legs. How can Tessa possibly cope when I can barely stand here listening to this... how is anyone meant to cope?

My best friend.

Someone nearby is sobbing. Despite everything, despite this being a wholly suitable place and time to breakdown and cry, the noise is embarrassing. I hold my breath to keep silent, mop away the marching drops, seek distraction, anything to take me away from this moment, this place; because Robbie is dead.

From outside, there comes the short flat whistle of oystercatchers coming up from the harbour, back to where the old shore used to be.

Do the birds somehow remember? Do they know what we have claimed from them?

Six men file into position around the coffin. On one side is Robbie's brother James, his father and one of the uncles who were in the line waiting to shake my hand as I entered the cathedral. In the shadows of the nave all the men look to have taken on some feature that reminds me of Robbie, high cheek bones, fine lips, muscular shoulders.

On the other side is Brian, Tommy, and Tessa's older cousin Neil. Neil's gaze never rises from the floor, his face is ashen and he looks ten years older since I saw him last.

Tessa's younger cousin Ronald remains seated. There's something about the way he sits that's too casual, more suited to a pub table than a funeral. Somehow, I couldn't bear it if he were to carry the coffin.

Does Robbie have to be taken out?

Stacks of bones are entombed in the red walls and pillars around me, bones and relics of saints and sinners. Sails were once hung to dry in the cathedral, markets were held, kids played in the high passageways and climbed harum-scarum on the rooftops.

I want to shout something to make them stop, but my throat is screwed shut.

I'd rather Robbie stayed here than go to the cemetery overlooking Scapa Flow, that fickle water scattered with wrecks from war and peace. Robbie didn't drown, but water took him.

The coffin moves, crawling from the chancel to the great

2

door, held up like an insect's prize. A guitar begins to play with a lone vocalist. The gentle reverberations spread into the high-vaulted ceiling. The spaces between the notes stretch longer and longer. Robbie always took a moment to find a comfortable resting place for his guitar; it was like an embrace.

A talent for music was one thing he and Tessa had in common. Even though she barely practised, she was often singled out for solo parts. When she was fourteen she stopped playing, just like that, to infuriate her father. It was the kind of thing she would do.

I picture the altar as it was for the annual school concert. I was in the second row with Ronald. Robbie shared a stand with Tessa who was first desk for violin. His face was calm as he played, like a smile was about to break open on his lips. At the time his hair was long, and now and then he had to flick it away with a shake of the head.

Always the clown, Ronald prodded Tessa in the back with his bow between pieces and she had grinned back at him. When Robbie looked back he caught my eye.

How long ago was that? Ten years? Fifteen years?

The guitar notes fade.

The pall-bearers pause and adjust. The reflection in the polish becomes coral tinted as they move, distorted arches and pillars drag along the box's surface.

Tessa and Jenna are the first to follow.

They are joined by Robbie's mother and sister, then by Tessa's parents.

The organ begins to play. A handful of bars of introduction then the singing starts, strong and brave. Among the singers are Robbie's colleagues from Flotta and fire-crews from mainland Orkney. There are sopranos from the festival chorus and everything else in between.

Lindsay slides a hymn book in front of me. Neither of us sing.

My gaze is glued to Tessa.

'She's doing really well,' Lindsay whispers, 'both of them. God, it must be impossible. Wouldn't it be impossible?'

It's impossible to follow the words of the hymn but I open and close my mouth in time with the music. When Tessa is close to us Lindsay raises her hand. She does a small wave and smiles.

Tessa does nothing except blink absently in return. I want to disappear. A strange croak escapes from my throat. The sound catches Tessa's attention, but her expression does not change. Her eyes are unseeing, as unresponsive as a sleepwalker.

I have an overpowering urge to grab Lindsay's hand and restrain it before she can attract attention again, but there's no need. She simply nods to the rest of the family filing past; her cheerful wave was reserved for Tessa alone.

Robbie's mother sees me. She looks me straight in the eye. With difficulty I control my expression until she passes then cover my face with my hands.

'Oh…'

An embarrassing noise and yet it escapes anyway. A fast current swirls around my knees, weight presses on my shoulders, squeezing my breath away. My knees are buckling. But nobody else is sitting down – not even the old folk.

Oh, Robbie. Why did we wait?

Lindsay drops the hymnbook into the niche of the chair in front and curls her arm around my waist. Despite the waving I'm glad she's beside me. Perhaps it's because she's my sister that she seems to know what to do.

'It's okay. You can lean on me,' she whispers.

The hymn finishes. There's a whisk of breeze around our ankles from the great door opening. Sharp light invades the interior of the cathedral, throwing into contrast the lines of pale mortar and the black cracks in the salmon-coloured stone. The skeleton painted on the Mort Brod hanging in the east aisle grins darkly. It doesn't move, yet in my mind I hear it squeaking on its hook.

People begin to file out along the rows of chairs. I slip free of Lindsay's support and sink onto the seat. I double over, winded, pole-axed. I lean over and busily push tissues into my bag.

Lindsay sits down next to me and swings a leg over her knee.

'Nice music,' she says. No one else is talking yet, but she goes on. 'Tessa looks very smart. You wouldn't think her hair long enough to be twisted up like that, I suppose she's had practice. By the way, I loved the way she cut your hair for the interview. Made you look like a proper teacher.'

My focus is drawn to the mouth of my bag.

'You look peaky, Christine. Why don't we skip the commitment and go straight to the Town Hall? They'll have all the food put out. Get you a cup of tea.'

Peaky – it's a word our mother would use, a southern word.

'We can go to the cemetery another time,' she says. 'It'll be easy enough.' She breaks off for a moment. 'Poor Tommy, he could hardly hold it together.'

'They were friends,' I mumble.

'I know. You all were. But he must feel so…guilty. Even though it wasn't his fault at all…guilty for being there…and what it must have been like afterwards I can't imagine…'

In my mind's eye I see Tommy's face as it was a few minutes earlier, his skin grey, his shoulders stooped. Yet his eyes had been determined. No one had expected him to speak. No one would have thought any less of him if he hadn't got out of his seat and gone to the front. He didn't stand behind the lectern.

He'd laid his hand on the coffin.

'Robbie, Ah'll miss you beuy. It's a poor day th'day, but there's no sense greetin in front of these good folk. They want to hear something aboot what kind o man you were, When I look back, it fair chokes me wae laughter the things we did.

'We had our scrapes, maybe one too many as bairns – there wis the time we got snared in quicksand on Scapa beach – and we were right scared for a peedie while, thought we'd never get oot. Never a peep to anyone afterwards because we kent it meant a skelping fae your dad – still got a row fae wur mothers for being covered in gutter, mind.

'That was a peedie while a go for sure. Ah'm heavier noo, but Ah'm maybe a peedie bit wiser. Still gettin plenty of rows one way or another. These days, you'd shaped up to be a fine fither to this peedie lass.' He'd nodded towards Jenna then had taken a deep breath. 'And Tessa…Ah'd have done anything to bring him back safe…if I'd kent what went wrong I would hiv done something aboot it…' His voice tails off. 'It'll no be the same without you, beuy. We'll miss you very badly.'

Tears slip down my cheeks again as I think what it must have been like for them. Lindsay chatters on, not minding that I don't answer back.

'…I never noticed how much Robbie looked like his father.

There's not much of him in Jenna though….she's obviously Tessa's little girl…poor mite. Who on earth found that dress for her? Can't have been Tessa…'

'I want to go.'

She's surprised at being interrupted, but says ,'You're right. I don't like it in here either when it's full of people. No wonder Dad goes to St Margarets'. Didn't you go with him when it happened? He told me he was going to see you, he knew it'd be a shock and you'd want to know whatever happened and that you might want to go to mass. I was going to come, but it's been such a long time since I went… and aren't there rules about keeping going? I think there must be. I suppose though, when there's nothin else you can do you might as well…'

Her words drift on.

She's right. Yes, when there had been hope,

I'd gone and I'd prayed. I'd watched the priest's hand raised in blessing, falling lightly through the air. I'd felt invisible threads knotted tight in the solar plexus as I knelt and prayed – not the heart, not the head.

Lindsay's still speaking, commentating.

'… Neil did a good job. Can't be easy being taller than everyone else. He suits a shirt and tie doesn't he? Oh, you do look pale, Chrissy. What about a real drink? Nobody would miss us if we slipped off for a sly one at The Catcher. The coffee would be better too. They've got a new machine and I hear that…'

My father had stayed with me during the afternoon while we waited for news. I was still unpacking boxes in the cottage. We worked quietly, it felt as if tiny moments of life and death were continually passing, and in no way could they be distinguished from each other, somehow they blurred into a singular feeling of timelessness. Later, Dad made a phone call. He'd returned with dull eyes and age embossed heavily on his features.

The news, already old, was passed on to me.

Robbie's body was driven to Raigmore Hospital in Inverness where there was a post-mortem. The police found no suspicious circumstances. They recorded the sudden death of a fit young man and his body was returned to the island.

'No. I want to go to the cemetery.'

'You really don't look up to it. Black's not doing you any favours today.' Lindsay looks at me squarely for a moment then says, 'I'm hungry.'

And I *am* thirsty. Perhaps it would be better not to go, but I want to be there for Tessa. I want to make the day more bearable. It gives me a purpose at least.

Lindsay zips her coat, a shabby red waterproof but equal to the squalls blowing up the cemetery hillside. My tailored woollen coat that was adequate for the weather in the south will not cope so well here. I'm not prepared for any of this.

It's an excuse and you know it, Christine.

As Lindsay edges along the row of seats I'm reminded of children leaving assembly in my previous school. In three days time I take up a new appointment at St Olaf's primary school a few streets away. Although I was used to autumn starting in August when I lived here, now it seems wrong.

She slips into the flow of people moving over the red and gold tiles. The closeness of the crowd reminds me of the London underground. Except here there is not a single stranger. Anyone I don't recognize instantly is familiar from somewhere. And it's likely, more than likely, that after a minute or two of conversation I'd find a connection that weaves us into the tangle of island life.

Lindsay is waiting for me, causing a ripple in the queue of people trying to move through the archway.

I shuffle, following the rhythm of other people's steps unaware at first that I'm directly behind Ronald. My nose is level with an acne scar on the flushed nape of his neck. For all the farm work there is still something unhealthy looking about him. He taps the chair backs with his fingers and nods to let people out of the rows.

It takes a while before I realise Ronald's not doing it out of politeness but to deliberately hinder my progress. He halts, forcing me to come to a stop then turns sideways and blocks my step when I try and move around him.

'Why are you back, Christine?'

'I've a job at St Olaf's.'

Ronald bends, so our foreheads almost touch. His breath is tainted by alcohol. He speaks softly into my ear, so no one else can hear.

'You'll no stay. There's nothing left for you.' There's a mocking gleam in his eye. He gives a tiny shake of the head, whistles air through his teeth then says, 'You're a liar, Christine.'

He straightens his back, putting a few inches of space between us. The pillars weave and rock, the colours begin to blur.

'What's that you're saying, Ronald?' says Lindsay, coming to my side.

'None of your business.'

She puts a firm hand under my arm.

'Come on, Christine. Let's go.'

I stumble out of the cathedral into the glare. Nothing is private here, every decision under a microscope before it's hardly been made, before it's been lived. Lives go past half-lived, half-decided and no one ends up getting what they want.

As we come down the steps my hair shoots upwards, caught in the wind spiralling up the front of the cathedral. It feels like standing on the edge of a high cliff with the frothy blue water below.

'What was all that about?' says Lindsay. 'I can't stand the way he talks to people sometimes…'

'I don't know. Nothing.'

'…he's always been a waste of space, but you can't choose your relatives, can you? Poor Tessa, what a filthy day it's been.'

Blood drums around my ears as we pass the worn out market cross.

'Maybe we could find somewhere… and have a drink,' I say. 'You're right about the cemetery. I shouldn't go. Not today.'

It isn't nothing. I am a liar.

I am a liar, Tessa.

Chapter 2

Six weeks ago I arrived back for the second time. Not an overnight stopover this time, but driving a car wedged with books and cheap household appliances, most of which could have been left behind. The already failing begonia from my school colleagues had tipped over in the footwell on the first corner.

At Lindsay's suggestion I'd applied for the job at St Olaf's. After an informal conversation on the telephone I had been invited for a further interview. The Headmaster had privately encouraged me to believe that the job was mine if I wanted it, so I made the decision to return. Robbie was alive. It's true you might make assumptions about him being the reason I returned, but Lindsay was the reason I came back. Earlier in the summer, when I came back for that first time, I'd failed her.

She'd done something stupid. She said it was a mistake, but there are always reasons. Mum and Dad didn't say anything. Nobody said it was my fault, but in the gap of no more than a heartbeat, I imagined the rest of my life without her.

So often my feelings towards Lindsay when we were younger were clouded by anger or embarrassment. I pretended her life was none of my concern. Perhaps events have made me more sensitive. It was a risk.

Was I thinking of her or me?

I came for her. Believe it or not.

Driving over the Tyne I became aware of how far north I'd come. I passed lines of rooftops and chimneys level with the bridge, slick with the grime of the industrial revolution. There's a multi-storey close by, inside are rows and rows of silent cars. There's nothing like it on Orkney – nothing like the bridge, the fly-overs and fly-unders, the circulatory lanes that switch and change. There is nothing like the lines of shops: pound shops, betting shops, tattoo shops, exotic-pet shops; Thai restaurants…some vast toy town, one shop after another.

A good chunk of what most other people call north was

already behind me, but Newcastle is still south compared to the Orkney Islands. I wonder at all these lives going on of which I have no awareness, all these places I have never been.

Occasionally, there are glimpses of landscape that resembles Orkney – the windswept coast of Northumberland where farmland stretches right to cliffs dropping down into the sea. It's not long before Edinburgh looms close. The density of cars and houses and multi-lane roundabouts increases and then diminishes. Another zone passed through.

Gradually, trees disappear. Between Golspie and Brora the change is marked. Swathes of spreading beeches and oaks give way to cantankerous lonely specimens. The remaining larger stands of trees are gloomy pine plantations, grown for slow profit.

There's a change in rhythm from Sutherland to Caithness. The brown signs indicating cairns or historic trails point to places I have still never visited, but they are familiar. I never visit, although I'm quite free to do so, because it would mean a detour from the way home.

Inverness, the long low bridges, the splay-legged oil rigs waiting in the firth were also left behind. I'd confidently swung the car around the invaginations of the coast. Views of cliffs and hills rear and disappear, a final rodeo until the land flattens and calms, swept clean by months of wind. There are miniature peat channels cut through the scrubby tussocks, dark banks fringed with rust-coloured heather. Even though it was August, last winter's bone-white grass has only an inch of fresh green at the base. The light is already waning towards the autumn equinox.

The process of recognizing vehicles heading to the port began hours before, delivery trucks driven with purpose. On the final twisting stretch of road from John o Groats to Gills Bay there's a clear view out over the water to Swona where the catamaran comes into view. Its white body is held high in the water. The split hull is painted bright red and heaves up and down through the swell. Two red lines are painted around the body of the boat, like go faster stripes on training shoes.

When beckoned I'd pulled forward and parked in the queue for the boat. I'd answered the man with the clipboard, smoking out one side of his mouth. He moderated his accent to be more clearly understood. It surprised me and hurt a little not to be recognised even though I know I don't sound like I belong. But I have never sounded properly Orcadian; at school I stood out as an incomer and my flat southern way of speaking has become more pronounced since I've been away.

There is never any ceremony to boarding, an instructing wave and nod to come forward. Passengers clamber out and are welcomed by the smell of diesel, rust and sea spray. After I'd ascended the steep stairs I chose the less crowded cabin where food is not permitted, but am still surrounded by the aroma of bacon rolls and chicken soup.

Few of the places in the bright purple rows were occupied. In a window seat of an empty row I'd rested my head on the scratchy nylon seat cover and stared out to sea. It has been two days of driving.

It's a twenty minute drive from St. Margaret's Hope to Orkney mainland. I know the road, each bend and field. The houses cluster like iron filings around the road. It is a relief that there are no trees to block the view.

There is a short causeway with open sea at one side and a brackish pond on the other. For a short distance I'd been flanked on both sides by water. One side was bright sea-blue, with miniature wavelets dancing merrily in the breeze, the other was a flat white, as pale as the moon, its surface protected by a high dune. Protruding rushes cast black lines of shadow through the water's skin.

There were oystercatchers at the shallow edge of the shore, the birds spaced quite evenly. They scamper with a sort of uneven hopping movement towards the drawing back tide, probing in the mud. One bird was caught out by a spume of spray as a ripple and wave collided. It spread its wings and shook, showing the black cross stretched across its back.

One of my first memories of Orkney came back to me, of my father taking Lindsay and I to the beach. It was a grubby beach similar to the one I had passed, more stones and clay than sand. My mother had been busy making a reconnaissance visit to a potential archaeological site, already too pre-occupied with the project that had brought us here to join our outing. Disappointed that she had not come and that there was no place for using our bucket and spades, Dad had encouraged us to search the rock pools. We'd filled our buckets with hermit crabs, piling them one on another. We watched our captives intently; they soon began to fight. When Dad saw he'd told us we must tip the creatures out and afterwards insisted that they mustn't be crowded.

He told us how the oystercatcher had been given its distinctive markings as a reward for concealing the child Jesus beneath seaweed when he was in danger. The idea conjured up monstrous images to two little girls. Lindsay and I had flipped over the leathery straps of kelp and shrieked, pretending to have found a dead body. Despite its irreverence Dad took our game in good humour. It was a happy afternoon.

I'd continued driving past the beach, over the causeway and then up the road on the other side. Memories now came quickly, a noisy crowd that pressed hard on my return.

I'd seen the wrought iron sign pole at the end of a turning rising up a shallow brae. The stout silhouette of a bull still balanced on the word 'Ayre'. It is the place where Tessa grew up and where her family still farm. Over the other side of the hill is The Brough of Ayreness, an ancient fortified settlement, now a ruin that juts out into the sea.

These were our places. This was our hill, our corner.

A wild heartbeat had risen in my chest when I saw them all and heard the oystercatchers' trilling cry.

I fled, but I have returned. Since the funeral Tessa and I have made a new start. Robbie's daughter Jenna will be brought up where the wind hurries you to shelter, to places where the door can be closed and a fire lit. Not that we have a real fire here, in this strip of converted outhouse that has been made into its own dwelling by bricking-up a doorway. We're kept warm by modern radiators, except the end room. It's too cold for anyone to sleep in there now. We've abandoned the room, moving the bed and shifting Jenna's books and toys. Now she has the big bedroom and for the moment, Tessa and I are sharing a wide double bed that almost fills the second smaller bedroom.

After the funeral Tessa didn't want to stay living in the flat above Robbie's parent's shop even though they wanted her to stay. 'Everything's changed,' she'd said. But there was no way she'd move back to the farm. The Blackhouse, the old farmhouse given to Tessa and Robbie by Neil, was only half finished. Robbie'd been renovating the building for years. It was no longer the wreck it had once been, but it wasn't ready.

So, I'd invited them to live with me in the cottage. I had more rooms than I needed; at the time we didn't know the end room wouldn't stay warm.

As you would expect it is plain and the furniture simple. The cottage is an extension of the original house and still enclosed by its garden wall. The wall is similar to the stone dykes around the fields, sturdy and lichen spotted, and there is a sense of privacy and enclosure in the strip of garden. There's a concrete path where Jenna scooters and a rectangle of lawn big enough for hanging laundry when the weather is fine and for picking daisies and setting out toys.

Tessa's endless bundles of toiletries and samples from work are banished to the bathroom; my lipstick and hairbrush sit on the window ledge in the bedroom. It's here that I rest her cup of coffee in the morning.

'Tessa, I'm off out to work.'

'Why d'you go this early?' She yawns. 'Don't you ever want more sleep?'

'Always. I've got to keep up a good impression. Jenna's awake, and remember it's Tuesday.'

'Tuesday?'

'Recycling.'

I turn away the cup's handle and pick up a lipstick.

Tessa rolls up onto an elbow, and squints at the steam rising from the cup. In the morning, unwashed, unwaxed and unstraightened, her hair is like a barley field tossed in a wind.

'Why do you never put it where I can reach it?'

'If you could reach it you wouldn't get up,' I say.

She smiles.

Jenna slips through the doorway waving a luminous orange bouncy ball.

'Mum, guess what I fund?'

'C'mon monkey, gae me a cuddle.'

Jenna flaps the duvet over her head and burrows underneath

like a worm.

'Argh! You're freezin,' squeals Tessa.

'I'm gaen,' I say. 'Bye, Jenna.'

Jenna pokes her head out from the duvet. She puckers her lips; they feel like a warm wet raspberry on my lowered cheek. I take it as a compliment that she hasn't said anything about my appearance today. Whether inherited or not, Jenna's instinct for style is like her mother's. This morning both have withheld opinions on corduroy skirt, roll-neck and boots.

Tessa gets out of bed. She stretches her arms over her head. The shape of her body beneath her T-shirt is revealed against the bright window. It seems so unlikely, so strange that it was once swollen by pregnancy.

'What's he keeking at?' she says.

Mr Sutherland's cap is pulled low, he's dragging a shopping cart and a dog with three legs and one blue eye jogs lopsidedly by his side.

'You standing at the window in yir nightie,' I answer, heading out of the room. 'I've got to go. There's a pile of clean washing if you need anything. See you at school Jenna.'

'I was going to borrow your white shirt,' calls Tessa.

'Help yourself,' I call back.

A wardrobe bursting at the seams and she chooses to borrow my things. It makes me smile. I walk down the corridor into the living room and through the kitchen. Outside, roses are still flowering around the window. There is a wide strip of crocosmia beneath the garden wall, orange trumpets nose through strips of flapping green. The path doubles-back past the bedroom window to the gate that leads to the street.

Tessa and Jenna tap on the glass as I walk past. Jenna squashes her nose onto the pane. A pair of dark nostril holes mist the surface. I can't help but crack a smile. Tessa is giggling; even without the squeaky chuckling it's infectious. As I lift and close the rusted gate latch I'm light at heart. Who could hold that against me?

Chapter 3

In the past St Olaf's always had more children and less composite classes than our school in the country. I never minded being in a mixed age group, although it meant I spent half of my primary years in the same classroom as my sister. Back then Lindsay had been noisy and forthright; she became more disruptive in her teens.

I was lucky to have Tessa, 'school sisters' we used to call each other. I greeted her every morning with hot gladness. There was always something new, something we *had* to talk over as soon as we met. While other children's bags skidded across the playground and balls span around our feet we'd catch up on everything that had happened since three-thirty the previous day. A weekend where we didn't see each other resulted in rapid simultaneous exchanges to convey our experiences. We shared everything.

The girls at St Olaf's are the same as they meet beneath the flags painted on the end wall of the junior block. The bright rectangles represent Orkney, Norway, Scotland and the United Kingdom and above them all is the Norwegian coat of arms, a lion rampant looking left holding a silver axe, the weapon used to martyr St Olaf.

Some of the pupils come from the countryside east of Kirkwall, many already set on farm work. It's true there is a limited range of occupations locally, but there is some variety: tourism, archaeology, fish-farming, healthcare, renewable energy, not to mention the oil platforms and the terminal on Flotta.

I see the father of a boy in my class who Lindsay used to hang around with before he settled down. Instantly, and involuntarily, I picture him in her room half-naked, sweating and grinning – Lindsay didn't even notice I was there. I wonder if he remembers.

'Whit like, Christine?'

'No bad,' I say, blushing.

It's the habitual exchange, regardless of the circumstance. His hands push into the pockets of his overalls, they are grey with concrete dust. He's wearing fawn-coloured steel toe-capped boots.

'I've to take morning lines,' I say.

He watches me walk away without comment.

Fine drizzle has been advancing from the north during the morning. My hair is curling. When I get home after days like these Tessa pulls my ringlets straight and laughs, 'You should carry hair straighteners in your pocket.'

I feel conspicuous since returning; although there are many more incomers now. It is noticeable how the Orcadian accent has become diluted in children compared to the older generation.

Today, I'm taking morning lines as a favour for Moira Gowrie. Poor Moira, bleary and coughing, smiling as if she were fine and being ignored by the other teachers in the staff room. She's from Westray, dark hair and dark eyes, and maybe she still feels like an incomer too. I like that she doesn't know quite so much about me as other people. She still tones down her accent when she speaks to me.

'Oh, thank you very much, Christine.'

'No bother.'

I lack the the soft, sing-song local accent, but it is the right phrase at the right time. It's certainly not recognizably Orcadian like it might once have been.

In the playground, a drain partly blocked by moss is being diligently filled with stones by two boys.

'Go find something better to do,' I call over.

One rubs the other's head with his knuckles and they both run away chuckling.

Two girls, linked arm in arm, rush up.

'Miss Marner, Heddle won't leave us alone.'

'Have you told him he's annoying you?'

They look at each other and break into a grin.

'No,' they both reply.

'Then go play somewhere else. I'll speak to him.'

The girls turn, clasp each other around the shoulders then dash over the wet concrete.

There's a tightness in my throat. I wipe away the droplets from my eyes and turn into the stinging wind, pushing my hands into my pockets.

Tessa will have her hands in warm water, soaping somebody's hair or she might already be snipping away, talking about this and that. It has to be hard for her, people expecting her to talk.

My fingers crinkle a wrapper in my coat pocket. The confectionary aisle in the big supermarket is the highlight of Jenna's week, despite having lived above a shop where she could pick and choose from the shiny display by the till without paying a penny. It's a pleasure to indulge her in little things after what she's gone through. I'm eating more chocolate too, must be the cold weather I tell myself.

'Sammy Dunnet, why are you always covered in gutter? Go inside clean yourself up. Mind you don't make a mess in the toilets either.'

Orcadian words are already creeping back into my speech. The bell rings, children stream like army ants from corners, benches, drains and gates into lines. Sticks warmed in the hand are relinquished sadly and shortly after forgotten.

'Morag and Sheena into line, please.'

Morag pushes her younger sister into the fidgeting queue of primary one children then skips over to where she belongs. Sheena keeps her eyes sullenly on the boy in front of her. Jenna is a few places ahead, smiling and fiddling with a reflector keyring on her bag. You wouldn't know from looking at her that her father died six weeks ago.

'Are we daen' human body?' asks Steven Drummond as he files past.

'Maybe in the afternoon,' I reply.

Stepping inside, the building is stuffy compared with outdoors.

'Canna go tae toilet, Miss?' says Amy Murray.

I nod and she skips away.

Her footsteps pat across the flecked lino towards the atrium joining the classrooms to the hall. There's a strong smell of garlic wafting along the corridor, signalling lasagne is on the menu for lunch.

At five years old Jenna has gone through everything Tessa has been through. I only saw Jenna and Robbie together a couple of times. At Anne and Brian's wedding they were laughing and sharing sweets. He held her fingers as she twirled to make her skirts spin. I think he must have hated being away on Flotta. I try not to be jealous.

What kind of person would be jealous?

The routine of going to school, the discipline, the busyness and need for concentration helps the day pass. Back in the cottage there is no privacy, yet being together has made it a place of solace, even if sometimes I must disguise my grief.

When I return today Jenna's watching television on her own. Her eyes are fixed tightly on the bright pink noisy screen. A half-eaten Jaffa cake rests on her knee, the underneaths of her white socks are grey from running somewhere without shoes.

'Where's your mum?'

Jenna sighs and rests her head on her hand, but doesn't reply.

In the unlit corridor the door to the abandoned bedroom is ajar. I walk towards it, past the closed doors of Jenna's bedroom and the bathroom. I pause, my shadow falls on the large glass panel of the half open door. It's patterned with michaelmas daisies, a net curtain is pulled across on the other side to give privacy.

Cold damp air flows out me as I push on the cool handle.

'Tessa?'

A chill settles on my skin as I step forward. It's dark and claustrophobic inside, the atmosphere compounded by the rows of cardboard boxes at the far side of the room. They are Tessa's possessions from the flat. One of the boxes has 'Funeral Cards' written on the side and is sealed with brown tape. Others are open; there is a rugby trophy poking out of one that must have belonged to Robbie.

'Tessa, what are you doing? Let me put the light on.'

'Leave it.' Her voice is unsteady. 'What do you want?'

Something slides and flops onto the floor. There are sheets of paper scattered over the carpet. The white rectangles seem to glow in the gloom against the dull brown.

Last time I found her she was looking at photographs. This time it's letters. It crosses my mind that they are something she doesn't want me to see or surely she wouldn't be secretive like this.

I close the door behind me, silencing the cartoon noise and

step further into the room. Even if Jenna understands, surely it can't be good for her to hear her mother crying. Or am I being naïve? Has Jenna seen enough to know adult invincibility is a myth?

I make out Tessa's tight hunched shoulders. The dim light reflects off her hair, a dull halo. The darkness presses around us like water.

'Shall I open the curtain a crack?'

'What?'

'It's warmer outside than in here.'

There's a small square window above an old writing bureau. It's thickly covered in maroon velvet. I pull one curtain aside. The glow of light, acid green from the leaves surrounding the window immediately changes the mood in the room. Tessa scoops the papers into her arms. She kneels on the floor holding them in her arms like a flower girl.

A box labelled 'Letters' has been pulled out of line from the rest. The flaps hang open backwards, like a spent flower.

'What do you want? I'm busy in here.'

'It's not a bad day. I'll let in some air.'

Gradually, the latch works free, paint flecks are left on the sill. A bus grumbles past and a tuneless chirrup drifts into the room with the scent of diesel and rain.

Tessa shuffles the sheets into an untidy pile. I step towards her.

'Need a hand?' I ask.

'I'm doing it,' she says.

'Let me hel—'

'Leave them! Jesus' sake…leave them alone.'

She rises, arms clutching the letters and envelopes to her chest. She struggles with the latch on the bureau, it slides open slowly, the wooden leaf not quite reaching horizontal and Tessa tumbles the papers inside.

There's no point being unkind, not when she's like this.

The musty air suddenly catches unpleasantly in my throat. I'd hardly noticed it before. Now, I return to the window above the bureau and push it open wide.

Tessa shoots me a hard stare. I move out of her way and stand with my back to the empty hearth. She pushes the flap closed then wipes her nose on the back of her hand. She breathes deeply, as if preparing to speak. I brace myself for what she might say.

Then I hear a little voice.

'Mum?'

Without either of us noticing Jenna has entered the room.

'Canna get another biscuit?'

Her cheeks shine green from the light reflecting around the room. There are smudges of chocolate in the corners of her mouth.

'Get one from the packet,' she says.

Jenna walks away, her shoulders bowed, bottom lip protruding slightly. It wasn't a biscuit she was after.

'Aways a wet blanket after school,' says Tessa.

'Are you all right, Tessa?'

She straightens her skirt and then runs a swift index finger beneath her eyelashes to correct her mascara. She changes her expression, her cheekbones somehow become more prominent, her lips fuller and her small straight nose more determined. Her blotched cheeks and dull eyes are banished. It is a well rehearsed trick

'I got some new tights from the chemist,' she says.

'New tights?'

'Patterned,' she says, 'only cost a few pounds.'

I follow her out, leaving the letters behind.

'Jenna, switch off that noise. Come have a look at mum's shopping.'

Tessa and I have been friends nearly all our lives. I like to think that we haven't secrets, but there are some things it's better she never knows. After all, eventually she and Robbie did get married.

Chapter 4

St Olaf's has changed, the way things are done has changed, but the children are the same. I hadn't realised before I came back how everything was linked together, how leaving had stopped me remembering my childhood; it was blanked out for survival.

'Can anyone tell me the ingredients of blood?'

Hands rise in the air.

Later, I hand out pens, paper, balls of red and blue wool, beads of different shapes and sizes. There is low chatter, the sing-song accented children's voices, the smell of roast dinner. A scene comes back to me from the past that is arrestingly clear.

Only on special occasions, on Christmas, Burns night and the last day of summer term, would Tessa be given money for a cooked meal. Otherwise it was home made bread, farm cheese and a slice of cake packed in an old ice cream box the lid held on with a rubber band. For days before special meals we would anticipate the pleasure of being able to sit next to each other. We'd debate which dinner ladies were most likely to give second helpings and plan how to select the biggest dessert. The morning before Christmas lunch we hardly attended to our lessons, too busy making lip-smacking faces or rubbing our tummies underneath the table.

Mr Blakemore had scolded Tessa, his suppressed native accent becoming more obvious as he spoke.

'Stop messing aroond or you'll get nothin but a piece of breed. Think you'd niver had a bite to eat.'

It was an idle threat, I know that now, but back then I was unsure. Tessa had started to cry at the thought of her slice of bread in place of Christmas dinner – Tessa who prided herself on never shedding a tear from any sort of pain. Anger boiled up inside me, thrilling and hot.

I'd knocked my chair back and stood up straight as a post.

'Tessa can have my lunch,' I said. 'I don't care. I'll have the bread.'

The class went silent.

Slowly, I lowered my gaze to my desk. I wished for invisibility, that the school would crumble into dust. I'd thought by speaking out that at least Tessa would get her slice of turkey and Christmas cracker. Now I realised it would make no difference.

'Maybe it'll do you good tae have a piece of breed as weel, Christine,' said Mr Blakemore, 'Sit doon, girl. Maybe it'll do you aal some good. Noo get these wirds written oot or there'll be nothin for any o you.'

Surely no one had that sort of power?

Tessa looked across at me miserably. Together, in the best handwriting we could muster and with shaking fingers we copied our spellings and nursed back to life the hope of Christmas dinner.

Apart from that one time, Tessa never blinked at being given a row.

There was one person in the class that Mr Blakemore seemed to dislike personally, we never knew why he chose Robbie. It was the same day, that another incident occurred.

After lunch, almost as soon as we were back at our desks, the slow blue gloaming of mid-winter drew on. The wind had been getting up, and was strong enough now to whistle air through the plug sockets. The shutters over the plastic ventilation fan in the wall clattered open and closed.

Mr Blakemore had given the class permission for art materials to be taken out for making Christmas cards. He'd demonstrated how to tip glitter sparingly onto dabs of glue and how to recover the excess on a sheet of folded paper so it could be neatly returned to the pot.

I daubed glue on the branches of a lop-sided Christmas tree while Tessa dashed blobs all over her paper without bothering with a drawing.

'It's a snow picture,' she'd said.

She went to Robbie's table to get the silver glitter. When she came back she was smirking.

'He's glued-up his fingers,' she'd said. 'Dipped them in all the pots.'

Robbie's multi-colour glitter-fingers waggled in the air. He warbled in a funny voice, 'I am a mum-my…a mum-my…' Everyone was giggling, pretending to be mesmerized by him.

Ronald had taken one of the white plastic spatulas and was beginning to paste glue over his hands when Mr Blakemore came in from tidying the art cupboard.

A sharp fizz of adrenaline ran through my body. Children paused open-mouthed, pens blotted paper, glitter-pots hovered in mid-air. Tessa and Robbie had their backs turned too engrossed in their ribald mock-horror role play to notice the teacher's return.

It was Tessa who noticed the change in atmosphere first. Her back stiffened. I could almost see the hairs on the back of her neck stand up on end.

'I am a mum—'

A precisely delivered whack knocked him half a pace sideways. Parallel red lines stood out on Robbie's cheek.

Mr Blakemore had in his hand an unopened packet of plasticine, the red, yellow, blue, green and white ridged strips visible through the cellophane window. He delivered a second, more purposeful blow to the back of Robbie's head, making him stagger forwards.

'Robert Muir, you tak things too far!'

At the third blow, again to Robbie's head, the pitter-pitter of glitter could be heard falling from his fingertips.

Mr Blakemore sent the plasticine packet across his desk through a pile of homework jotters.

'Put it aal in the bin,' he said. 'Everyone in your seats. Arms folded. Heeds doon!'

I'd sloped up to the wicker basket and dropped in my half-finished card. I'd already written in my neatest hand, *To Mum, Dad and Lindsay. Merry Christmas from Christine xxx.*

Robbie stayed hunched over his desk, his face bright red, eyes bulging slightly as he tried to hold back his tears.

'Noo, hands oot,' said Mr Blakemore. 'Let's see who else thinks it's funny to waste wur school's val-u-able resources.'

We all thought he was going to give us the cane – the whole class. Margaret Clitheroe wet her knickers and had to change into her PE kit, which didn't improve Mr Blakemore's temper. He checked our hands and sent us one by one to the toilets. Re-inspecting and making everyone wait their turn. The rest of the afternoon was spent sitting in silence, except for Ronald. He put a pencil up his nose and escaped to the sick room with a nosebleed.

I don't know why Mr Blakemore reacted to Robbie the way he did. He wasn't naughty or mean, not at heart; perhaps it was because he was so well liked by everyone.

There are some pupils who you can't help feeling more sympathy for than others. Each child butts up against their classmates in different ways; we accepted Tommy's nose bleeds and laughed at Margaret's weak bladder without thinking twice. But I remember Ronald sneezing on the back of Margaret's head during the nativity and hating him. She'd dropped the baby Jesus and sat on stage in tears. At the Grammar he set off the fire extinguisher in the music room, everyone who was waiting to go into the changing rooms for swimming saw him, but he always denied it was him. Robbie had charm; Ronald was plain annoying.

Back in the present the grey drizzle is being driven against the windowpanes. It has almost turned to rain when the bell goes.

'Coats on,' I say. 'How's it you're always such a raffle, Owen Harvey?'

Kaitlin Menzie is scratching the plastic bag full of sugar in a display warning about tooth decay from fizzy drinks. She shrugs when I tap her on the shoulder and wanders into line.

In the next room Moira is suffering another coughing fit. There was a box of chocolates from her on my desk this morning with a thank you card. She seems to want to get to know me, to be my friend.

I parade the class to the main doors and into the playground. They disperse quickly, apart from a handful who've no one waiting for them by the gate. Owen Begg starts kicking stones against the wall.

Jenna's class comes out next. I'm about to speak when someone by the gate catches her eye, she gasps and grins.

'Granddad!'

A van door slams,the engine left running. Owen's father, Irvine, walks towards the iron gate, his hand outstretched.

'C'mon boy. Unless you're stayin the night.'

'Who?' I say.

'I've no seen him for ages.'

Alfred waves at Jenna. The same Alfred who threw Tessa out when he found out she was pregnant. Jenna runs ahead of her classmates and easily overtakes Owen in her excitement.

I call after her.

'Your mum's picking you up. Come back.'

It's like watching a boat slip its moorings, a rope uncoiling too quickly to catch. I see what's going to happen. A metallic thud rings out in the playground as Jenna runs full pelt into the gate. The impact knocks her off her feet.

Chapter 5

For a second I'm rooted to the spot; everything moves slowly.

'Jenna!'

I streak across the playground, crouch down and make myself a barrier against the rain. There's grit splattered across the side of her face, a dent on her forehead. Her eyes flutter open, her lips draw back and she realises a throaty, choking cry. I carry her into the foyer to the secretarial office. Alfred stumbles behind, holding his arms out as if he is transporting an invisible child. I see he must have been waiting outside for a long time because his clothes are drenched

Owen and his father also follow. They stand by the photocopier staring at Jenna. The school secretary, Cynthia Greenwood, activates a cold pack busily rustling it to and fro.

'Shouldn't take a moment. They're marvellous things once they get going, can even be a bit too cold. Best to wrap it in some paper towels. What a thing to do, eh Jenna?'

'Ran heed first intae the gate,' says Owen's father. 'Canno have seen it.'

'She didna see where she was going,' throws in Owen, staring at Jenna's forehead.

'It wasn't her fault,' I say. 'It was an accident.'

A quiet high runs round the room, the pinch of excitement that comes from an accident or a storm.

Jenna is pale, her cheeks grey-green, tiny pink blotches on her neck. A lump now stands out proudly in the centre of her forehead. It's like some embryonic Cyclops eye that could open at any moment. I feel sick at the sight of it, pathetic for not being more practical.

'She wis running tae me,' says Alfred. 'Ah've not seen her since her dad's funeral. Poor peedie wife. When's she going tae come up and visit? Eh, Christine? Cheust wanted to pick up the peedie lass from school. Whit's Tessa daen living with you? Why doesnae she come back home?'

'Alfred, if you could give us some space?' says Cynthia. 'That's it, to let some air through.'

He shuffles backwards. His cheeks are flushed, his eyes rheumy.

'She's me grandbairn. Ah've a right to see her. '

There's an electronic ting from my pocket. It's a call from Tessa. It's difficult to hear what she's saying over the background noise.

'Chrissy, I'm running late,' she says. 'Can you hold onto Jenna for ten minutes?'

I must tell her what has happened.

'Jenna's had a bump. In the playground, on the gate.'

'What's she done?'

'She might have to go to the Balfour.'

'Sorry, I canno hear. Say that again.'

Cynthia looks up from attending to Jenna. Clearly she is listening to the conversation.

'Oh, no. I shouldn't think she needs to go to the hospital, Christine,' she says. 'It's already swelling out nicely. I'm not allowed to have any arnica cream here, which is quite ridiculous, but you need to rub some on as soon as you get home. Maybe Tessa will have some? My mother used to rub on butter. Every time we'd have a knock she'd say "I'll get the butter." I couldn't bear it…so greasy…'

Her voice runs on as I explain what's happened to Tessa.

'She was running to your dad.'

'What's he doing there?'

'He wanted to pick her up. Do you want to speak to him? Did you know he was coming?'

'I've no idea what he's doing there.'

'Don't bother coming up here I'll bring Jenna back.'

'Sure you can manage?'

I say yes and end the call, my fingers clumsy from adrenaline.

All the while Alfred has his eyes hungrily on Jenna. His shoulders lean forward slightly towards her like an animal recently out of harness. Yet, there's something bewildered about him that I've not seen before.

'She wasn't knocked out at all was she?' says Cynthia. 'Keep an eye on her that's all. If she feels sick, or sleepy then take her to the doctor by all means, but there's no need to overreact.

Children are always banging their heads. I've seen far worse. Look, I'll stay with her while you collect your things – that is, I heard you were going to take her home. Now, now Jenna, you're over the worst of it. No need to start crying all over again.'

'Ah'll gae you a lift,' says Alfred. 'I can tak you.'

'Isn't that kind Christine?' says Cynthia.

I don't like the idea of being driven anywhere by Alfred.

'No, Alfred. Go back to the farm.'

He stares at Jenna as if he hasn't heard.

'Let me tak you,' says Irvine. 'Owen'll go in the back of the van, no bother.'

'I don't want a lift from anyone,' I say.

Cynthia darts a sharp look in my direction.

'I don't see why you would turn a lift down, Christine?'

'We'll walk. It's not far.'

As I step out of the door I can hear Cynthia apologising to Alfred and Irvine for my refusal of their offers in a tone that clearly implies I'm being unreasonable.

Back in the classroom, the desks are strewn with beads and wool, and half drawn pictures. I sling piles of books into a bag and grab my coat. The thought of Jenna's injury brings a sickly taste to the back of my throat.

Moira rises from her seat as she sees me pass by.

'Cheerio,' she calls.

I say nothing. My strides are swift, energy floods my limbs.

In the office, Jenna is holding the cool pack to her forehead, eyes fixed solemnly on Cynthia. She slides her feet to the floor when I enter, leaning for a moment on the seat. She blinks, re-focuses and then stands upright. Alfred is gone.

'The fresh air will make you feel better,' I say to her. 'You'll be all right.'

Jenna nods. I take her bag. The bump on her forehead is like a massive blister, growing before my eyes.

'I'd let you take the cold pack Christine, but we've lost so many lending them out,' says Cynthia, 'and you never know when someone might need it tomorrow. Children are always having accidents.'

Jenna shrugs and lets the blue pouch flop onto her hand.

'It's not the worst I've seen, Jenna. Although it is pretty bad.

See how it's bulging out, Christine? Coming out nicely now.'

'We've got to go,' I say.

I take Jenna's hand and we walk together down the steps and pass cautiously through the gate.

Indecisive streetlights flicker in the gloom. flashing neon pink light into upper rooms of houses lining the street. Starlings flit between gutter, windowsill and twig. I imagine Robbie holding Jenna's other hand.

She points out the tall ships in the harbour and the new white lines along Main Street.

'Do you think Mum'll give me a row?' she says.

'Not for a moment,' I say. 'It didn't happen on purpose.'

When we reach the gate I lift the latch and Jenna goes ahead. Her light footsteps ring between the garden wall and the side of the cottage, she strokes stones loose from the harling with her trailing hand and they patter softly to the ground.

When she sees Jenna, Tessa does not blanche. She kneels down and cuddles her tight, pressing their cheeks together.

'Oh, you poor peedie wife.'

'S'all right, Mum.'

'Let me see…poor peedie thing.'

Tessa reaches into her pocket and brings out a tube of cream.

'I ken it's sore but I'm still going to rub this on, sooner the better.'

Jenna squirms away and covers her forehead with one hand.

'Sure, it'll look better come the morn.'

Jenna moves her hand, and looks at her mother with clear sea-blue eyes. After she's rubbed on the cream Tessa surveys the injury again.

'Holy mackerel, it looks cheust like an egg,' she says.

The corners of Jenna's mouth turn upwards with a little glimmer of pride. Tessa

continues her inspection.

'I'm gaen to have to kiss it better. Hold still you little monkey.'

Jenna flinches, but she lets her mother kiss the bump. Tessa wraps her arms around her daughter. Jenna's whole body relaxes, fitting into the shape of Tessa's body. I have an inexcusable stab of jealousy.

I turn away from their embrace and reach for the kettle.

I want tea and a change of clothes. Tessa can take over now. Then I hear the sound of a man clearing his throat in the bathroom. It's a sound that has no place in the cottage. A sort of announcing of presence cough that could be followed by the sound of a zip-fly and a belt buckle.

My gaze now alights on several items that I hadn't noticed before. There's a giant tube of smarties on top of the fridge, a children's magazine on the table and a leather jacket hanging on the back of a kitchen chair.

'Who's here?' I say.

Jenna and Tessa separate.

'Where?' says Tessa.

'Who's in the bathroom?'

There's no flush, no sound of hand-washing. Tessa pulls a face, but she's got no choice except to reply.

'He arrived as I was coming in the door.'

Soon afterwards, Ronald steps into the corridor. His shadow stalks along the wall as he comes towards us.

I can tell he's making an effort not to smirk.

'Whit like?' He looks at me from under his dark eyebrows. 'Saw each other at the funeral didn't we Christine? Stepped oot together.'

'Did we?'

'Course you might not ken, being so cut-up aboot Robbie.'

He glances at Tessa, who doesn't seem to be paying attention to what he's saying. The smirk grows.

'Looks like you've had a spot of bother, Jenna,' he says.

Jenna's fingers are exploring the edges of the mound on her forehead.

'It was on the gate. Canna have some noo?' she says, pointing at the chocolates.

'If that's all right by your mum,' says Ronald. 'Your dad, ken he loved chocolate near as much as he loved beer.'

Tessa smiles

'Nearly.' she says, passing the packet down. 'Staying for a cuppa?'

Ronald catches my eye then reaches for his jacket.

'No. I'd better get back. Neil's fixing to shift the kye. Funny peedie hoose this, canno be much room. You ken Uncle Alfred wants you to come back to the farm, Tessa?'

'I'm fine stopping here.'

'Up to you. Think on it though. Christine might like a peedie bit o privacy noo and then.'

Ronald brushes against me as he walks to the door. A shiver runs across my shoulders. I have an urge to have it out with him, to tell him what I think of him. But I don't want to rock the boat with Tessa. Not today.

'Weel, noo I've found you, I'll drop in more often.'

He winks at me, lets himself out and is gone.

In the next room Jenna flicks on the television.

'He's no that bad,' says Tessa, noticing my expression.

'I've nothing against him.'

Tessa frowns.

'Come on, you've never liked him. It's good of him to drop round. I don't ken what Dad was doing at school, but it's nice to see some family once in a while. God, I'm sorry I was late. We were cheust fixing up Mhari's hair for this evening…I don't ken what happened to the time.'

I'm pouring milk into the cups when there's a shout from the living room.

'Mum, I feel sick…'

Apart from the blue bump on her forehead Jenna's face is very white. Tessa crouches by her side.

'You're boiling,' says Tessa.

'I'm going to be sick…'

'Did you eat *all* the chocolate?'

There is a deep gurgle from Jenna's throat. She leans forward and her head flops down. Tessa gently eases her backwards. Her skin is shiny and silver-grey, she doesn't move or speak.

Chapter 6

I hold out the basin and tea-towel I've brought through from the kitchen.

'Perhaps she's in shock,' I say. 'Maybe we should take her to the hospital? She wasn't knocked out…but…'

Tessa slides the basin under Jenna's chin and looks up at me.

'It's too much chocolate.'

'How can you be sure?'

'She can't help herself. Mind on the state she go' into at Anne and Brian's wedding?'

There is a moment of silence between us. Of course I remember.

'Ronald shouldn't have brought those chocolates,' I say.

'She needs a warm bath and a early night, not a doctor.'

'Are you sure?'

'I did use to manage without you.'

The comment is delivered sharply. All of a sudden it's not natural for me to be there, I'm not needed. I should leave them alone. She has a mothering instinct, a way of telling this is not serious that's alien to me.

These intimate moments between mother and daughter upset my temper; I know it's irrational because I love them both. I go back to the kitchen, the low comforting murmur of Tessa's voice still audible through door.

I pick up my mobile and call home, for distraction more than anything else. After one ring there's a click and the call goes to the extension in the gallery.

'Northshore Gallery.'

'Hi Dad. Busy?'

'Not really.'

'Sold anything?'

'Couple of woodcuts….and one of those old paper boats to a retired couple from East Oxford, a nice couple. How's school going? All settled in now?'

'Getting there. Jenna bumped her head on the gate at home

time – Alfred had come to meet her.'

'Alfred?'

'He wanted to take Jenna back with him to the farm.'

'Oh? Are he and Tessa on better terms?'

'No. He's just causing trouble,' I say. 'Ronald was here too and on about Alfred wanting Tessa to move back to the farm.'

'Jenna seen a doctor? Best to be on the safe side you know. Plenty of ice if you can get her to hold it on. I can come over if you want. I've pulled the sign in.'

'No. Tessa says she's okay. How's Lindsay?'

'All go today. Having a big sort out. She wants to re-vamp her room – make a fresh start. I keep going over to make sure she doesn't demolish the rest of the house. She's happy.' His voice is cheerful. 'That couple from Oxford knew the street backing onto the canal where we used to feed the ducks.'

'I don't remember,' I say.

'You know the bridge? We went nearly every day.'

'Oh, vaguely I suppose.'

'You do know how much Lindsay wants you here – Mum and I were sorry you moved out.'

'It's better like this. But Lindsay's okay isn't she?'

'Taking her pills and kept her appointment to see Doctor Carnegie yesterday. It's a shame he's retiring, but the investigation after the accident was very stressful. I think it made up his mind. Lindsay trusts him and you know...I don't know who'll take the position on after he goes.' There's a short pause. 'Your coming home scared her a little bit.'

'Why?'

'Well, that she got your attention.'

I don't reply. Whether she admits it or not Lindsay is responsible for the events that drove me to leave in the first place.

'I'll come over soon, okay?' I say.

'I'll tell Mum you called. You know she sends her love.'

I hang up feeling there was something else that my father wanted to say. Does he know I lie about remembering Oxford?

The smell from the overripe bananas in the fruit bowl catches sickly and sweet in the air. My head swims, overtaken by unexpected emotion at the memories of twenty years ago. The kitchen tiles sway and I have to clutch the counter to steady myself. Ronald's leering grin rises up at me from nowhere. The men in Tessa's family all seem to be bullies. They think people can be possessed, that they have no more right to decide what happens in their lives than a plough decides where it cuts.

Alfred used to say, 'It's fur your own guid,' to justify everything he decided. The big rent came and Tessa stopped believing him. It'd been coming for a while.

Chapter 7

The morning comes again. Moira stays outside with the children; even though she looks no better, I'm too exhausted to offer her a break.

My phone rings. Rather than Tessa it is my mother's picture that flashes onto the screen. It's not easy to find anywhere private, certainly not the staff room. I settle on the classroom.

Her voice gallops down the other end of the line, I can hear she's typing as she speaks.

'I'm off to Edinburgh tomorrow. Shall I stop by before I go? I can squeeze it in once I've the grant proposal sent off, which I'll do first thing. It's been a nightmare getting all the collaborators to send me their sections. Anyway, Dad said Alfred was at the school. He sounded concerned. Should he be? I think you should be careful.'

'About Jenna?'

'About Tessa's family.'

'I don't know what you're getting at, Mum. Anyhow, what's Lindsay up to?'

'She's fine. Don't worry about her. You've your own life to get on with.'

Her tone is condescending.

'Why're you being like this? Have I done something wrong?'

'I told Lindsay she'd be doing more good if she worked on your room…good grief is that the time? I've got Historic Scotland coming to look at our hole in the ground. Livingston this time, knows as much about the neolithic as your father. Listen darling, people… they can be very selfish at times.'

'Who? What are you getting at?'

'Give Jenna a kiss from me and tell Tessa not to worry. You fell into an exploratory trench when you were a toddler, thought you'd been abducted by tourists, but there you were, huge cut in the centre of your forehead, happily playing in a two thousand year old midden-pile.'

'Okay, thanks Mum.'

She ends the call. The school bell rings and play time is over. Hurriedly, I select Tessa's number. When she answers I can hear Jenna giggling in the background.

'You didn't get much sleep,' I say.

'Sorry. I was checking on Jenna. I mind on the doctor saying to check on her when she fell in the store room of the shop learning to walk. What people must have thowt when she was peedie, soon as one bruise healed she'd knock herself again.'

'I wanted to see how you were.'

'We're fine,' she says. 'It looks awful, but she's fine.'

The class rumbles into the room. The smell of puddles and the faint musk of incipient puberty comes with them. On the table in front of me something catches my eye.

'I have to go, see you later.'

'Cheerio,' says Tessa.

'Abby and Steven, is this your poster? What are these?'

'Tubes gaen to the bladder.'

'Really?'

Abby's cheeks flush. Her hair falls over her face.

'Steven did tha' bit,' she says. 'I thowt it looked a bit…'

'Do it again. You can work on it at break if you can't get it finished this morning.'

I scrutinize the remaining posters for 'accidental' representations.

To avoid the staff room I volunteer to take Moira's playground duty at lunchtime.

The leaves will not be on branches much longer. The few trees that grow here have turned from belligerent grey-green to wind-burnt brown . The street cleaners sweep up the fallen leaves with irritation, annoyed at their temerity to grow and their double temerity to fall. This leaf fall is nothing compared to places that *really* have trees – where they grow upwards rather than bent over like crabs trying to scrabble away from the wind.

The largest woodland glade in Orkney runs for no more than half a mile in a shallow cleft between two hills. In winter the empty branches barely conceal the flat sides of the worn away hills.

When we moved, I carried north memories of hedgerows that grew fast and dense in spring, country lanes full of scent and edible bounty that would mark the turn of summer and the arrival of autumn. They would not have withstood the battering of wind, salt and hail that pays no regard to season here.

My memories have fault lines, like the sloping slabs of granite that mark the edge of the land. There are incidents from before we moved that I don't want to remember : the time my mother burnt my father's paintings, the day there was a policeman in the living room, the day she locked herself in the bathroom and we had to go and tell a neighbour.

Remembering the streets is safer territory. Often they were lined with chestnut trees, their generous skirts providing shade in summer and a bounty of conkers in autumn. The houses sometimes had two, three or even four levels if you included the basement and attic. They had tall wide windows designed for letting in light rather than withstanding gales. Many were built of vibrant terracotta bricks with fancy coursing around the windows, others were grander made from large sandstone blocks. My mother would take us to the archaeology faculty behind the Pitt Rivers museum and we would have to wait patiently while she collected her papers and talked to colleagues. It was freezing and foggy much of the time and I remember stamping my feet to keep warm while we waited at pedestrian crossings.

The fields outside Oxford turned to water for months on end, bright blue against pea green fields, dotted with the white plumes of swans. I remember my mother being furious when I refused to walk through a puddle by the river. Mallard ducks escaping the current were making themselves at home on the water and I didn't believe we could make it across. The ducks became curious, quacking and bustling, they scooted towards me in a strange comical race that made me scared and want to laugh at the same time.

The ducks had squabbled around my red-wellied feet. Lindsay, older and taller, stood above the rubbery beaks and merrily scattered the remains of her snack, giggling at the riotous fray.

Dad took over caring for Lindsay and I when Mum went back to work. I can't remember a buggy or pushchair, maybe they were too feminine. It's definitely more acceptable now, even Orcadian men push prams up and down the snaking shop-lined street, doing their duty, passing the time of day.

We were expected to walk until truly tired and even then we could only be carried one at a time.

The pay-off for my mother's speculative collaborations, meetings, site visits, free advice and trips away was the chance to work in Orkney. We left Oxford behind and started again.

A voice jolts me out of memory.

'Heddle pushed me over.'

It's Lucy with Rosie again, her face red with tears.

'I don't think it's cut, but it looks sore. Go and get cleaned up,' I say. 'I'll speak to him.'

'We're no playin with him anymore,' says Rosie.

Lucy leads Rosie carefully away. Something is in the air. In the next half hour there are tears and recriminations between children who are usually fast friends.

The afternoon is taken up with assembly practice and passes quickly. On the way home I step into our nearby convenience shop, like the one Robbie's parents own, perhaps more down at heel. It sells everything from superglue to fake flowers. The lino is liver-red and engrained with dirt and it smells of bread and sausage rolls. The sight of the ice cream counter is surprisingly tempting despite the cold weather, but I leave carrying only a bottle of wine and a loaf of bread.

A tractor carrying round bales of winter fodder rumbles past as I reach the cottage gate. The driver turns his head. I recognise the open face, flat cheeks and bright eyes. Unhurried by the queue of traffic behind Neil raises his hand in acknowledgement. For a split second we make eye contact.

Despite the road noise I close the gate with care. The cottage is dark, no flickering blue in the living room window. I leave my shopping on the kitchen table and go through.

There's a pair of crumb-covered plates, a half-finished glass of milk and a mug of cold coffee on the floor. White paper cuttings are heaped on the arm of the sofa. On the cushions are chains of miniature figures holding hands, the folds creating the illusion of movement as I walk past.

I soften my footfalls. They are together, asleep beneath the quilt of the double bed, the shapes of their bodies echoing each other. In the deepening twilight I can still make out the contusion on Jenna's forehead. The lump is the same colour as a greening potato. Jenna had run her fingers over the bruise at breakfast time, exploring the changed dimensions of her forehead.

'A real egg, like Granddad said.'

I had to agree. It looked stuck on her forehead by a special effects department testing out designs for an extra-terrestrial.

I turn away from the bedroom. They're catching up from the physical tiredness caused by the emotional shock. I can understand, it was the same when Robbie died.

In the corridor the dimly lit glass panel catches my eye. I'm drawn towards it. It would clear the damp musty smell that's started to linger inside if I opened the window.

The handle is cold, rough from tiny splatters of white paint. I notice black spots of mould are bleeding through the whitewash by the bricked up doorway that once gave access to the main house.

Inside, the curtains are half drawn. I reach for the light switch. It's more beakish than those in the modern extension. The dim, environmentally friendly bulb reveals the leather sofa, patterned rug, glass coffee table, cheap bookcase and old bureau in the corner.

My shin scrapes the edge of the coffee table, the sharp itchy pain of broken skin making my senses keen. I step past the hearth to the deep set window above the bureau and force it open. The sea-salted air wafts into the room.

I notice that the grain of the bureau is deep and nutty. A rose and leaf motif is carved on the sloping cover and on each of the neat drawers. The four legs are spindly, colt-like beneath the boxy top half. They finish without flourish in a delicate taper and are embedded in the carpet. The key in the bureau lock turns easily.

Chapter 8

The hidden brass runners slide, there is a gentle bump as the ledge reaches horizontal. Sheets of paper shuffle and slide over each other until they rest in a heap like bleached autumn leaves. There would be no harm in straightening the papers out, making them tidy. If there was anything Tessa really didn't want me to see then she would have taken the key.

The letters on the top page crouch on the line, a row of neat curls, Tessa's handwriting. The letter is dated February twenty-fifth. The address of the flat above Robbie's parent's shop is written neatly in the corner as Mr Blakemore instructed us to do at school.

The barrier between reading and not reading is broken into small manageable transgressions. My gaze dives onto the page.

Hi Robbie,

> *Jenna's party went just fine. She's done a drawing of everyone eating cake. The boy with the large head and three legs is meant to be second-cousin Lenny – not a bad likeness if you ask me. She wrote her own name (squiggles at the bottom) and <u>loved</u> her princess castle, wanted to sleep in it last night.*
>
> *Mum came to the hall, didn't approve of buying the cake – but at least it was edible – not like anything I'd have made.*
>
> *I'm going out with Anne tonight celebrating her engagement to Brian. She wants the whole 'big wedding' deal and is already in a raffle.*
>
> *Your dad came up to the flat and gave Jenna <u>another</u> packet of sweeties. I expect the weather's just as bad on Flotta and nothing to do either.*

Did you get the DVD player working? I
can pick up a couple of films on special if you
like. Give us a call if you can get a chance.
Shame you weren't at the party. Jenna's
missing you.

Tessa

A small heart crosshatched with blue pen is drawn after her
name. There's a note at the bottom of the page.

PS Anne wants the wedding in summer. She'll
give me the date ASAP so you can book time
off. She plans to invite everyone she's ever
known (in her dreams if her father's paying!)
Sure, it'll be a good knees up though.

I put the letter to one side and look again at the pile
underneath. I tease out a card decorated with roses. My heart
flutters at the sight of the handwriting.

Sorry about the rugby Tessa. I won't ask
again. Rob x

I know straightaway what the note is about; tears prick in my
eyes and at the same time a laugh forms in my throat.

Tessa and I had pledged that should either of us have ever
ended up involved with a rugby player we would *never* make
lunch for the team. It was sexist – not to mention Tessa can't
cook to save her life, even sandwiches are a dubious affair. We
were fourteen at the time we took the pledge although Tessa
was easily passing for older. Robbie was already on the rugby
team when I left.

There is another letter in Robbie's hand, tidily printed capitals
with an occasional flamboyant 'T' whose top line overflies entire
words. I suppose he became quick at it. The paper looks the sort
put in a photocopier.

My back aches from standing – I could carry the letter over
to the sofa, but then it'd be no longer taking a quick glance. I

couldn't pretend to anyone I was tidying. It's odd, given Robbie is dead and Tessa is asleep in the next room that I experience a bigger prick of conscience before I read his letter rather than hers.

The note is a reply or near reply to Tessa's earlier letter.

> *Hi Tessa and BIG HI to Jenna,*
>
> *I don't suppose there's any birthday cake left? Tell Jenna I've put her drawing next to the one of the Christmas Tree. It looks great. I hope she likes the postcard.*
> *I'm not sure about getting more time off this summer. I thought we had plans to go away? Anne and Brian aren't going anywhere.*
> *I'm on the twelve-thirty boat.*
>
> *Rob*
>
> *PS Maybe we can go out when I get back. It's been ages.*

I remember Anne's invitation propped on my mantelpiece, with its gold embossed patterns and fancy lace edge. My name was formally printed inside with the details of the service at St Magnus Cathedral and the reception at the community hall. I pictured everybody there, all my old friends.

Among a crowd of so many people I'd calculated that it was unlikely I'd be pressed into speaking to Tessa or Robbie. By going I could keep my promise of visiting Lindsay. And why shouldn't I go?

From the note it sounded as if Robbie wasn't bothered about going to the wedding, that he was more interested in going away. I re-read the last line and wonder what it means. I'm still speculating when I realize I'm being watched.

Chapter 9

I'm exposed, as if a lighthouse lamp has me in its glare. The paper shivers in my hand. It feels unconscionably heavy.

'What do you think you're doing?'

'I came in to open the window…then I thought I'd straighten things up.'

'You cheust canno help it, Christine.'

'Help what?'

'You have to know everything.'

'That's not true. I was tidying.'

Tessa marches towards me, whips the letter from my fingers. She looks briefly at the writing then screws it up.

'Don't do that, Tessa.'

'Why? I don't want it anymore. What does it matter anyhow? People keep telling me that I'll move on.'

'It was only six weeks ago, Tessa. It's been a hard time for you. You must still be in shock.'

'Must I?'

Her face is pale, angular shadows fall across her skin. Her lips are bleached, faded to almost nothing.

'I should get rid of it aal,' she says.

'No.'

'Why not?'

'I should never have looked…please, don't throw it out. It's the handwriting…I recognized the handwriting.'

'Perhaps I'll have a fire,' she says. 'Then nobody can read them.'

Tessa throws the screwed up ball of paper into the empty grate. I picture her scooping up the letters and throwing them onto a fire. It's the kind of thing she'd do.

'What about Jenna? You should at least keep something for her,' I say.

My voice strains, plaintive.

Tessa doesn't notice. She's not listening to me. She scans the muddle of papers and cards, like giant confetti sprinkled on the bureau. Maybe it's because she knows I'm suffering and wants to prolong it, or perhaps she's undecided about what to do. The more time passes the more difficult it is to resist the temptation to look at the letters even though she's right next to me.

'Shite,' she says. 'Robbie wouldn't have cared. What am I getting so worked up for?'

Her taut anger collapses, her hands flop limply and she half-heartedly shuffles the papers around then pushes the bureau flap. There's the hollow slide of the hinge, the dirty metallic smell of brass.

It's harder on the heart, seeing her like this.

'Don't do it again,' she says. 'Who minds if it's a mess? Nobody comes in here anyway. Too bloody cold for one thing.'

She doesn't even bother to push the bureau properly closed before walking away. I'm left alone in the room.

I follow her, my gaze fixed on the carpet, shamed.

Tessa pads down the corridor. Grey sweat pants and zip-up hoody hang limply around her slim body.

'Where's Jenna?'

'Playing on me phone. She's definitely gaen to school tomorrow.'

Tessa stares at the oven door, twiddling a fork between her fingers puzzling over the temperature dial, excluding me from her thoughts, her eyes dark and limpid. I think she hates me.

Jenna is fed fish fingers and put to bed early. As I wipe down the kitchen table before starting marking there is the muffled whoosh from the boiler as the shower starts running. I imagine the floral scent of her shampoo, an antidote to the smell of fish and burnt crumb.

When the bathroom door opens my attention is on the jotters. I hear the hair dryer and presume that when I see Tessa she'll be in her pyjamas. I'm half way though marking a comprehension on blood when there are footsteps in the living room.

'Thowt you'd be working. I'm gaen oot.'

'Out?'

'You don't mind?'

'Yes. I mean no, I've got loads to do.'

'Jenna's asleep. I looked in.'

'Are those new?'

'No, I've not worn them much. They're a bit small.'

Her trousers are tight rather than small, wrinkling at the seams.

'Where are you going? Meeting someone?'

'No plans. I cheust need a night oot,' she says.

Tessa adjusts the edge of her top, creamy shoulders peep over the tightly stretched black fabric. She doesn't want to talk to me. She wants to go out.

When we were teenagers my outfits were never as striking as what Tessa put together. Tonight, I look a generation older than my school friend.

'When will you be back?' I say.

'Not sure. I'll bed doon on the sofa if it's late.'

'Don't worry about waking me.'

'You've got work,' she says, opening the door. 'All I do is cut hair.'

She's gone before I've a chance to reply. Tears well up. Why did she have to go out? Why can't we have a proper argument without the past hanging over us? What does she want from me?

My tears reabsorb, and I carry on working through the pile of books. The blue-lined jotters diminish and are replaced by ones with orange covers and squared paper. Marking columns of numbers requires less attention and signals permission for wine.

I check on Jenna, she's breathing easily, both arms lying flat out above her head as if she is floating downstream. In the kitchen I pour wine. It is bitter-sweet, with the colour and taste of blackberries. Blackberries don't grow on Orkney. One of those weedy side-of-the-road species you take for granted, but it's missing here.

I switch off the main lights and mark by the lamp on the table adding red ticks, squiggles and question marks. Those who do not work tidily are already unlikely to change.

I drink the remains of the glass and mark with more of a flourish, my mind becoming occupied with memories of moving up to secondary school rather than the work in front of me.

Tessa came into her own at the grammar school, joining groups quickly, adapting her speech and posture to mimic the older children. After the first week I was surprised by the number of children who'd stop to speak to her, or acknowledge her in some way, whereas I still felt as if I knew nobody at all.

I scrub out a score and take away a mark. My final tick is nearly a half the length of a page. At the bottom of the empty glass black flecks gather in a tight circle in a small burgundy pool. I push back from the table and seek out the remnants of the bottle on the kitchen counter.

Tessa rarely drinks wine, she reverts to sweet fizzy alcoholic bottles on a night out. She didn't have alcohol at home when she was a child. My parents have offered me half glasses of wine and sips of beer since I can remember. Boxes of wine and beer were stacked under the stairs until Lindsay proved herself untrustworthy again and again. It didn't stop her drinking – as long as you knew someone who drove there were certain places in west mainland where you were always guaranteed a drink, never mind being underage. There used to be 'Thirsty Thursday,' in The Catcher, a pint and a half for the price of a pint, but it's definitely more of a coffee place now, trying to shake off its image. There's only one place that can really be called a club, 'Blend' . It's been re-furnished, but remains the same place in spirit, slow service at the bar and the whole place reeks. Close to nothing happens every night in Kirkwall.

My head swims. I should eat something but the smell of Jenna's singed dinner has ruined my appetite. Instead, I pour more wine. There's something slovenly about marking with the bottle sitting on the table. It makes me think of Mr Yorick who taught us geography at grammar school and smelt increasingly of beer as the term went on.

The next comprehension is abysmal, barely a correctly spelt word or properly punctuated sentence. Donald Donaldson, writing's not his thing. His thing is birds; bird watching, bird shooting, sea birds, bird eggs, geese, geese migration, bird feeding, bird diseases, anything that relates to birds and he has a story to tell you as long as you don't ask him to write it down.

When I reach the last book I glance outside. I'm sure there's a shape that wasn't there before, a shoulder amongst the mass of twigs and leaves of the fuchsia. I look harder, squinting into the dark. Surely, the lump must have always been there. Something makes me feel uneasy.

I pile everything up, refill my glass again then stroll into the living room. I curl up in the partially dismantled nest where Jenna and Tessa have spent the day. A green felt-tip has been resting on a cushion leaving behind a ragged inkblot. I flick on the regional news '…in broad daylight, only yards from his front door…' I don't want to hear any more, but watch anyway and wonder why an attack is more awful for being close to home. Homes are dangerous places.

There is a draught shooting under the door to the kitchen. I pull up Jenna's discarded blanket to cover my knees.

The local and national weather bulletins give different forecasts for the weekend. Low pressure systems coming from over the Atlantic, dumping rain on the Western Isles then the swinging, coiling tails sweeping over Orkney and corkscrewing northwards to Shetland.

The next programme offers dispiriting political discussion. Soon, I become aware of something knocking, vibrating with a dull persistent rattle.

I check the windows in the room Tessa and I share. Clothes are slewed across the end of the bed. I pick up a bottle of her fragrance and absentmindedly sniff the nozzle. I have a flash of empathy with my sister, of how she can be over taken by the world around her, led by instincts. I seem to be becoming more susceptible to these feelings. I drop the bottle quickly back on the bed.

In Jenna's room she has thrown off her blanket and changed pose from floating to studiously holding her chin. I replace the cover, tucking in the far edge. At least her bump is more rounded now, rather than some strange vertical eruption.

The rattling is louder further down the corridor. The door of the cold room is knocking against its frame. The contours of the Michaelmas daisies etched into the glass door pane gather the light into curved slivers. The glass vibrates beneath my fingertips.

I stand, my mind blank for several moments without doing anything then remember I need to close the window. I didn't promise that I wouldn't go in.

There's resistance then the wind tugs the door open. The air inside is making a violent circuit of the room. I grope forward and catch hold of the swinging window latch.

Tessa must be mad. Who'd want to be outside tonight? She was always doing crazy things, always the last one to pack anything in and go home. The wind whistles shrilly as I pull the window closed, whooping in protest until the catch is down.

Papers have been dislodged from the bureau, others balance precariously, about to fall. If Tessa sees them she might think I've been in here again.

Using the streetlight to see I gently rearrange the overhanging sheets. My heart beats quickly. There is a page of Robbie's writing, no date at the top and no signature at the end. I lift the sheet and tilt it towards the window to see more clearly.

My mouth is dry. I want to know everything, collecting new facts like cuts made close by one another. If I could I'd go back and watch, I would watch.

Chapter 10

The upper case lettering is easy to read but still I read some sections several times.

> *...Jenna should see more. The boss'll give me a decent reference if I want it. The hands on stuff's no bother — engine & all the gear — and I'll get my head around health and safety regs soon enough. There's plenty on the oil platforms I could turn my hand to.*
>
> *There'd be theatre things in a city, you can get Jenna to a childminder and do something different with yourself. Some people enjoy being south. Can we speak about it without a row, just because you've never been...*

I reach the end of the page and scan the desk for more of Robbie's writing, anything to ease the disappointment of stopping reading mid-flow.

Again it's only a single sheet.

> *...no point coming to see a load of men yawning, smoking and waiting to get on a boat.*
>
> *I don't much think about it, but the big oil tanks can give you a funny feeling. Like you said, if it ever went up — and I shouldn't say this — we couldn't do much about it, not half a dozen of us, not anyone. The bunds are meant to stop oil leaking away and there's direct pumps into the tanks, but until it's happened you don't know if it's all going to work. I couldn't live here.*
>
> *There's a emergency drill next week. The Flotta folk get all made up with blood and*

burns – and get a chance to nose round the place. We're on triage duty while the boss puts his feet up in the emergency control room and makes pretend phone calls with the other bosses.

I'm getting used to being here – catering's okay, rec. room's depressing – nothing but a telly and a few chairs. No mobiles allowed out of the accommodation because of spark risk. It's not worth mucking about, since we'll be putting out the fire.

Deploying air monitors this afternoon, then out to the helipad. Not much else. Give peedie lass a kiss and tell her thanks for the new picture…

A loop of nylon cord slips out from the pile. The words Flotta Fire Service are printed across the top. There's a photograph beneath the laminated cover, passport style on a white background. I tilt it to see better.

He's looking me straight in the eye, his cheeks flushed. The image is so alive – Robbie, about to say something that will make me laugh. I run my finger over the top of it, tempted to bring it to my lips.

I'm taken back to a particular moment years ago. Tessa and I were at the sports centre making decisions at the vending machine. I was thinking salt and vinegar crisps followed by a Topic, Tessa was undecided on spicy Monster Munch or a packet of Polos.

'I want crisps, but Polos'll last longer,' she'd said.

'I'll give you a bite of my Topic if you give me a Polo.'

'All right.'

She pressed the stubby black buttons, the machine whirred then the grey spiral turned and dropped the desired items. Robbie, wearing a bright purple football strip, squirmed between us and the machine. His hand dived inside the flap.

'Gae it back, Robbie!'

'Finders keepers,' he said.

'They're mine.'

Tessa stamped her foot, grabbed his shirt and reached for his backwards stretched hand. Most of the boys were still struggling to get on level terms with the girls height wise, but Robbie was tall. He was already half a foot taller than Tessa, a couple of inches taller than me.

'You wanting these?'

'Give 'em back to her,' I said.

'You saw me put the money in,' said Tessa.

He jinked around, pleased with himself. While he's got his eye on Tessa, I'd snatched at his raised right hand, hot and satisfied as I'd taken back the crinkly packages. Tessa and I had turned and run.

'You're a bugger Robert Muir, a real bugger!' shouted Tessa at the top of her voice.

We skipped away, waving our sweeties. Robbie grinned like a monkey, not bothered about following us and stayed at the machine searching his silky nylon shorts for money.

A shout from outside brings me back to the present. 'Come on, beuy!' is followed by other loud voices that fade into jocular conversation. A can being kicked along the pavement ricochets off our wall. There's no tapping of high heels.

I calculate how to close the desk and leave the room without being discovered if I hear the back door open. If Tessa looks through the living room from the kitchen she'll see right down the corridor, so I will have to be quick.

My fingers return to the bureau. I find a short note dated two years ago, this time in Tessa's writing.

> *I was having a dance and got carried away. I thought you'd gone for a chippy and were off back to the flat. You know what Tommy's like, and he knows he was out of line. You've got to be crazy to think anything really went on between us. I don't often get a night out. It won't happen again. I told Jenna you had to go back to work early, but she's confused. She expected you home for the whole weekend. Come back to the flat.*

My heart pounds. I don't know anything about the incident, but I know Tommy.

When he was younger Tommy had bright red hair, he had freckled skin too – not peely-wally though like most of the lads, he always looked like he'd been outside. By the end of grammar school he'd lost his boyishness, grown square-jawed and if you hadn't put up with him for a decade you might think he wasn't bad looking. Even his hair was less red.

Tommy's face was gaunt and grey at the funeral, even his hair looked grey – but you'd expect that after what he'd been through.

Tessa's name at the end of the note is written in looping letters, flamboyantly underlined with a large 'x'. There are tiny shadows where the paper has been indented from the pen being pressed so hard.

It must have done the trick. Robbie wouldn't have wanted to be separated from his daughter. The few times I saw them together I could see he loved Jenna.

The shadows seem to move slightly, I'm drowsy and crave another glass of wine, yet the thought of more alcohol is repellent at the same time. Getting a drink would also mean leaving the room. At the moment, I'm still here by accident; happening to glance at the leaves of paper before they are tidied away.

It must be the back of eleven by now. Kirkwall, midweek in the rain, there can't be anything to do.

What are you doing Tessa? Who are you with?

A leaf of paper different to the rest catches my eye. I pick it out with finger and thumb. The handwriting is different with an old-fashionedness that is out of place with the other letters. The strokes are light, hardly making a mark in places.

The letter is to Tessa from Marion, her mother.

In character and appearance Tessa and Marion are opposite to each other. Marion's dark curly hair is always pinned up in a bun, buoyant strands escaping around her ears. Her features cluster together timidly in the centre of her face. She already had the appearance of a grandmother when she was in her thirties and she still wears the same collared shirts, plain sweaters and knee-length skirts with knitted tights that she always has done.

Her mother's clothes perhaps inspired Tessa's outlandish fashion sense. I find it hard to fathom that Marion's only a handful of years older than my mother.

'She hates living here,' Tessa told me once. 'Hasn't got a proper driving license even. Not that it matters unless the traffic police come on the ferry. She's always wanted to go back to Westray – there's still land that could be farmed. But Dad'd never go with her, sour-faced about the fare even when we go over in the summer.'

The date in the corner of the page is three years old. The letter begins *I always wanted to speak to you the night before your wedding. I imagined you'd still be at home…* I squint, adjust the angle of the paper and read on.

> *… I never thought it would be hard to see you, but that's you away for nearly two years. Sometimes I don't ken you well at all these days. I can't help thinking you're still a teenager away having a adventure rather than with a bairn of your own. She's a fine peedie thing.*
>
> *I'm not used to talking about myself, so I'm penning it down for you. Sorry if I should have told you more about myself before, but nothing's a secret that's happened.*
>
> *My life was set before me as soon as I was on the boat from Westray. Your father, he'd followed me back from the county show to Westray, stayed for three days and wouldn't let me out of his sight until I said yes. There wasn't any choice after that. He brought me back to his mother's farm, for his father had already died.*
>
> *I'd no experience, no way of knowing that I could have said no. That there was no <u>need</u> to marry him because he came after me.*
>
> *I thought myself lucky to have a jealous man – my friends had done nothing but grouse*

*about the other type. 'A jealous man doesn't
stray' they'd say. I knew what I was getting.*

*So I followed him, glad at the thought of
being a farmer's wife. But his mother was
always the farmer's wife right up to the day she
died.*

*Even standing at the kirk ready to marry
your father I was terribly homesick. It was a
fine day, sky bright and clear, the sun warming
the skin of the land.*

*I'd hoped I'd be happier on the farm as time
went on, but I wasn't – even after having you.
And you were the best thing.*

*Your granny couldn't bear you greeting, said
she couldn't bide hearing any baby cry. Sure,
she never took to you as she did Neil and
Ronald – she spoiled Ronald something rotten
and he's turning out worse for it.*

The letter continues overleaf, the script leaning backwards, its
hanging tails overlapping the tall strokes in the line beneath.

*She told us we'd be better off by ourselves
after you were born. The Byre was hardly fit to
live in back them – what a raffle it was, no
proper heating, half-fitted windows.*

*I folded your blankets and toys into the baby
bath. In a few trips I'd carried everything over
and then tucked you into your basket. It was a
new thing, the one thing I told your father I
couldn't do without and that had to be newly
made.*

*We were in sight of the farmhouse, but he
missed being there badly, it was something he
dwelled on a great deal. Even after we moved
to The Byre, every morning he still crossed the
yard to have breakfast in his mother's kitchen.
I made light of it when you were young, but you*

should know it made my life so very lonely that he kept to her table.

Alfred caught and married me without asking her approval. She never forgave him that. It was the one thing he'd ever done by himself.

He was never away at sea or working for anyone else. He was here, but not here, always working on the farm. I kept you indoors as much as I could, I didn't want you roaming with your coarse cousins. I wanted to press you in a book like a flower, to keep you how you were. But you found ways to escape.

Your father'd do anything to make you happy. But he's a jealous man, that's his nature. God, don't I know it. He can't stand the thought of what you've done. All the shotgun waving nonsense and throwing my mother's clock, all that was because he loved you.

I've seen temper from my father — it's one thing I was glad to get away from — I can see it coming, but they never mean to hurt you.

I can't tell you how much I miss you and the peedie lass. I stand at the top of the brae looking over the water and I want to hold her the same I held you.

Some days the few miles over the causeways feel like the other side of the world all because I don't damn well drive.

I'll do my best to persuade your own father to be there tomorrow — it'll be the first time he does anything I ask him. There never was any standing up to the man. I'll do my damnedest to be there.

You and peedie Jenna are always in my mind. And Robbie looks like a fine father. Good luck. Maybe as time goes on we'll get to see each other more. Mumxx

The letter ends abruptly as if Marion was interrupted. I'd never thought of her as a person, how she came to be at the farm doing the things she did.

What would Tessa have thought of the letter? Can explaining the past excuse what is happening in the present? Tessa used to care for her father's approval as a girl, but it's all changed. Their relationship was always close, coddling when she was younger. She never saw anything bad in him at all then all of a sudden she saw everything, and all the good was gone.

Along the corridor Jenna coughs in her sleep, a dry tickle caused by dust on the oil heater. A gust of wind diverts rain onto the windowpane.

My thoughts drift, I think about my own mother and father. It wasn't really economic logic or feminist principals that drove my mother back to full-time work. It was what she wanted to do. Sometimes I wonder if she would have been happier without us, that we took more than we gave.

Tears gather in my eyes, my vision blurs and the room distorts; drops roll down my cheeks. This isn't the past that I want to think about. I try to refocus and replace the letter. I should leave; whatever I'm searching for, I'm not going to find it here.

An envelope addressed to Mr and Mrs Muir slips to the floor, inside there is a card.

Chapter 11

Outwardly, it's nothing special, two balloons tied with white ribbon. A simple design on lightweight card.

Reading a card is nothing really compared to a letter. After all, it's meant for display, often impersonal and marking an occasion more out of duty than anything else.

'*To Tessa and Rob, Congratulations On your Wedding Day. Best of Luck in the future. Tommy.*' His name is underlined diagonally, with a tweak at the lower end that forms the shape of a question mark. It seems deliberately overstated this line, cocky somehow.

Everyone who was invited would have sent a card. Even I sent one.

There's no other cards in the bureau. Why has Tessa kept this one?

I remember my parents bringing my invitation down to me on one of their visits south. I was in my second year at university, renting a room in a red brick terrace in Guildford backing onto the A3. The tide of cars rolled past. Grey ceaseless noise became an internal rhythm of my day and night. I'd not been back to Orkney and had no plans to return. I'd become used to the close horizons where trees saluted over the roads and marauded thickly over the hillsides.

The invitation to the wedding, so solid and definite: the date, the time and the place, sat sandwiched between textbooks on my bedside table. Before they left my father recommended I send a card, even if I didn't attend. He'd brushed a loose hair from my shoulder and smiled.

'Course she'll attend,' interrupted my mother. 'They're best friends.'

'No,' I said. 'Dad's right. I won't go.'

After they'd left I trekked over the railway bridge, past the river and across lanes of traffic to the ugly maroon brick shopping centre. It was airy, bright and metallic inside, a consumer cathedral. I went into the biggest card shop with fluffy white bears and balloons in the window. Inside, after

'Sympathy', 'Get Well Soon' and 'Special Birthdays' there was a section devoted to 'Weddings.'

It was the first time I'd bought a wedding card: champagne and roses, bride and groom on a cake; they were all so crass. Surely Tessa and Robbie wouldn't have a plastic couple on top of the cake? They'd have to have a toddler in a buggy as well. You see, I'm not above being cruel.

I wanted to send a photo of a drunk Saturday night huddle wending its way home from the extortionate clubs. That's what I spent my time doing – and smoking. I'd taken up smoking in the evenings. I was something of a novelty because of where I'd come from, I was different, but not too different. Without Tessa by my side I'd changed; I'd become a bit more like her.

In the end I chose a card with a close-up photograph of two hands interlocked. Not laid over each other like in wedding ceremony, but holding hands like you would walking on a beach. They could have been anybody's hands.

The tap, tap of high heels brings me back to the present.

Quickly, I slot the card back between the letters. The contents of the bureau looks too organized, as if someone has been picking up and putting down items with care. I waft my fingers over the top to create a more jumbled effect.

The gate squeaks. A murmur of voices reaches my ear. Tessa laughs, her heel scrapes then the gate clashes shut. A few seconds later a shadow falls across the window. When it is gone I whip the curtain closed, plunging the room into darkness. My movements are awkward from being still so long, but I'm out of the room long before Tessa fits her key in the lock of the back door.

There's a bitter aftertaste of wine in the back of my mouth, my skin is clammy after the exertion. Yet the relief that my trespass is undiscovered swiftly turns to bad temper. I go into the bathroom and squeeze a too large blob of paste onto my brush and wish I had simply gone to bed. Between brushing I hear Tessa talking to herself in the kitchen.

'Gee-whizz,' she says. 'Glass o water, glass… okay…water.'

There's a whoosh from the tap. A glass knocks against the counter.

'Steady noo. Take a breath…water.'

I rub a flannel over my face then step into the corridor.

'Still up?' says Tessa, tilted glass in hand.

I flip my watch off and produce a yawn.

'Watched a film,' I say. 'Have a good night?'

'No' bad.'

'Meet anybody?'

'Canno keep up any more. No used to it.'

'Cuppa?'

'No. Yes...don't...I'll do it. Go to bed. No, wait is Jenna okay?'

'Not a peep.'

'That's fine...tol you she wis...hold on... a minute. Gotta get some fresh air.'

She fumbles the latch briefly then opens the window. She crooks her body at the waist and leans on the windowsill then folds her arms to make a pillow and turns her face to the night air. She hiccoughs loudly.

'I'm fine...thanks for...for takin care of peedie wife.'

Other times I'd have made her tea, stayed up to talk. Tonight, I want to fall asleep without her by my side.

In the bedroom I hear the remote fall and the lamp jitter. The TV comes on loud then quietens. I shut the door and block out the sound then switch off the light.

The strange deflated sensation returns. I puzzle over phrases from the letters. The block capitals of Robbie's writing dances inside my eyelids. I lie with my eyes open, staring at the orange cut in the curtain.

Were you happy Robbie? Did you love her?

I'm still awake when Tessa comes in. But almost as if her presence flips a switch I fall asleep before she's removed her make-up and clambered under the duvet.

Chapter 12

The next morning Jenna returns to school. The disfiguring bump rapidly transforms from an embarrassing source of sympathy from adults to a badge of honour among her friends.

In the staffroom at morning break I receive a text from Tessa.

'Thanx for coffee. Hangover no too bad. Will make dinner, T.'

Cynthia peers over my shoulder.

'How's that little niece of yours?'

'Niece?'

'Oh sorry, I forget you're not related, it's just with you and Tessa living together.'

'Jenna's back to her usual self,' I say.

'My sister-in-law saw her and said it looked as if someone had knocked her on the forehead with a hammer. She was always covered in bruises when she was a toddler, but you wouldn't have seen her then, would you? Who'd have thought a gate could leave such a mark? She's a delicate thing isn't she? Mind you, there's not much to Tessa – not like you, Christine.'

'What do you mean?'

'Well, there's a bit of something to you. Tessa's always wearing those tight black clothes, you'd hardly see her if she stood sideways. Is that her uniform? I mean, does she have to dress like that?'

'What?'

'Being a hairdresser. I always think wearing black makes dyed hair look very unnatural. Agnes always does my highlights, she's very careful. One thick heavy shade can be so unflattering. I mean, do you ever think of a change?'

'No.'

'I suppose Tessa could do it for you easily. I expect she'd be happy to and no inconvenience to do it at home.'

Cynthia pauses and waits for a reply. I need an excuse to leave.

'There's a coat up on the scrap store roof,' I say.

'Where? No, I think your mistaken, Christine I don't see any...'

'There's something up there.'

I'm out of my seat and heading past the noticeboard before she has time to say any more. I'm not hungover, but not quite right. I have to slow down when I'm out of the door to catch my breath while some dizziness passes. The staffroom door opens behind me.

'Christine,' calls Cynthia. 'I really don't think there's any need to go out.'

'I'd best be going back to class anyway.'

Cynthia is not deterred.

'I thought it was nice of Alfred to make such a fuss of her this morning,' she says.

I stop and turn.

'A fuss?'

'Didn't you see him? I thought Tessa was a bit ungrateful personally, shooing him away like that. All he wanted to do was give over a bag of sweeties.'

I don't reply and resume walking.

Once around the corner I pause again by the 'How to Care for Our Planet' display and collect my thoughts. There's cut out pictures of lions in a cage juxtaposed with a view of open savannah with a lioness contentedly resting her paws on a kill.

'Feeling okay, Christine?'

'Oh, Moira. I'm fine, just admiring your art work.'

She smiles and begins to speak but is overtaken by a coughing fit. Her eyes water.

'How are *you* feeling?'

'Better today, thank you. So many bugs aboot.'

She raises her handkerchief then weaves towards the entrance of the female staff toilet.

Alone in the silence before the bell, I stare at the lions on the poster and wonder what Robbie thought of Alfred. He never would have stayed at The Byre, maybe once or twice in the farmhouse because he was pals with Ronald. Alfred did not like many people. In fact, begrudged silence was the closest he came to approval of anything whether it was winning first place at the County Show to Tessa getting the lead in *Grease*.

There were plenty of occasions when I slept over at The Byre and in return Tessa would come and stay at Northshore. At these times I became most embarrassed of Lindsay's erratic behaviour. It didn't matter if she was high or low; she always made herself the centre of attention.

Once, Tessa had come around for tea before a play rehearsal – we must have been eleven or twelve at the time, Lindsay would have been fourteen. There'd been a terrible scene. We'd been dropped off by the bus outside the studio. It was still a building site back then. Mum was away at a conference and there was no sign of Dad. It was early spring and light enough to play outside before tea. We'd started running around the house holding our coats open over our heads to catch the wind then I'd found a couple of tennis balls in the old plant pots and we counted how many bounces we could catch off the kitchen wall.

Lindsay arrived on the grammar school bus while we were mid-game. She shrugged off her bag and coat and began leaping up and down in front of us. She'd squealed, 'Can't get me! Can't get me-e!' Over and over again.

I ignored her. Tessa followed my lead.

'Come on, get me. What's your problem?'

She started to pinch us, nipping wherever she could. Small mean pinches that dug in, her fingers closed tight enough to leave a bruise.

Tessa bent sideways in pain as she was caught in the side. She appealed to me with her eyes.

'Leave us alone, Lindsay,' I'd said.

'Lea–ve us alo–ne,' she chanted, skipping around us.

We put our backs together so at least our bottoms were protected and we could see her coming, guarding each other as best we could, slapping her hands away. Sharp laughter shot from Lindsay's mouth, she let out a goose-like whoop every time she was slapped or successfully landed a pinch.

'Oieee!' she'd grinned. 'C'mon get me! Can't get me-e!'

Lindsay's taunting grew wilder, now accompanied by a weird prancing dance.

'Oieee! Does it hurt? Can't get me-e.'

She landed a pinch on my forearm. It smarted enough to bring tears to my eyes. I hated her when she acted like this, especially in front of Tessa. I grabbed a loose crock from a broken pot and hurled it towards her.

'Stop it Lindsay! Stop it!'

She bent down, gathered up the tennis balls we'd been playing with, drew back her arm and with exceptional strength flung them towards us. The first hit my chest, the second struck Tessa's cheek bone, leaving a livid red blotch. Tessa clasped her hands to her face.

'You see…you see what you make me do? Little bitches! Not letting me join in. Pair of f-u-c-k-i-n-g scrubbers, scrubbers!'

She'd shifted her balance then surged forwards, fingers outstretched. I grabbed her wrists and held them at bay while she started to kick out, jerking, scratching and swearing. Tessa began to scream for help.

The attack couldn't have lasted more than a few seconds before Dad rushed out of the door.

'Lindsay! Stop!' He threw his arms around her. 'Stop it now. What is all this?' He pinned her arms against her squirming body. 'Stop…okay? Stop. Come away.'

He held her, absorbed her blows. When she realised he would not let her go her fists uncurled and hung limply at her side, her knees buckled. Dad lowered her to the ground.

Lindsay started sobbing.

'Dad, Dad…she…'

He patted the back of Lindsay's head while she buried her face into his chest. She pointed an accusatory finger at Tessa, garbling nonsense into Dad's sweater.

'Everything's okay,' he said.

I held up my arm showing him the scratches.

'Look what she's done and…Oh my God, Tessa, you're going to have a black eye.'

'She's going to need an ice-pack,' he'd said. 'That'll stop it coming out so bad. I'll explain to Alfred. Come inside and get yourselves a snack. Christine, pick up Lindsay's things.'

It was cold now, everything was grimy and dull, the thrill of the high wind was gone. I trailed Lindsay's bag and coat along the ground. Dad led her upstairs. A few minutes later he returned.

The orbital of Tessa's eye was pink and swollen and not much reduced by the bag of frozen peas. Above, the ceiling creaked as Lindsay moved around in her room, radio noise beginning to filter through the floorboards.

The rehearsal was dull. No one except Tessa knew their lines. The drama teacher responded by taking away everyone's scripts and making us tediously repeat after her anything we couldn't remember. Any time we were not on stage was spent chewing over strategies for bleaching Tessa's hair for the show. Even though she was a blond already she was determined to look perfect.

By the time Dad picked us up we were weary. The green-grey horizon rose and fell like the sea as the car swung towards the barriers. It was low tide and masts of the sunken blockships that had once ferried the concrete cubes that topped the causeways stood out of the water. Greylag geese crowded together in the fields, cropping the new shoots needed by the pregnant ewes. Hands of daffodil leaves shivered at the foot of the stone dykes.

Dad drove past the abandoned farmhouse. Old iron letters spelled out 'The Blackhouse' on the cracked wall by the front door. Few slates remained on the roof, the windows were blank apart from the branches of the sickly sycamores that had taken root inside. Tessa already had a fantasy about renovating the building. She told me how she would have a wall of glass looking down onto St Mary's Bay.

The current farmhouse hunkered down into the land protected by the natural dip between two hills. There were changes happening on the farm.

Tessa's granny had died at the turn of the year. She'd taken a store of knowledge with her – homemade recipes to poison leatherjackets, diarrhoea cures for calves brought home from the Mart. She'd collect moss then boil it up in a great vat on a fire outside. The mossy soup was poured into a cloth tied over a big funnel to fill plastic bottles onto which she'd push red teats and go round dosing every calf. If they shied away she'd put a firm hand under their chin give the bottle a squeeze and make it shoot down their throats.

Tessa wanted to please her granny, but she favoured the boys, Ronald in particular. Neil helped with the kye; Ronald did as he pleased. After her granny died Tessa's uncle Owen invested in a new combine and earned money doing contract work, something that had never happened before.

Gravel chips and sand were heaped in the farmyard. Inside the barn there were lengths of timber for the extension. A structure made of second hand windows and corrugated iron where Tessa's mother grew tomatoes and cucumbers was soon to be demolished to make way for the new building. Tessa cried the day they pulled it down even though it was nothing but junk with a few dried up old pots, because Marion gave up on her plants as soon as she knew it was to be levelled. It had been a rare place of earthy smells and warmth, and I think the only place where Tessa's mother enjoyed working on the farm.

Dad pulled in next to the three-quarters empty shelter for winter fodder. For a moment he remained holding the wheel staring at the empty yard. Not that I think he was afraid of Alfred, but he was cautious and he didn't want Tessa to take any blame for what had happened. In the passenger seat Lindsay sat biting her fingernails.

'I didn't mean it,' she said. 'I went a bit mad.'

'It doesn't matter,' he'd said.

Time had passed, we had all cooled down.

'God, I was awful. I know I was. I had a crap day at school, everyone on at me. But you must have said something. You must have done something.'

'Nothing.'

'I wouldn't just do that for no reason. Will you get in trouble Tessa? I hope you don't. It'll be my fault. I'll make it up to you.'

'He'll never let her come round,' I said. 'She'll be the first Sandy in Grease with a black eye.'

'I was miscast anyway,' said Tessa, smirking. She touched the swelling on her cheek bone. 'Never had a black eye before.'

I squeezed her hand in the dark, stroked her fingers.

'Let's go and talk to your dad, Tessa.'

'See you the morn,' I said, an expression I wouldn't normally use.

'I'll be fine,' she said.

Shrill barking had erupted as soon as the car door opened.

The two of them walked past the winter vegetable patch, past the spherical seed heads of leeks left from last winter tilted over on the sodden earth. A section of old carpet had been laid down to smother the weeds but was being pushed upwards around the edges by determined arrows of dandelion leaves.

The scratched door of The Byre opened from within and Dad went inside. Two minutes later he was striding back down the concrete yard.

I'd asked what Alfred said as soon as Dad was back in the car.

'I told him what happened…and he wasn't happy about it, but…' his voice faltered.

He had looked at Lindsay. She was unaware of his attention, staring into the gap between the barn doors.

'…it's all fine,' he finished.

But it wasn't all fine and it wasn't long afterwards that Doctor Carnegie referred Lindsay to the Adolescent Psychiatric Unit in Aberdeen Hospital.

Staying at each other's houses never provided complete escape, but at least we were together. Outwardly, we've returned to supporting each other again now Robbie is gone. In the present we're providing shelter for each other. Unlike when we were children though, when afternoons held the promise of an infinity of togetherness, our current arrangement surely cannot be anything other than temporary.

The school bell rings and when the class settles I set them the task of completing their posters of the circulatory system.

'Miss, why do we have twa kidneys?'

'Pardon?'

'But no twa…' begins Steven.

'Okay, settle down.'

There's a sprinkling of laughter.

These impromptu questions could lead to a discussion, but today it's hard to be interested, hard to keep my eyes open.

At the end of the day I spot Tessa at the gate. Jenna skips over. She eyes the gate as if it were an unpredictable dog before side-stepping and, once clear, rushing to her mother.

I return to the classroom and hurriedly tidy and make preparations for the next day. When I'm finished other classrooms still have their lights on; I see Moira is putting up a display of acrostic poems.

The cleaners, Mrs Malcolmson and Mrs Walls, move in convoy along the corridor, one with a brush the other with a mop and bucket. The purple tabards they wear remind me of the robes worn by the catholic priest when I've gone to mass with my father.

'Whit like, Miss Marner?' says Mrs Malcolmson.

'Sorry about the footprints.'

'No bother,' says Mrs Walls.

They lean on their equipment and watch me leave.

How do the days keep going past?

My breath keeps moving, but little black lines of loss and hate are drawn over my day, like vertical blinds that can flip and block out the view at any moment.

A minibus filled with boys from primary four and five is parked outside the school gates. They are all wearing red and white football shirts. Michael and Andrew Biggings are squirting water bottles at each other, dodging out of their seats.

'Whit like, Christine?'

The voice takes me by surprise.

Neil is on the street behind the bus. He's in blue overalls and smells of diesel, but there's no farm vehicle in sight.

'No bad,' I say, without thinking.

There is a muffled thump from the minibus. We move on together.

'Shame aboot Jenna,' he says. 'Always been a peedie monkey. How's Tessa?'

'Fine,' I say. 'She was here half an hour ago if you wanted to speak to her.'

'No. I didna need to see her. You seen Ronald?'

'In passing.'

'He say anythin to you?'

I shake my head.

He nods. Our eyes meet then he looks away and scuffs the toe of his boot against the curb.

'See you aroond then, Christine.'

He glances back at the minibus then walks away up the street. When he disappears around the corner I'm still staring after him. With his figure gone the render on the houses looks doubly grey, the withered vegetation doubly depressing. It's as if the street isn't complete anymore without that blue.

Chapter 13

'He just asked after Jenna,' I say. 'How d'you get through the day?'

The cup of tea I'm handed is scalding.

'Bit rough this morning. Mrs Sinclair's colour went a shade orange, but she didn't say anything. One of those folk who's too good for that.'

Tessa drizzles an extra spoon of sugar into her brew.

'Maybe your dad asked him to go over.'

'What?'

'Neil wouldn't just turn up at school to say "Whit like?"'

'Well, I don't ken.'

Tessa peeks through the doorway into the living room.

'Are you all right, Jenna?'

The canned giggles of a children's TV show drift through to where I sit at the table with a pile of quizzes about the human body.

'The secretary said she's seen your dad…' I say.

The sound of retching comes through the doorway.

'Mu-um, I've been sick.'

Tessa is straight through the door. The mess is everywhere, brown vomit dashed with yellow and green. An acidic smell fills the room. Tessa crouches on the floor. She bears little resemblance to the young woman who went out last night.

'Does your puggy hurt?' she says.

I open the bay windows then go to the bathroom and return with towels, tissues and cleaning products.

'Thanks Christine. Can you get her some fresh clothes as well? Might as well get you changed here rather than spreading it around the place.'

However, when I return she is speaking less kindly.

'Why did you do that?' she scolds.

She turns around and takes the clothes from me.

'She's fine. Get up Jenna.'

'She's very grey. It might be the bump on her head,' I say.

'I don't think so,' says Tessa.

'But she looks awful.'

Jenna emits a groan, turns her head a fraction then releases a mouthful of liquid onto the tissues. Tessa flinches but doesn't move away.

'Gae us a towel.'

She props the towel under Jenna's head, hooks an index finger around a stray hair slicked across her daughter's cheek and tucks it behind her ear.

The smell catches in my nostrils. On television, someone is about to do a bungy jump from a tall bridge and the sight of the swinging view from the camera combined with the unpleasant odour bring on a feeling of sea-sickness.

'She shouldna have eaten them all,' says Tessa.

'What?'

'Mum dropped in a bag of sweeties to cheer her up. Said Dad was sorry for all the trouble he'd caused. No doot she's feeling all guilt-ridden as well. God's sake, I've got to get some new clothes. Can you stay wae her a minute Christine?'

Tessa holds the bottom of her T-shirt out in front of her like an apron to avoid making more mess on the carpet.

Jenna retches again. This time nothing comes out except a deep burp. She puffs her cheeks out and stares blankly at the television.

'Come on Jenna. Let's get you changed,' I say.

'No. I don't want to. I'm watching.'

'You're covered in sick. You'll feel better wearing something fresh.'

'I don't want to.'

She refuses to move. I tidy up around her, scraping, sponging, and rinsing. The draught from the window is cold, claggy and damp, and a chill settles on the room.

When Tessa's out of the shower she orders Jenna to her feet. She gets her showered and changed into pyjamas. Jenna returns to curl up on the remaining dry patch of the sofa. She watches the television in a strange crab position, her head pushed down into the fold of the cushions, one leg bumping rhythmically up and down. The swelling on her forehead is mushroom-brown except for a blurred green crescent in the centre.

Tessa rinses clothes in the kitchen sink then carries them to the washing machine leaving a line of drips across the floor.

'She fund them in the cupboard and then I had to tell her they were from her Granddad…then she was on at me wanting them…I was on the phone to Tommy for a bit afore you came back and in between she's scoffed them all.'

'You didn't have to give them to her,' I say.

'I ken.'

'Your dad wants you to go back to the farm…'

'I don't care what goes on in his heed.'

'Mum, I need a wee,' calls Jenna.

Tessa sighs heavily. Her eyes are bloodshot, her skin almost the same sickly tone as her daughter's.

'I'm going to put her to bed.'

Jenna doesn't offer resistance this time. She rises, totters slightly then shuffles down the corridor. I picture Robbie helping get his daughter ready for bed. I imagine Tessa, Robbie and Jenna sauntering around the harbour, licking ice-creams by the Peedie Sea. Whatever problems they might have had I didn't share any part of their life and I do regret this.

I hear taps, flushes and doors then it becomes quiet. Even outside the breeze has dropped.

I add ticks to the answer sheets. The washing machine spins and whines. I find myself staring at the wall, sapped of strength, without any inclination to eat or drink.

A click from the machine interrupts my blankness. I fill a basket with the wet laundry and carry it to the end of the corridor and unfold the clotheshorse. Tessa's underwear resembles tiny Speedos. My underwear is larger and more similar in shape to the pants that Jenna wears.

I busy myself with domestic chores, sweeping crumbs from under the toaster, wiping the surfaces. I pass the time. I want Tessa's company tonight but she does not re-appear.

Peeping through Jenna's doorway two shapes are discernible on her narrow bed. Both are sound asleep, eyes lightly closed. A book rests on Tessa's chest. I have the urge to stir them in someway by rearranging something, but I resist. I draw the curtains to block out the streetlight, switch off the lamp then retreat.

The smell in the living room is enough to send me to bed as well. I close the windows switch off the lights and lock the door. The lines of shadows, the varying depths of darkness heighten my sense of hearing and touch.

In the bedroom I pull the curtains slowly; the plastic runners slide and click. I imagine that someone might be watching me from outside, seeing my body silhouetted against the light. I undress where I stand, screened from the outside by nothing more than a thin layer of cotton curtain; perhaps my silhouette is still visible. I choose a clean T-shirt from the drawer and pull it on over the red lines that remain on my hips, shoulders and back from the elastic in my underwear. I remain conscious of the feeling of nakedness.

I press in the sliding switch of the lamp and remember the night of Anne and Brian's wedding, the event that finally brought me back to the island. I visualise the view from The Blackhouse.

It was the deep dusk that passes for night in summer. There are oystercatchers calling from the shore, curlews and lapwings trill and warble across the still air. The young black steers are getting fat, already weened from their mother's milk. On the low hillside opposite tractors are working in pairs, harvesting. They cut and bale, keeping sure to the line of mown grass, up and down. They work through the night because it is summer and the time doesn't matter.

The night is still. Clouds of black winged insects emerge from the scrub and mud, and dance together where the air is warm. The water seems thick, moving gently, mollifying the foreshore. Bold and round, the chalk penny moon shrinks as it rides into the blue. Close below the horizon the sun denies the moon its chance to cast shadows. The stars are very near and the clouds moored to a ceiling of glass.

There is stillness and silence; it's all so close. Robbie is next to me, and he holds me.

By the time we rise there is nothing left in the field except stubble and bales.

Chapter 14

I turn onto my side, there's a cool triangle between my back and the space where Tessa usually stays.

I've not had many partners.

By the time she was sixteen Lindsay had a packet of condoms in her going out bag and in the drawer by the bed. I found them one day whilst rifling through her childhood keepsakes. Because of the location of the gallery you could see who was coming and going for miles, privacy could be more or less guaranteed from our parents. She took advantage of the situation.

There was something about Lindsay when she was a teenager – a boyish unconcern for the admiration of female peers that attracted boys and older men. She has darker hair, greener eyes, more external advantages than I.

If Dad was in the workshop she'd flirt with any man who came into the gallery. She'd while away the time flicking through magazines until a car pulled up. Then the game began.

The challenge was to persuade every male customer to buy three items. Couples walked back to their cars with men smiling and women glancing with irritation at the neat brown paper parcels they inevitably carried. Lindsay'd stand at the window, waving and smiling. I tried to copy her unconcerned toss of the head; she was a master of the trailed fingertip.

I walked into her bedroom once, accidentally disturbing an act I'd only just begun to understand from the pulled up sheets and eye-popping female expressions on films. She released the duvet top with one hand letting it droop over the moving figure beneath and flicked her fingers while mouthing the words, 'Piss-off.' I hadn't realized she even knew the fella who'd come to fit the new washing machine. Later, Lindsay explained they'd met each other through the Youth Club years ago. It seemed sufficient explanation at the time.

Tessa and I had also gone to Youth Club, and enjoyed the giant sumo wrestling suits, ping-pong, and creating messy home-made chocolates, that kind of thing. There were a couple of discos, a mixture of dancing, dim lighting, loud music and ginger beer. One time, Mark Dunnoch, who was in the same year as Lindsay at school, engineered me into a corner by the stage and managed to put his hand under my shirt. His parents owned a snack wagon and he smelt of chip fat. Afterwards, he told everyone. It felt like the end of the world – the ultimate embarrassment. I hated him from then on, and all opportunistic intimacy.

It was different with Robbie. I wouldn't have cared if someone had turned a flash light on us. I wanted it.

There were other boys. Calib Spence, a thin dark boy from Stromness who'd played Danny in Grease. When he came round my mother always insisted on asking if he had European ancestors and took extraordinary interest in his hands. He would pick me up in his dad's van and take me into town. The smell of sawdust reminds me of him.

There was a brief thing with Sam Waddle, a couple of get togethers at parties. He was mad about rugby. I told him straight out he could stuff the honour of baking for the whole team. In the end he took up with Agnes Saltwater, the niece of the frozen fish shop owner.

In retrospect, Sam and Calib's fumbling efforts were not the era ending events I labelled them at the time. This was the reason my anticipation had grown about Tessa's eighteenth birthday party. It was to be held on midsummer's eve – the day after we graduated from the old Kirkwall Grammar School. All I thought about was Robbie.

On the last day I'd sat with everyone else in the main hall. Blunt slashes of sunlight cut across the hall. It was the only room in the whole school with the potential to be light and airy and was decidedly prevented from being so by the dirty-green curtains with mustard ovals that hung in limp strips either side of the tall windows.

The Headmistress, Ms Weston, with forced sincerity, had spoken about how much progress we'd made. We weren't what was called a 'good' year; few students had applied for university places or higher education courses on the mainland. Ms Weston had spent the majority of our previous gatherings saying how disappointed she was with our behaviour.

We sat in worn, tight-fitting uniforms. Robbie was in the row in front of us. He'd had his hair cut short, clipped around his ears. It made him look younger. Now and again, when he turned to whisper to Tommy the hairs on the back of his neck caught the sun and looked golden. I longed to feel the soft bristles with my fingertips. Tessa had nudged my knee and pulled a lipstick out of her pocket.

Ms Western finished reading the list of sporting achievement and gave us permission to applaud our classmates. She raised her hands as if calming troubled waters. Her nasal voice cut through the noise. She apologised that the invited speaker, a poet from Glasgow who the head of the English department knew, had failed to show up at the last minute. She told us she was very grateful that his place had been taken by Fraser Ponting, the head of the Parent Council.

He was a stocky bulldog of a man with four daughters and ran the Boy's Brigade. He had a brusque Yorkshire accent despite having lived on Orkney for twenty years.

'It isn't the fashion to talk aboot heaven and hell. You'll not be thinking much about it at your age. You think you're invincible, you lot. All that future ahead of you and not enough past to drag your hopes down. I've not so much time left – perhaps that's why they're giving me a turn standing in front of you lot.

'I was young once, handsome too. I'd be lying if I said I didn't put it about a bit. Saving the blushes of my daughter in the front row I'd tell you a few tales that'd make you whistle. No laughing matter, Tommy Rendell and Robbie Muir. Don't believe everything you hear – there's some of it that'll be true, but more often than not it won't be.

'What I want to say, what I thought was important to say, is that you must *think* about what you're doing. Don't be just a doer. All doers do, is *do*. They follow behind the crowd and say, 'yes.' They carry on against common sense that's in front of them because it's the thing to *do*. Doing without thinking – too much of it goes on. *Try thinking*.

'You may not have done too much of it before – too busy *learning* to try thinking. It's not the sort of thing anyone can teach you. It's not the sort of thing you can write on a CV or that'll ever get written on your headstone, but you lot aren't planning on dying anytime soon, are you?

'*Try thinking.* I can't promise it'll make your life easier, or better, but at least you'll be responsible for what you do. It'll need some practice. You'll have to start with small things – like thinking wearing a belt'd save a-hoisting your breeks up every two minutes, Sean McGavin, like thinking lessons'd be a good idea before taking your test, Glenda Morris. It'll take some practice. You'll not all be good at it to start wi', especially if you prefer catching and kicking a ball to anything else…'

There was a ripple of laughter. Mr Ponting was famous for the lively abuse he scattered on the boys he enthusiastically coached for football.

'…or if you've never had much going on your head except thinking how to make that bonny face of yours look even bonnier, Tessa Hewison.'

Heads turned Tessa's direction. She pouted and finished her lipstick with a flourish. The scowl on Ms Western's face that had grown during Mr Ponting's speech deepened.

Mr Ponting stood square, newscaster-like, with his hands lightly clasped in front of his tie. The noise settled in the room and he continued.

'*Try thinking.* You'll get in the habit if you practice. Then, one day there might come a time for choosing. This way or that way, fast or slow, stay or go. Most of the time it won't matter which choice you make. You're still young, still busy doing. And it won't matter for the most part to anyone else. We don't want to see your underpants Sean, but it doesn't really matter one-way or the other, Glenda'll take her lessons and sooner or later you'll see that what you look like doesn't matter one jot.

'But sometimes the choice you make, the road you decide on, *will* make a difference. It will *matter.* And what you decide *will* change your future and it might change other people's lives as well. That is not something to be undertaken lightly.

'So, even if you haven't made a strong start in it yet, and maybe today you feel you'll live forever, I want you to *try thinking.* Prepare yourself for those big decisions by getting those small ones right.'

At that Mr Ponting gave his audience a sharp nod, turned slightly to Ms Western and performed a neat bow then returned to his seat. He stared out at us with his bright beady eyes, his arms folded across his chest.

The sudden end to his address and its short length took the headmistress by surprise, and the fact that Ms Weston was lost for words was enough of a reason for us to give a hearty round of applause that escalated into cheers and cat-calls.

Ms Western blinked like a confused hen. Mr Ponting beamed.

When I told my mother about the speech she laughed out loud. I didn't understand exactly why and I won't say that the speech changed my life but on occasion it comes back to me. The words are with me as I drift off to sleep. The image of school hall fades. I'm in The Blackhouse again. Robbie is there.

'Move up. I'm freezing.'

Tessa flaps open the duvet and lets in a draught of cold air.

'Wha?'

'Budge over,' she says.

'I was asleep.'

'You were muttering…Jenna needs another heater, it's freezing in there tonight. Sorry about earlier. I don't ken what to do…I slip into this way of being with Dad.'

'You've got to get on with your own life,' I murmur. 'Night, Tessa.'

'Night, Christine.'

Chapter 15

In the morning, I skip breakfast and leave while Tessa and Jenna are still getting up. A look in the rearview mirror shows unruly hair. I find a hair band and tie a ponytail. The effect is to make me look younger.

The calm of early morning is stirred by a westerly breeze. It's due to strengthen during the day. At this time of year more leaves can be stripped from their branches in a single night than will fall in a month down south

The empty spaces in the car park promises a chance to catch up on marking. Juggling folders, I head around the side of the hall. Behind me the pedestrian entrance gate squeaks. There are hurrying footsteps.

'Christine? Bit keen comin' this early are you no?' says Ronald.

He's more recently shaved than usual, even at the funeral he had stubble. Underneath his overalls he's scrawny, small-waisted.

'What do you want?'

I transfer the folders from one hand to the other and adjust the strap of my bag.

'Alfred wants to see you,' he says.

'Why? Why does he want to see me?'

'You should go if you ask me.'

'I didn't.'

He chuckles, enjoying my irritation.

'Calm doon, Christine.'

'Why're you his messenger?' I say.

'You and me hiv always got on?'

'Have we?'

'Don't be so moody,' he says. He reaches into his pockets and rifles around. 'Mind on, can you give somethin' to Tessa for me?'

He hands me a keyring engraved with the number eighteen.

'Did she lose it?' I say.

'It's the key to the annex,' he says. 'Neil wanted me to pass it on. Ken we were there on Tessa's eighteenth – whit a night that wis.'

'Really, I have to…'

His tone changes abruptly.

'Did you miss us when you were away, Christine? Why's it all of a sudden you canna stand to be away? Tessa's taken you back. God knows why.' His eyes flash. 'But then I'd tak you back if you came to me.'

'You never had me.'

'Even efter all you've done. '

He turns and slopes away across the playground, hands in pockets and whistling The Bride's Lament. The gate swings hard behind him. From somewhere out of sight come the sounds of children voices, echoing around the walls.

The automatic doors swish open and I am inside. A dry lemony smell of cleaning product wafts from the toilet area. My stomach heaves.

There are still a few minutes remaining until people arrive. In the classroom I begin pulling apart a plastic model of the eye and force down a few chunks of chocolate from my desk drawer to ease the feeling of emptiness.

Between morning break and lunch an incident occurs.

'Why's it filled with jelly?' asks Sorcha Finlay.

'What do you think?' I ask.

'Light couldn't get through if it were blood,' puts in Abby Jameison.

'Why not water?' I ask. 'Why wouldn't water do?'

'Dunno,' says Steven, twanging the end of his ruler.

'Think about it,' I say. 'I'll get the model.'

As I stand the classroom spins, I'm light headed again. I reach for something to hold.

When my vision returns to normal Robbie is leaning back on his chair, nearly tipping over backwards. Ronald saunters behind him. He places two fingers on the seat back and pushes down hard. The legs shoot beneath the table sending Robbie plummeting downwards so his back thumps the floor.

'Ronald Hewison, what do you think you're doing? Robert could have seriously hurt his head.' It strikes me as strange that I should be their teacher, but I carry on regardless. 'Robert why is it impossible for you to have four legs of a chair on the ground? I've a mind to send you both to Mr Blakemore.'

'Miss?'

'I haven't given permission for anyone to speak.'

There was something so deliberate about how Ronald made the chair overbalance, and insolent about his attitude. My neck itches with irritation, hot patches flare and disappear over my skin.

'But, miss.'

'I really have had enough of this class today.'

There's a tap on my elbow.

'Miss, are you aal right?'

'Of course I'm all right. Go and sit back down.'

'But...who's Ronald and Robert? Aal Owen did wis walk into Steven's chair. It wasn't on purpose,' she says.

Owen turns his face away, a smirk on his lips. There's a hint, the contours of his hairline, something about him that is enough to remind me of Robbie... A murmur rises in the classroom. The air is full of muggy breath. I have a strong urge to walk out and leave them all behind.

'I was thinking about another class...my class back at St Mary's, in the south. Return to your desks. And... take more care in the future please.'

The boys gather winks from their friends. Abby Jamieson whispers something to Niamh Fletcher. They look back towards me with serious faces.

'Turn to the section on optical illusions,' I say. 'Page forty-six.'

While they are busy finding their books I walk over to the window. I want to press my forehead onto the glass and feel its sharp coldness. Instead, I twist the handle and tilt the window open. My fingers are shaking, tears threatening. I draw in a deep gulp of rain softened air and steady myself.

The classroom gradually cools, the children become less excited. I sit at my desk sipping water watching the breeze lick the corners of the work stapled to the wall.

Ronald's invitation weighs on my mind. His insinuations are so far from what our relationship has ever been, I wonder what he's thinking about. What does Alfred want to speak to me for? Ever since Jenna bumped her head things seem more chaotic, the past infringing more on the present.

By three o' clock I resort to clips on the smart board to keep the class busy. Moira is coughing next door. The clock hands move slowly.

First out, my class quickly disappears out of the gates. Niamh Fletcher glances back at me. She says something to her mum as she reaches the railings and I realise she could be retelling what happened earlier in the day.

Children are good lie detectors – I always knew when Dad was covering for Mum not coming to school events. The children might ask their parents who Ronald and Robert are. Perhaps they'll get nothing in reply. Perhaps they'll get my life story. Perhaps they know it already.

Tessa collects Jenna at the gates. I wave then turn and go back inside. On the surface everything is normal.

A few minutes later, Moira's eager round face appears around my classroom door. The edges of her nostrils are glowing red.

'All done, Christine?'

She puts on a bright smile.

'Sorry, Moira, I've got to dash.'

'Of course. See you the morn.'

Poor Moira. She keeps trying. As I bend into the wind, it strikes me, perhaps she thinks I need a friend – someone apart from Tessa. But where would I start? How could I begin with someone new?

The key from Ronald drops to the ground as I fish out my car keys. The embossed numbers are surrounded by golden stars. It is heavy and surprisingly cold in the palm of my hand. I tuck the key into my pocket, it makes a sharp, circular, imprint against my thigh. The plastic smell of the car creeps inside my nostrils, my senses over-alert even to the electrical impulses as the ignition turns. However much I want to stay away from the farm I think it will be more dangerous if I don't to go and hear what Alfred has to say.

Chapter 16

In the lengthening autumn dusk a depressed spirit surrounds The Byre. In the walls, the maze of horizontal cracks and fissures disguises the original identity of the stones cracked by wind, rain and ice. A track separates the low building from the main farmyard.

The wind forces through the narrow opening of the car door when I release the handle. I grab at it to prevent the door swinging uncontrollably.

The brisk air is moist and mild, arriving from the south-east. It seeks out untethered pieces of clothing, purposeful in its search for flesh. The landscape is losing grip of its greenness, succumbing to blue and grey. The sun dips below the horizon behind a bank of cloud. There is no reprise of colour, no peach or gold.

A tractor rumbles past. Ronald stares down at me from the cab above.

'I kent you'd be back.' he calls.

He smiles to himself then turns away and drives into the gloom beyond the faded red doors of the barn.

At the bottom of the brae the ferry traffic from St Margaret's Hope streams past the entrance I took a minute ago up to the farm. This section of road descends and rises around the shallow hills through a series of scooped blind summits. It's a stretch I fear to trust my judgement, even though if you can look ahead far enough it is safe to overtake; there are flowers marking the spot of a recent fatal accident.

A dented Land Rover is parked in front of the lean-to that serves as a porch to The Byre. The structure serves as a dumping ground for outdoor clothing and equipment. Inside, Marion's plants are wilting and yellowing as the nights lengthen. The complex musty smell is instantly evocative of spending time with Tessa.

The bell has always been out of order. I rap my knuckles on the glass panel of the inside door. It is in Victorian style, a mosaic of tiny glass webs without their concentric threads. Black mould has invaded the uneven surface of the glass spoiling the effect of the refracted light.

The door is opened by Marion.

'Hello Marion. I've come to see Alfred. He wanted to speak to me.'

'Best come in, Christine. Mind oot your feet.'

There's a car battery and a pair of clay encrusted boots on the doormat. Inside, there's the musty smell of animals, but no sign of the dog.

'Where's Freki?'

'Gone,' she says, without regret. 'Aye, weel his legs got too bad last winter. He'll no be biting anyone agaen.'

The kitchen is freshly scoured. It smells of frying beef and onions, cut through with the sharpness of chopped swede.

A table is pressed up against the window overlooking the barn. Alfred occupies the seat with its back to the boiler. A blue flame bulges and thins behind the round window that guards the pilot light. An old-fashioned oil lamp converted to an electric light hangs over the table.

'Christine's come to see you,' says Marion.

She sits down opposite her husband near to a pile of manila envelopes. There are bundles of white ribbon with names embroidered in red cotton on the table. Alfred has nothing in front of him, no newspaper, no book; his hands rest palms down on the table.

'Who?'

'Remember you wanted to see her.'

Alfred turns his eyes towards me, their rims are salmon-coloured, the whites tinted pale pink.

'Wheel, Christine is it?'

'Ronald said you wanted to see me.'

Marion picks up one of the bundle of ribbons. She lowers her eyes to her work and begins to roll them neatly into an envelope.

'Jenna was sick after the sweets you gave her,' I say.

'Sweeties'll not harm her. I ken she's had Bru since she wus in her pram. Then whit'd I really ken? Ah'm cheust her granddad. Poor peedie lass got a reel scare bumping her heed.'

He speaks in a deep baritone and I'd forgotten how strong his accent was. It's hard to catch everything he says.

'Why did you come to the school?' I say

'It'd be no buther fur me to walk her home once in a peedie while,' he says. 'Wan grandbairn, only wan. An' I niver see her fae wan year to the next. More o a stranger…' The small pink circles on his cheeks deepen and a flush spreads over his face. He looks down at the table and rubs the fingers of one hand over the rough grey back of the other then starts up again in a quieter voice.

'Is she feelin better noo? Tell me.'

There's gentleness in his voice I've not heard before.

'It wasn't a concussion or anything,' I say. 'She'll be fine. But you can't turn up at the gates to take her home like that. We're not supposed to release children to just anybody.'

'Ah'm no cheust anybody. Ah'm her granddad. And this is her Granny and we've a right to see her some more.'

Marion doesn't say anything.

'Aal Ah've ever done wis for Tessa,' Alfred says. 'Workin an makin sure she'd everything. Whit do I get? She niver cared aboot anybody except hersel.'

'That's not true.'

'You ken whit Ah'm sayin? It's no a bad job lookin efter Tessa while the weather's fair, but it's no easy on a poor day.'

Alfred stares at me, opening his eyes wide for emphasis. The capillaries in his eyes seem to run right through his iris into the tight black pupil at the centre and through the other side. His face is red from the effort. He coughs deeply, bowing his head and grappling a handkerchief from his pocket to cover his mouth. His forehead is glassy with sweat, his long nose blue-purple and punctuated with dark red pores. He turns sideways on his chair, pushing on the edge of the table with one hand.

'I'm going, Alfred.'

Marion looks up at me; tightly clasped in the fingers of one hand is a bunch of stiff white ribbon.

'Wait, Christine,' she says. 'Cheust bide a minute. He's no wantin to make you upset. Are you, Alfred?'

Alfred looks over to his wife. He shakes his head, gestures towards the third chair at the table. It's Tessa's chair that faces the window and the farmyard.

'Sit doon, Christine,' he says. Then more softly, 'Will you sit doon?'

He wipes his lips and folds his handkerchief away. He still has that power of an adult commanding a child and I obey.

'Niver can howld his temper,' says Marion.

She tuts between her teeth making a sound just like the birds in the cliffs around the brough.

'I wanted to say,' says Alfred, '…to ask if you'd tak a word to Tessa fae us? Mind on that we've not seen her…'

'He wants to say he's sorry,' says Marion, interrupting her work.

'Aye.'

He turns to me. The hardness in his eyes disappears, there's a searching, hopeful expression on his face that's hard to bear.

Instead of meeting his gaze, I stare at my reflection in the window and out into the darkness. The dusk has run out and proper blackness has descended, the high barn doors are no longer red. Somewhere out of sight a bright light illuminates the walls inside. There's the shadow of a man working, tall with wide shoulders. The kye will soon be brought in from the fields and the stalls are being prepared for their arrival. The shadow turns and bends then disappears.

'I mean to say it to her mesel,' he says. 'Robbie wis gaen to help me.'

The sound of Robbie's name brings my attention back into the room. Alfred strokes the table with his index finger, rubbing at the grain.

'He came to see me.'

'It wis the day o the accident,' says Marion.

'What did you say to him?' I say.

'The same Ah'm telling you. He wis spaekin to Ronald in the yard an I called him in here. He didna seem in the mood to hear at first, but he settled doon after a dram and fell to listenin.'

'What about?'

'I niver thowt he wis a bad beuy, Christine.'

A hot flush creeps across my skin. I steal a glance over at Marion to see if she's watching. She has her eyes down, conscientiously winding ribbon around another cardboard square. Skin spots cover the back of her hands.

'He had his faults mind,' says Alfred.

'Did he?' I say.

'But he kent I wanted to mak amends, to get Tessa more forgivin an see more o the peedie lass.'

'I can't help you, Alfred.'

'Tell her whit Ah'm thinkin aboot, Christine. I canno speak tae her. Niver could withoot loosing me temper. Do y' ken?'

'And that's what Robbie said he'd do?'

'He did. And I widno been so generous wae the Highland Park if I'd kent he was gaen for a dive. But I wis in the mood to hiv a glass, an he didna say no.'

'He should have known better.'

'Aye,' says Alfred, shaking his head. 'A demned pity.'

'And he never spoke wae Tessa,' says Marion

Alfred glances over to me. There's a curmudgeonly spark back in his eye. The warmth of the room and my tiredness has make me forgetful of my reluctance to be here, never mind listen to what Alfred has to say.

'I'll think about it,' I say.

I rise from my seat, suddenly conscious that the brightly lit kitchen is visible to anyone in the farmyard outside. Marion shuffles her work and rises to see me out. Her gaze rests for a moment on the empty chair I've left behind.

'I went to the boy's funeral,' Alfred calls out,

His voice rolls around the dark hallway, bumping against the dresser, sinking into the carpet and walls. I'm about to answer him back but Marion shakes her head.

She opens the door and lets me past, but before I step through lays her hand on my arm. Her grip is tight, her eyes tiny bright pricks of light in the gloom.

'Don't mind on. He's forgotten you wir there as weel,' she says. 'He's no a cruel man, and…he's no whit he used to be, Christine.'

I nod. After reading her letter I know she'd say anything to heal the family rift. She lets go of my arm and I step into the porch.

Again the muddle of shadows transports me back to other times, to games with seashells, to collecting shed fleece from barbed wire and twisting out strands of thick greasy wool, to dozing on canvas sacks pretending to be on a beach in Spain, to being curled up against Tessa listening contentedly to the long wind-filled summer afternoons.

The lights on the barn float in the darkness, disorienting after the bright domestic kitchen.

I'm struck by a sudden stab of grief at the memory of tender-friendship. All the moments blurred together into an intense longing for my friend.

Hardly aware of what I'm doing I twist the slack door handle this way and that until finally the latch opens.

I fumble for my keys, without thinking where I am going.

'Mind oot the road!'

Two moons seem to hurtle towards me. The ground shakes beneath my feet. I raise a hand to shade my eyes from the lights bearing down on me.

Someone catches me as I fall and drags me clear. Metal glints, high black wheels roll thunderously past. The imprint echoes of the lights jig across my eyelids.

'Whitna she think she was doing?' hollers a voice.

'You must've seen her, Ronald.'

'She shouldn't be wanderin aboot. Why'd she no get oot o the road?'

'Move past. You're blocking the light.'

'She's fine. Look here's her keys. Get her in the car.'

The wind whips away their voices, but I know who's speaking. Wetness seeps through my skirt from the ground, the cold anchors me physically, brings me back to where I am.

'We've to bring her inside,' says Neil.

'Put her to Marion. She'll tak care of her. '

'No. Up to the hoose.'

'Do whit you want. Ah've work to do,' says Ronald.

'Fuckin bales can bide.'

Neil's voice is angry.

'Serve her bloody right,' says Ronald at a distance.

A moment later the idling tractor engine revs and the headlamps swing away. The farm yard is dark again. I lift my head away from the arm that's supporting me. Neil's body shelters me from the wind.

'Ronald said he didna see you.'

'It's my fault. I wasn't looking where I was going.'

'Bide a minute, you fairly went over.'

'Really, I'll be okay.'

At the bottom of the track two flashing orange lights wink round and round in the dark. Neil moves his arm a fraction so we're no longer in close contact. I lean forward, the blood comes back to my head, my thoughts are clearer.

'Ronald had to get on,' says Neil.

'I forgot, when I was coming out. I forgot where I was that's all, but I'm not hurt.'

I rise slowly, loose gravel sticks to my clothes.

'You must come up to the hoose, Christine. Ronald will be sor–'

'No. It's okay. I shouldn't even be here.'

He hesitates then holds out my keys.

'You'll be needin these.'

As I take them he notices the eighteen key-fob.

'How d'you get this?'

'Ronald gave it to me for Tessa.'

'It's for the annex.'

'I don't know why he gave it to me. Honest I don't. You take it.'

'Sure you're okay?'

'Thanks.'

Neil stays and watches me get into the car. There's a tingling numbness in my fingers that makes gripping the steering wheel difficult. I force my breathing to be slow and regular, to appear unshaken. It takes three tries before I can get the car turned around.

He stands patiently waiting, as if he's got nowhere else to go. Memories, separated by decades, collide together. Back then it all seemed so inevitable. And now nothing is inevitable, nothing at all.

Chapter 17

Gradually, the car warms, yet my hands hold the steering wheel awkwardly, my fingers shake when they dip the headlights. I picture Alfred and Marion sitting at the kitchen table. His words sound over and over in my head. Why would Robbie take a drink with him?

The scruffy edges of the roadside sweep away towards the barriers. As I drive back to town my mind strays back to the days before Tessa's birthday party. The whole term we had been preoccupied by the event, never mind upcoming examinations and important events like driving tests.

Even Lindsay's mini-breakdowns were squashed into second place. At the time, she always seemed to recover. I thought my parents took her problems too seriously – a reaction to the guilt they felt because they were away so often. Dad had started to accompany Mum on her conferences. This seemed to coincide with us getting older yet I sensed something had to have changed for the man who could happily spend all afternoon drawing a shell to say he enjoyed going to European cities. There must have been a reason. I suspect it was something Mum said or did.

He went even though he knew that left to her own devices Lindsay's behaviour became more extreme. When she'd left school the summer before Dad had given her more responsibilities at the gallery to show he trusted her, but it wasn't working out well. Money had gone missing and several expensive originals had been sold at the wrong price.

The weekend before Tessa's party my parents were away again, a trip to Edinburgh where my mother was giving a lecture on 'Neolithic Ritual – Evidence of Animal Sacrifice from Mainland Orkney'. This time the gallery closed.

On the first day they were away Lindsay loped around the house in a camisole and ate nothing but chocolate – sugar highs and lows, chocolate in particular, exacerbated her mood swings. On the Saturday night she invited friends over.

I'd stayed in my bedroom on the telephone to Tessa for most of the evening, engrossed in party planning without caring what was going on downstairs. At least company gave me a break from Lindsay trying to get my attention for a while.

I always found, still find, Tessa's voice addictive on the end of the line. There is a strange magnetism that keeps me in place. I promised Tessa I'd call back. However, eventually noise started to intrude upstairs. The sound of music bounced through the floor and heavy footsteps came up the stairs and stopped outside my door. Whoever it was eventually went away along the upstairs corridor to the bathroom.

Male voices ricocheted around the house like billiard balls, punctuated by Lindsay's high-pitched chatter and laughter.

Images of the likely desecration occurring below flashed through my mind. I imagined my mother's Ethiopian bowl, handcrafted from red clay, fired on the communal pyre and gifted to her by a woman whose son had shown her to the archaeological remains, now teetering on the table edge. I pictured my dad's postcard sized canvases of sea and sky being used as beer bottle coasters.

The image of Lindsay in her camisole earlier in the day stuck in my head.

I stepped slowly down the stairs, giving Lindsay a chance before I walked in.

When I'd entered the living room a brilliant copper-green dusk filled the windows. Later, it would bleach and fleshy peach stretch across the long low horizon.

Three men were sprawled like starfish over the furniture. I knew Neil and recognized one of the Isbister brothers, the third man was older by at least a decade and I had no idea who he was. A pack of cards was strewn across the table, loose change arranged in piles around the edges.

'Lindsay kent you were upstairs,' said Neil.

'Come to join us efter aal?' said the old guy, tipping up his cap. He stretched out on the sofa one elbow propped underneath his head.

'Where's Lindsay?' I said.

'Come on, tak a seat. Ah'll show you the rules.'

'I'm not joining in. What are you doing?'

'Cheust a peedie bit o fun.'

'Where's Lindsay?'

'In the kitchen,' said Neil.

'Sorting herself oot a piece,' said the older man.

'What d'you mean? And who are you?'

'Call me Wriggles. Your sister fair lost the last roond. But she's game fur another.'

He made eye contact with the Isbister boy and both sniggered.

I'd turned and walked through into the kitchen. Lindsay must've heard someone coming.

'Give us a minute.'

She was trying to tug her shirt down over her bra without undoing any buttons.

'What're you doing?'

'Oh it's you, give us a hand,' she said.

I took hold of the fabric under her armpits

'Push, no not up, outwards. God, this is tight.'

'Whoa…you're pulling my hair.'

'Didn't mean to…why don't you undo the buttons? There. God, what were you doing?'

Lindsay had reached for a scarf that belonged to our mother lying over a chair. It was deep red and sat well against her hair.

'How's that?' she said. 'You've not got any money lying around have you? Pay it all back. They keep giving me penalties when I run out of money. '

'Strip poker? Really?'

'Loosen up, Christine. I had a great hand, but I ran out of change and they kept raising the stakes.'

'If I had any money I wouldn't give it to you. Who's that old guy? Tell them to go home.'

'Piss-off. I can do whatever I want.'

'Lindsay, c'mon.'

'Have a drink and come and join in, or get back upstairs. Jesus, you're such a baby.'

Isbister came into the kitchen and collected a can of beer from the counter.

'Whit like, Christine? Any better at poker than your sister?'

He winked at me. Lindsay broke into giggles.

'Come on, tak a drink wae us,' said Lindsay with her best

Orcadian mimic.

I couldn't help but smile.

She took down two glasses and returned to the living room. I went with her, nudged Neil's feet off the table and sat down next to him. Wriggles tipped a dram into everyone's glasses. Lindsay tidied the cards on the table, then began to shuffle.

It turned out that Isbister and Wriggles weren't bad company. Wriggles was from North Ronaldsay and had endless stories of returning drunk over the fields, tales of being chased by trows and old women and kids making money driving drunk folk home from parties. They became more hilarious and more unlikely as the cards went down.

The bottle dwindled. Neil fetched a jug of water to add to the whisky. In the end he gave up trying to explain the rules and helped me play my hand so I didn't go broke. He didn't seem to mind losing his own money. We played through the brief blue night until the horizon was visible again between the sea and sky.

At three o clock Lindsay made bacon rolls, coffee was brewed and drunk. At four-thirty Neil said he'd better get back to the farm.

He had eased himself up from the sofa and I'd walked with him to the door. As I let in the dawn we heard the first whistles of the black and white birds overhead.

'What're you up to today?' I said.

'Silaging.'

'Always working.'

'Sure enough. But…'

He'd paused and looked at me. His eyes betrayed no trace of tiredness or of the drink he'd taken. He waited for a moment in the doorway, gently tapping his fingers against the frame. There was the slightest movement, a change in angle of his body in relation to mine. For an instant I thought he meant to kiss me.

There was a noise from inside.

Neil's gaze had darted back into the corridor and the moment was gone. His hands slipped back into his pockets.

'I'll see you at the party,' I'd said, my voice soft.

'Aye,' he said.

Footsteps came from behind us. Wriggles appeared out into

the daylight looking much the worse for wear.

'Drop me along the road, beuy. Ah'm fair needing me bed.'

The yellow tractor cab sea-sawed between the stone dykes as they drove away, the knock of the engine fading. Its path lay over the causeways that took the road away from East mainland over to Lamb Holm, Glimps Holm, Burray and South Ronaldsay, back to Tessa's family's farm.

I didn't feel drunk anymore, just sleepy. I left Lindsay and Isbister finishing their drinks and went to bed.

Wriggles came back six weeks later to fix the dishwasher for Dad. I didn't bring up the poker evening. It didn't seem I could have anything in common with the man wearing a boiler suit with a brown belt around the outside who was talking to Dad about valves and pumps, and the shortening longevity of white goods. Lindsay seemed to have forgotten about Isbister too.

By then everything had moved on.

I wasn't speaking to Lindsay or Tessa.

Neglecting my father's offer of paid work at the gallery, I employed my time lying on my stomach staring at grains of sand on the beach, isolating the blackest, the whitest and the reddest in my field of vision, squinting so that each pinprick grew in identity and importance. The high sun through the clouds warmed my back and the shore breeze cooled my side.

If I looked up I could see the Italian Chapel, a Nissen hut converted into a church by the prisoners of war who helped construct the barriers. From this viewpoint it was impossible to know that the hills were on separate islands which had only recently been linked, grey arms across the azure water. But there was nowhere I belonged except staring at the sand, no escape.

I'd secured a last minute place on a teaching course at a town somewhere in Surrey and was preparing to leave.

Chapter 18

On the day of the party Lindsay's spirits caught in a low. After a week of very poor weather for June a summer gale was coming. The dig site was flooded and Mum was holed-up in her study trying to re-arrange work for her volunteers. Dad had been busy with browsing tourists, keen to stay out of the wind and horizontal rain. When he finally came back into the house Lindsay was slamming doors and irritated with everything.

'It's your fault. Keeping me here. Never letting me go anywhere. Stuck on this stinking island. Stuck in bloody Orkney. You never think about me and what I want to do…'

'Now, Lindsay you know that isn't…'

'You do everything for Christine. Fucking miss perfect.'

'There's no nee – '

'Piss off. Leave me alone.'

There was a slam and the house went quiet within. Outside the storm was rising. My heart beat hard in my chest, eager with anticipation at the evening ahead. The poker night had whetted my appetite even more for the party.

I'd looked over again at Tessa's gift. It was a photograph Dad had taken of us when we were in primary three. We were both dressed as cats for the school Christmas play. I was wearing tan-coloured tights, brown knitted jumper and a bobble hat from brownies with sewn on felt ears. Tessa had a black leotard, and a black Alice-band with cut out cardboard ears. Our whiskers and painted noses matched, as did our smiles – we had one front tooth missing a piece.

I'd gathered driftwood from the beach then shaped the edges to make a frame. Finally, with Dad's help I'd used a tool to burn our names and an inscription into the wood, 'Happy 18th Birthday!'

The picture was wrapped in gold paper and I was tying red ribbon around the parcel when Lindsay pushed open the bedroom door.

Rain tatted against the window, air squealed through gaps

around the glass.

'You can't make Dad take you over the barriers in this. It's completely fucking selfish.'

I didn't want to start a fight with Lindsay, not if I could help it. I'd tucked my bra strap away and looked in the mirror. I'd held up two nail varnishes.

'What do you think, silver or gold?'

'You're a selfish cow,' she said. 'Who d'you think's going to look at you anyway? The whole dress looks squint.'

She reached out for the hem. I ducked backwards out of reach.

'Dad says he doesn't mind taking me,' I said.

'Stay still,' she said. 'I'm trying to help you.'

She advanced steadily.

'It's fine.'

She moved forward, her eyes glinting with mischievous intent.

'Lindsay, don't. I like it the way it is.'

Directly under the light her face had been thrown into sharp relief. Her eyelids, the tip of her nose and her cheekbones bleached like old ivory, the rest was green-grey shadow. She scraped her hand across the dressing table knocking Tessa's present to the floor.

'Why are you being like this?'

My voice was low, I tried to get through to her, but she pushed me sharply in the chest. It was hard enough to make me stagger against the bed. Her pin-prick pupils were tightly fixed on me.

'It's Tessa's eighteenth,' I said.

'Don't fucking care do you? Don't care about me. Don't care about Dad. Don't care about risking people's lives.'

'What are you talking about? Can you even hear what you're saying?'

She pushed me again, her fingers rigid. They could hold such horrible spiderish strength. The next shove sent me onto the bed.

'The wind's not going to get really bad until tomorrow mor–'

'Sel-fish bi-t-ch.'

She sang the words, sweet and high.

'You're a sel-fish bi-t-ch.'

Her eyes flashed. She drew back her hand and brought it down hard on my upper arm. A fat handprint stood out on the skin.

She raised it again to land another blow. This time I blocked the arm. In response, in one fluid motion she brought up her forearm and began pushing into my throat.

'Get off, Lindsay.'

She pressed harder, forcing the back of my neck into the mattress

'Dad…!'

Her weight was full on my chest. Even though she was lighter, thinner than me, she was incredibly strong. I flailed with my free hand and grabbed for her hair, twisted in my fingers and pulled hard.

She reached backwards grabbing for my hand and released my neck. I rolled away from under her and stood up on the bed.

'Bitch! Bitch! Bitch!' she yelled.

She scooted away and yanked my curling tongs out of the plug socket.

At that moment the door flung open. I'd never heard my father shout so loudly.

'Stop. Lindsay, no!'

She launched herself, curling tongs in one hand, flex held tight with the other. She became a whirlwind, screeching and flailing, attacking my arms.

'Get her off me.'

Dad reacted rapidly. He positioned himself behind her and as she stretched up her arms for a fresh assault he reached over and grasped her opposite wrists. She tried to twist away, but he held her fast, arms folded across her chest.

'No, no. no! Let me go! You can't take her. Don't go. Don't you see what she's doing?'

'Lindsay, stop. There's no reason to be so upset. Think. Everything's going to be okay. You need to calm down.'

'I won't fucking calm down. She hates me. She does. She thinks it all the time. She thinks I ruin everything. I….I. Don't go. Something terrible, something terrible's going to happen. I know it is. Make her stay.'

Her voice started drifting, babbling, justifying, blaming other people in an incoherent monologue. I couldn't bear to hear. I couldn't bear the sight of her.

There were livid scratches down my arms, feathers of skin

lifted away with gathering red dots of blood beneath. The purple crescents reddened where she had sunk her nails more deeply.

Lindsay had rarely deliberately hurt me when we were children, and perhaps that's what made these physical attacks harder to bear; harder to forgive. It wasn't long until I would be eighteen too. Lindsay was close to turning twenty. I thought we were adults. Adults didn't do this to each other.

'I could press charges,' I'd said to my mother downstairs afterwards. 'I could take photographs of the marks. You'd have to be witnesses.'

'How could you? It's not her fault.'

'Of course it's her fault. She starts everything.'

But if I was honest, it was Lindsay who suffered most after our physical fights. My father took any wrecked possessions out to the gallery workshop to be mended or disposed of, but I never concealed my cuts and bruises. Lindsay would stare at them as they healed as a sort of morbid self-punishment.

The night of the party a sort-of compromise was reached. Mum had driven me over the causeways while Dad stayed at home with Lindsay. I'd wanted him to drop me off because he'd helped with Tessa's present, I wanted him to see her open the parcel.

When we arrived my mother immediately performed a three-point turn so she was ready to leave as soon as I was out of he car. Gusts of wind threw rain at the windscreen.

'Wish Tessa a happy birthday from all of us. I'll pick you up at one.'

'I'd rather stay over,' I said. 'It'd save you coming out so late.'

She shook her head.

'I'm working late anyway. You might not get back tomorrow with the weather that's forecast. Anyway, you've not got any things. It's a compromise. Okay?'

She double-checked her watch. A fresh squall was coming, it dragged the door open when I released the handle. I climbed out; the wind was instantly through my clothes and over my flesh.

My mother had called, 'Tights would have looked more elegant.'

'It's summer,' I said with a smile.

I let go and the door slammed itself closed. Mum bumped down the track and was gone.

It *was* cold for mid-summer, barely ten degrees. It was not warm enough for a short black dress, but if I didn't wear it now when would I? We'd be inside anyway, Alfred had banned parties on the beach after Tessa's sixteenth had got out of control.

Through the kitchen window of The Byre I could see Marion arranging a tray for the oven. She was wearing a carnation pink jumper in honour of the day. Tessa came into the room, followed by her father. They stood face to face, hardly a foot between them, Tessa speaking, her hands clasped to her chest. Alfred pointed a finger first at Marion and then at Tessa then turned around and stomped out of view.

When Tessa saw me she cracked a grin and did a little stamping dance on the spot. I met her in the lean-to shelter by the door. Tucked away from the wind the smell of sausage rolls mixed with old rubber things, silage and wet carpet enveloped us. I gave her my present.

'We look so young.' she'd said and hugged me. 'C'mon. Let's get oot of here. I'm gaen to fix us some fuckin delicious cocktails.'

That was how the evening started. Tessa high as a kite.

Chapter 19

Behind the clouds the sun was still high in the sky, occasionally showing through as an eerie white disc like a blind eye. The pick-up time of one o' clock already felt too early.

Tessa was wearing a tight orange dress. It had a sheer pink over-layer and was three inches shorter than mine. Our nails were matching blood red.

'Neil's cleared out the annex. Dad's a pain in the arse saying we can't go up to the brough or doon on the beach. What's the point of having all this land if I can't do anything? Oh, niver mind, did you get the balloons and streamers?'

I nodded and held up a bag.

The annex had been added to the farmhouse much to Alfred's disapproval. It was meant to earn extra income from holiday lets, but it was often empty. The building work had stretched out for years and had for the most part been carried out by people who owed the family favours rather than by professionals. The one person who'd been paid anything was an electrician recently come over from Caithness – the fuses tripped if too many sockets were used at once.

Neil and Ronald weren't bothered about keeping the place turned out nicely. There were scrapes and scratches on the walls and few furnishings to make the rooms feel homely. Marion had offered to look after the housekeeping, but Alfred had forbidden her from getting involved.

Even that summer the annex had only been booked for a few weeks during the St Magnus Festival when everything else on the mainland was taken. The drive over to Kirkwall put many people off, but in festival weeks people were desperate.

Neil had readily agreed that Tessa could use it for her party.

He was in the kitchen when we arrived, still in his blue working overalls, smelling of salt and grass, stashing a roll of black bags under the sink.

'Mix you a drink, Neil?' said Tessa, sauntering over to the cupboards.

She pulled out some old-fashioned smoked-glass tumblers and wiped out the dust with her fingers.

'Ah'll stick to beer, thanks.'

'Christine?'

'Whatever your having,' I replied. 'Can you push this in for me, Neil?'

I'd handed him a streamer pierced with a drawing pin and he followed me into the living room.

'Where do you want it?'

'Over in the corner. I'll twist it then…there…if you hold it up… Pretty good hey?'

Curls of red paper swung against the magnolia wall. Neil glanced back at me. My skin warmed under his gaze, a glow of pleasure rose in my cheeks. Our eyes met and the room seemed to grow voluminously large, as if the walls were made of fabric that stretched and grew with Neil and I at the centre like some tiny seed.

'Bet you can't wait,' called Tessa from the kitchen.

'For what?' I called back. 'It's your party.'

Neil kept his eyes on me.

'I ken, but…tah dah! White Russian. My version.'

Tessa came and stood next to me, her eyes shiny and bright. The glass looked as if it were filled with chocolate milkshake.

'What do you think, Neil? Sophisticated? Beautiful? That's us you ken, no the drinks.'

I glanced at him over the rim of my glass. A feeling of gladness swept through me like I'd not experienced for years – like chasing waves on the beach, or lying on my back and being able to see nothing except blue sky.

Neil held my gaze for a moment.

'The boys won't know what hit them,' said Tessa, clinking our glasses.

'Dead right,' he said quietly.

His eyes had darkened. I held out another streamer, but he moved his hand away. Instead of helping he went and brought through a chair from the kitchen. He placed it against the wall.

'You'll reach weel enough if you can manage on a chair,' he said. 'Ah'm in the hoose if you need anything.'

'You're not coming later?'

He shook his head.

'No.' he said. 'No dressed fur it. Maybe Ah'll see you the morn.'

His footsteps faded along the corridor that joined the annex to the farmhouse. I felt self-conscious standing on the chair after he left, my dress too short, too tight.

Tessa clattered around the kitchen taking out more glasses. Creamy, rich and heavily laced with vodka the drink she'd given me warmed my insides and chased away my doubts about the evening ahead.

I'd finished the decorations and was concocting another drink when Dora Holloway arrived. She was in a tight red halter-neck and silver hot-pants. The skin on her shoulders was strap-marked from a fine day back in May, but it wasn't the sort of thing to deter her from wearing what she wanted.

'Gee wiz. What a wind oot there. Is there a mirror? Are the loos through-by?'

She pointed to the door out of the kitchen. I nodded.

Tatty Edwards arrived next. She'd always been tall, stopping shy of six foot, and was wearing tight jeans and a flowery shirt, her hair loose around her shoulders. She'd lived on Sanday for ten years before coming to the Kirkwall Grammar and staying in the boarding houses. Her parents were English and she spoke with an unashamed home-counties accent.

She plonked down three bottles of red wine and some peach schnapps on the table.

'Mummy said I could take the schnapps as long as we drank it with plenty of lemonade. You haven't got any limes have you, Tessa?'

'Might be able tae stael a lemon.'

'That would be perfect.'

'Can you get plates out, Christine? Mum's been baking all the day. Back in a blink.'

The draught as she'd opened the door threw the streamers upwards and rocked the lampshade.

'Start with the good stuff, I think,' said Tatty. 'Unless you need me to do anything, Chrissy?'

I shook my head and she selected a bottle of wine and took a glass through to the living room.

After she'd gone the interconnecting door between the annex

and the farmhouse had slammed – trust Dora to become disoriented before she's even had a drink. I'd left the kitchen and gone to find her. A single poor window, barely the size of a piece of paper threw light into the corridor. There was the faint smell of stale water from the place being left empty so much.

I ran my fingers along the wall searching for a switch. They made contact with someone who had concealed themselves in the darkness.

'Dora? Is that you?'

'Aye-aye, Christine.'

'Jesus, you gave me a shock. What are you doing here Ronald?'

His hands slipped around my waist.

'Come on, Chrissy. I won't tell anyone.'

'You're kidding? Get off me.'

'Give you a orgasm…and Ah'm not speakin aboot a cocktail.'

I pushed his hands away, but he pressed against me. He pushed himself against my hip and breathed close to my ear. His grip tightened.

The bathroom door opened, light flooded the corridor. Dora paused from adjusting her shorts when she saw us.

'Why don't you give Dora an orgasm?' I said, shoving Ronald aside.

'Ooh, Ronald,' she cooed. 'You're soooo sexy.'

She wriggled her little finger like a worm, blew him a kiss and turned away. She knew how to deal with attention, flirted and bitched her way out of it without so much as a blink. Ronald grabbing me had been so unexpected I'd lost my composure. For a few seconds he'd felt like a real threat, a man rather than a boy who I'd gone to school with for ever.

'Keep your hands off me,' I'd said, finding my nerve. 'You fucking loser. Not even if you were the last man left on the island.'

His stupid grin dropped.

I copied Dora and swung my hips as I walked away.

In the kitchen I saw Dora still hadn't got her shorts quite straight, but nothing dented her confidence. I pushed down the laughter that followed the relief from being away from Ronald and poured myself another drink. Alcohol and adrenaline skidded around my body. Every sensation was rapid, sensual, fleeting, my consciousness sharp.

Tessa was drawing some of the curtains in the living room. In the distance, out over Scapa Flow, the bright gas flare on the flue of the Flotta oil terminal glowed brightly. The fluorescent orange flame hovered over west mainland. Beyond the low green fields rose the lonely elephant-grey of Hoy's hills, fading and reappearing behind the wind chased clouds.

Brian had been fiddling with the stereo since he'd arrived and suddenly succeeded in making it ten times as loud as Tessa had managed.

Soon, there was a line of rust-scarred cars and semi-feral farm vehicles parked along the lane up to the farm. Robbie arrived late after finishing work at the shop. He turned his eyes to the window as he approached and saw me. I glimpsed a smile.

I'd tried to convince myself that there was plenty of time, smoothed my hair and went through to the kitchen to find him. The back door wheeshed closed, making the room feel pressurised. The streamers along the walls slowly drifted back into place and the storm was left outside.

Robbie pulled a four-pack from under his jacket and slid it onto the table. It joined a motley crew of bottles, cartons and cans. Brown bottles with ceramic caps signified home brew, to be drunk with great caution or with reckless abandon. Clear bottles of unheard of spirits clustered near the cartons of orange juice, coke and lemonade. Someone had brought half a bottle of port and there was a chlorophyl-coloured liquor with only three words in English on the label saying 'Product of Hungary.' There was a picture of a skull and cross bones embossed in gold on the back. Cans of beer leaned against each other, supported at the neck by rings of plastic. A slab of Tennant's that Tommy and Brian had lugged in from the van sat on the floor beneath.

I was unscrewing the vodka when Ronald came through the outside door.

'Thought you were going to make an orgasm?' I said.

A queer look of want flashed in his eyes. He took a pair of cans from the table and went towards the noise in the living room without saying anything in return.

I poured an inch of vodka and a splash of gin into a glass then added orange juice and a dash of lemonade.

Robbie leaned in the doorway between the kitchen and the back corridor talking with whoever was seeking refuge from the music or making cocktails. He looked taller, the muscles on his arms more defined from the physical work in the loading bay. I barely measured up to his shoulders anymore. All I wanted was to be alone with him. In the kitchen even speaking to him privately was practically impossible.

'What d'you think of the decorations?' I said. 'I got them in your dad's shop.'

He raised an eyebrow and took a can away from his lips.

'No bad.'

Dora pattered into the kitchen. She adjusted her top then bent over to examine the labels of the bottles on the table. She unscrewed a bottle with a tall ship against a navy blue background. The words 'Dark Rum' were written in red block capitals. The contents looked poisonous.

'What d'you think Robbie? Rum and coke? What're you having, Christine?'

'Not rum,' I replied. 'Not after Christmas.'

'Any ice in here?'

'Might be.'

'Sorry Rob, can I get by?'

Dora made a show of squeezing past him to the freezer then bent over so her bottom nudged against his leg.

'God, you've gotten so tall, Robbie,' she said. 'Go on, open this for me.' He opened her can of coke and she poured some into her rum. 'What else's through by?' she said, pointing down the corridor.

'Bedrooms,' I told her.

'Oh?'

'There's not much in them. It's all been cleared out.'

'I suppose you'd know,' she said. She looked from me to Robbie, took a glug of her drink then said, 'I want to dance. Comin, Rob?'

'No yet,' said Robbie. 'You get started.'

I'd moved aside to let Dora past. Why she thought Robbie would want to dance with her I'll never know. The silver shorts were really too much.

People drifted in and out, pouring and spilling drinks, fetching glasses, stripping off clothing. Occasionally, a shrill whistle sounded through a minute opening somewhere to remind us of the rising gale outside.

I gave up on speaking to Robbie and went to look for Tessa. She was squashed between Tommy and Brian on the sofa. The three of them were sunk deep in the cushions and Tessa was busy showing them the butterfly pattern in the top layer of her dress.

'You ken it's a butterfly.'

Tommy smirked and shook his head.

'I cheust can't see it Tess. Show me agaen.'

Mary Butterquoy and Barry Wick were on the other sofa, in close bodily contact and barely moving apart from their lips and fingertips. Next to them, sitting cross-legged on the floor, Tatty was reading the sleeve notes from a CD. She sipped her glass of wine and tapped along to the tunes oblivious to what was going on behind her.

'Come and dance, Tessa.'

'Noo?'

I swung my hips slowly from side to side.

'It's your birthday. Let's dance.'

I pulled her up and we took to the floor, cheek to cheek. It didn't matter that it was a dimly lit living room in a farm annex, it was our turn to shine on the dance floor.

A handful of girls joined us and there were a few whistles from the boys. We waved, skidded, swung and rotated our way through our favourite tunes. Time passed quickly.

Between the squalls a scallop pink line appeared on the horizon. It widened to a strip of flat gold and without fanfare the sun slid into its foxhole in the north-west.

Soon afterwards, the darkness which had held off so long, finally came. There was a crash against the window as the storm rolled in. The music played on in a tuneless hollow sort of way, but all conversation stopped. When the song finished the hiss and roar of the wind outside drowned out the introduction to the next song, lengthening the strange silence in the room.

Brian levered himself out of the sofa and fiddled up the volume even further. The dancing recommenced, although it was more muted now, its energy dissipated.

In the big west window I saw the reflection of the party flex inwards from the force of the wind. I'd thought of Lindsay; her violence; her fragility. There's really no point dwelling on it, but if the storm had arrived later everything would have been different.

Tessa started doing some weird hip-banging dance with Dora and I left them to it, eager to be away from the flexing window. En route to the bathroom I mixed a fresh vodka and orange in the kitchen and drank it down in one. The alcohol hit like a seventh wave.

I could hear someone crashing about inside the bathroom. They begin swearing loudly when I jiggled the door handle. I worked my way down the corridor to where I knew there was a separate toilet.

After I'd peed I took a moment to fix my smudged mascara. As I'd looked in the mirror my eyes became darker, a soft pearlescent glow grew in their centre. They were like Tessa's eyes, and my lips held themselves in a pout rather than a smile. It made me laugh at myself. Even when I stopped laughing the same look returned to my face. It was as if I had turned into someone else.

I switched off the toilet light and opened the door, determined to go and dance, but someone opened the door of the bedroom adjacent to the toilet.

'Robbie?'

'Is that a toilet? The other one's a fuckin mess.'

Rather than going away I'd waited in the grey light of the bedroom doorway. Storm clouds bowled across the sky, grainy and brown, washed with faint traces of green and pink from the oblique rays of the returning sun. The gloom was reminiscent of midwinter at two o' clock in the afternoon when the light that never really arrived starts to wane.

I leaned on the doorframe – enjoying being away from the party, knowing that at any moment I was free to return. I didn't hear the toilet door when it opened.

I'd felt hands reaching around my waist.

'Robbie.'

'You looked lonely.'

I pictured the girl in the mirror and said, 'Going to keep me company?'

'Weel, if I don't then…'

My arm slipped to his belt. We kissed. A soft, slow kiss, melting into the shadows, drifting away on the distant tails of the wind.

At the end of the corridor a hullabaloo kicked off about the wrecked bathroom. Somewhere a light was switched on. We stepped inside the bedroom and closed the door. We kissed again. He pushed softly against me, his fingers brushing over the scratches that he didn't know were there. The tingle of pain felt sweet. It was something I'd been longing for without knowing.

The shine of a car's headlamps encouraged us away from the door to the bed. I reached my hand out to keep my balance as I leaned backwards.

We were kissing again, hands seeking the edges of clothing, finding fresh places to touch.

This is why Lindsay has those things in the drawer by the bed. She's not as stupid as I thought.

Chapter 20

'Christine, your mum's here.'

I heard the voice clearly. There must be another Christine whose mum had come to pick her up from the party. Poor girl.

'Christ-ine, your mum's here.'

My body and the cascade of messages from its nerve-endings were in control. It was so unexpected, so delightful, like the building blocks of who I was were being utterly changed.

Robbie froze.

'Someone's callin,' he said.

'So?'

I started kissing the edge of his mouth, where his lip met the smooth curve of his cheek.

'You've got to go.'

Where his hands had moments ago been stroking and exploring they stiffened against my ribs.

'What?'

There were voices in the corridor, slamming doors, giggling and scraping heels.

'Ignore them. No one knows we're in here.'

I pinned him with my knees either side of his hips.

'What're you doing?' he'd said.

I pressed my palms against his shoulders and pushed him backwards.

'I want to.'

'No. You're going.'

He grabbed my wrists firmly and then almost lifted me into the air and put me on the bed. He swung his legs down over the side.

'We'd better no,' he said.

'What do you mean?' I said.

He shrugged and looked away.

'Nothing,' he said.

I'd been a bubble ready to burst free from its hoop…now… now I was nothing. Indignation rose in my chest.

If he didn't want me then I didn't want him. I didn't want to be in the same room as him. Didn't want his taste in my mouth, didn't want to touch him. That was what I'd thought at the time. Where my blood had raced to the surface seconds before it now drew back. My hands, feet and cheeks became cold.

'Nothing?' I said. 'Is that what I am? Just someone you were going to get off with?'

Robbie reached for my hand. Outside the door my name was being called again. The voice became clearer and closer. I drew my fingers away.

'Christ-ine. Your mum's here.'

Tessa was in the corridor, knocking on the toilet door, thinking I was inside. Calling me like a child.

'Chrissy, are you in there? You've got to come oot. Your mum's here.'

Robbie stayed next to me, his shoulders curved like a boulder in the darkness.

'You're wrong…luk…Ah'm going to open the door.'

He straightened his back, adjusted the waist of his trousers and stood up. Standing there, even in the dim light, he was the best looking boy at the party. At that moment, I was desperate. I wanted to hurt him for making me suffer.

'How am I wrong, Robbie?' I'd said.

He shook his head. His whole face was in darkness except for the reflection in his eyes. I could see he was looking at me steadily. My heart pounded high and hard in my chest, waiting for what he would say, but his lips didn't move. There was no time for long silences, no time for feeling each other's thoughts. He needed to say something, but he didn't. It ignited a sort of self-righteous fury at what was happening

'Then you'd better find someone else.'

That's what I said. I couldn't stop myself.

There was a knock on the bedroom door. Tessa must have heard our voices.

'Are you in there, Christine? Your mum's here to tak you home. Canna come in?'

'You don't mean it,' said Robbie.

'Don't I?'

I wouldn't give way. I couldn't be any other way. I couldn't see how things might be different.

The handle of the door turned. A slit of bright yellow light invaded the room. I ran a hand through my hair and straightened my dress.

Tessa's cheeks were flushed from dancing.

'Come on, Christine. I left your mum spaekin to Brian. I'd no be surprised if he made a pass at her he's so far gone.' She paused. 'Everything all right?'

As they walked out of the room Tessa and Robbie briefly exchanged a look.

'D'you get lost coming back from the toilet?' said Tessa.

I thought she was speaking to me, but in the second it took to compose myself to reply Robbie spoke.

'Somethin' like that.'

Mum was talking to Brian in the living room, tapping her foot to the musical beat. She didn't seem anxious at all about leaving. She had put on a gold and electric blue scarf. It was silk and reserved for summer, something a colleague had given her.

'Hello, darling. Ready to go?'

'What are you doing here? You're early.'

'I did call… I spoke to Marion. If we don't go now you'll never get back home and Gill wants you in the gallery tomorrow. They'll stop cars going over soon. Had to time my run as it was, waves crashing right over the top of the third barrier.'

'I could have stayed. You didn't have to come.'

'Marion thought we'd be okay if I came before high-tide. Anyway, Lindsay was concerned about you.'

Brian looked like a drunk gerbil.

'I wis tellin your mum hoo Ah'd seen this trick wae Sambuca ower in Stromness…'

'Shut up, Brian. No one wants to know.'

He stopped in his tracks and blinked rapidly.

'Christine, don't be so rude,' said my mother. 'But we do have to go, Brian. I'm sure it was a great trick or whatever it was. Do you have everything?'

'Jesus, I'm nearly eighteen. You let Lindsay ruin everything.'

'Really, it's only a party.'

'Do you see anyone else leaving?'

'Come on darling, you see each other all the time. I do think you're over reacting a little. Careful Brian, you'll spill your drink.'

Everything about the scene was humiliating.

Tessa had met us at the kitchen door with my coat.

'I'll call you tomorrow,' she'd said. 'Don't forget lunch on Monday, my first full day.'

'Sure. Sorry I've got to go.'

We hugged. Tension rose in my throat, I squinted to see into the shadows. There was no sign of Robbie.

'Happy Birthday, Tess.'

I kissed her on the cheek then turned quickly away.

Air shot over the farmhouse then flew back in an downdraft that twisted in chaotic circles among the weeds and farm machinery. Anything not heavily secured was moving in the scarified farmyard. Black plastic snagged on the stock fences flew like witches bunting. All around flowers were being stripped of their petals, leaves wind-burnt, scorched by an invisible torch. Everything from trampolines to shed roofs were fair game to the lick of the wind.

Out of the corner of my eye I'd seen Neil dodge into the barn. He braced himself against one of the doors and began to slide it closed. The squeal of the metal rollers was drowned out by the wind.

The tangled shapes and shadows blurred as my eyes watered. I felt miniaturised, thrown into a seashell, trapped in a pocket of endless echoing, whistling air.

It was far colder than when I had arrived. The belt and buckles of my coat whipped against my body and it was hard to catch my breath as the gusts quickened and dropped.

Robbie…who did he think he was? Did he feel anything?

The indicators of the car flashed and I hustled into the passenger seat and let the wind shut the door. Inside, the car was instantly claustrophobic. Gusts of wind pounded the windows like an angry mob. The blow and suck as the driver door opened and closed made my ears sing with a high pitched note.

The car was repeatedly side-swiped by the wind, an invisible cat's paw playing with it as we drove, switching and patting us between the verge and the white line. Mum adjusted her steering and slowed whenever the road was exposed to the surging wind and rain.

There was a row of cars stopped before the second causeway. The first car waited then accelerated, dashing between the crashing waves. Water slammed against the blocks spewing up against the breakwater. A surge flew over in a giant arc, the great weight of water narrowly missing the car in front and slewing across the tarmac in front of us, tumbling over the giant concrete cubes back into Scapa Flow.

Mum was pensive, shifting gear crisply and adjusting the rate of the windscreen wipers constantly. Once we were over the barrier and protected again from the waves she spoke.

'Lindsay's been shouting a lot. Shouting and slamming doors is her thing tonight. Gill said it's a good job you were out of the house.'

'She won't thank you, or be glad I'm home. She just wants to get her own way. That's all it's about.'

She glanced at the scratch marks on my arms then said, 'She got hold of a bottle of brandy and locked herself in the bathroom. There wasn't much we could do. I mean we can't call the police. I thought she was having a shower, I heard running water, anyway. There aren't any pills kept in there. Eventually, Gill managed to persuade her to open the door. It was a complete mess, everything tipped out, torn up – like a toddler tantrum. She was soaking wet and had drunk half the bottle – two star Metaxa brandy of all things, someone gave it to me on a dig years ago. At least the taste put her off drinking too much. She could've killed herself.'

She didn't speak again until we were safely over the next barrier and had caught up with the traffic.

'She's calmed down now. She's been copiously sick so I expect she's feeling better. Not before she kicked in another kitchen cupboard. I don't know where she gets her strength from. I mean, she's lighter than you.

'Gill didn't want to leave her. She's very low, Christine. I don't know what set her off really. It was something about this party, something you said to her. She said a whole lot of stuff I didn't understand. Gill says she needs quiet. Proper rest. No one visiting the house. No going out.'

'Take her back to Doctor Carnegie.'

'I can't force her to the doctor's anymore. I can't make her do things she doesn't want to do.'

'I didn't want to leave the party.'

'That's different, and you know it.'

She rested her forehead on her hand, elbow propped against the window as she drove, adjusting to the wind with one hand on the wheel.

Clumps of red campion flashed past the beam of the headlights, the green barley was whipped low, bending its back against the punishing storm.

As we pulled into the turning for the gallery she said, 'Anyway, it looked a quiet do.'

My heart swelled as I thought about Robbie. Leaving him behind like that hurt more than I knew was possible.

Chapter 21

I come back to the present. I've no recollection at all of the drive between the farm and the outskirts of town. Steam rises like incense around the towers of the whisky distillery. The streetlight orange glow is briefly flat and diffuse before the vapour is spirited away.

There are few cars. A mobility scooter wobbles up the hill driven by a hunched figure in a faded high visibility coat; leaves scuttle along the gutter.

I pull onto the concrete slab outside the back of the cottage. The car door crunches into our neighbour's wall caught by a gust of wind. I should know better, but I don't care about the wall or the door. My reactions are dull, overloaded from visiting the farm and the relentless stream of memories. I bump the car door closed and trail a bag of exercise books to the door.

A meandering trail of rose petals dislodged by the wind leads me to the door. There are no lights on.

'Anyone home?'

There's no reply. No sound from the bathroom, nothing from the bedrooms.

'Tessa?'

I push open the doors and stare a while at each of the empty rooms. Jenna's school bag is on the floor by the sofa, her sweatshirt thrown down nearby. There's half a glass of blackcurrant squash on the windowsill and Tessa's black ankle boots are leaning near the television. Our bedroom smells of recently sprayed deodorant.

When I return to the kitchen I notice a piece of paper torn from Jenna's scribbling book. Tessa's rounded script fills the page. '*Gone to the hotel to meet Tommy. Getting Jenna fish and chips for tea. Join us when you get back. T*' There's a smiley face and two kisses.

I'm far from in the mood to mark exercise books. Yet, I hesitate. There'll be people who know me in the bar. My hip hurts from the fall and I feel out of sorts after the visit up to the farm.

I want to speak with someone who'll comfort me. I pick up the phone and press in the number for the gallery.

'Northshore.'

'Hi Dad, it's Christine. Did Mum get back yet?'

'Not until tomorrow morning – weather permitting and aeroplane functioning.'

'I've not heard from her at all.'

'Tried her mobile? Mind she's been having trouble with it lately and you know how remote these sites can be.'

'How's Lindsay?.'

'Full of energy. Started trying out tester pots on the walls.'

'On my room?'

'You don't mind do you? There's no harm in what she's doing. I mean, you seem settled in town and now that Tessa's helping pay the rent – I presume she's paying you something – you won't be needing your room.'

'Settled?'

'Well, you won't be moving back any time soon will you?'

'No.'

'And Lindsay's right, it could do with repainting. I told her to put all your things into boxes. Although anything that's obviously rubbish she's getting rid of.'

'I suppo–'

'Why don't you come up to the house? She'd love to speak to you about what she's doing.'

'I'll try, but I want to be here for Tessa, you know Jenna had this fall and I've got lesson preparation.'

'Yes, yes of course, you must be busy.'

A yawn escapes my lips.

'It's all catching up with me a bit. I'll call back tomorrow.'

'Bye for now then, Christine.'

I have no intention to go out, but my gaze wanders back to the phrase, 'fish and chips' on Tessa's note and my stomach pinches.

The splatters of farmyard muck on my skirt and ache in my side recall the events at the farm. Something happened the day Robbie died, but the pieces don't fit together…there's something I'm missing.

The rose bush scatters shadows over the sitting room as I walk through. In the bedroom I take off my top. Grey bobbles of thread cling to the straps of my bra, the lace over the bust is stretched. I take a shirt out of the cupboard, pull over a grey tank top then squeeze into my better pair of jeans. I swipe over lipstick and run a brush through my hair. Regardless of the effort my reflection is still that of a schoolteacher. I imagine how I look sitting next to Tessa. There never was any contest over who attracted more attention. I never used to mind.

I set off for the St. Kilda Hotel. Through the bedroom window I see my discarded clothes lying on the double bed. I wonder what our life looks like to outsiders, my clothes next to Tessa's dressing gown and in the next window a mess of puzzles and dolls and trails of tiny stickers along the furniture.

The curtains of the abandoned room at the end are open. A crooked cross of shadow falls over the carpet. The wrinkled leather sofa glows softly and in the corner I make out the bureau. On the writing flap there are piles of neatly arranged letters as if someone has been going through them carefully.

The urge to return and indulge in trespass tingles briefly, but I pass on through the gate.

At the foot of Clay Loan there is a new water leak. The temporary traffic lights glow red and a man in a yellow mini-excavator is digging a thin trench parallel with the pavement following the etched lines of a pneumatic drill. Another workman in bright orange overalls throws me a crooked smile then pokes a cigarette into the centre of his mouth and picks up a shovel.

The wind ushers leaves from their hiding places, twisting their tattered brothers from the sycamore trees above. Mrs Dornoch passes me at the mini-roundabout, her battered shopping trolley obediently skittering at her heels. Mr Donaldson is parking his van outside the Salvation Army, his jacket tightly buttoned over his paunch.

The hotel's side entrance is through a grey rendered extension. The three square windows belonging to the toilets look out over the carpark. Two men are smoking by the disability access slope in the company of a ginger-haired boy shaking a half-empty bottle of Irn Bru. I half-recognise all of them. In the south it might be reason enough to start a conversation. I pass on without speaking.

Despite the uninviting exterior it's warm and welcoming inside. The walls are decorated with red paper embossed with gold fleur-de-lis. My hair has been tossed and muddled by the wind – I have wasted too many hours on hair styling in Orkney to be fussy any more. I'm only here to eat fish and chips.

In the saloon a well banked peat fire glows in the nook one side of the bar. Wood panelling lines the walls, painted a rich meaty brown. Cocktail menus sit squint in their perspex holders. The barman leans over the local paper, cocktail stick between his teeth. There is no sign of Tessa and I head upstairs.

Tessa is sitting in the bay window. The view behind overlooks the harbour. In the darkness beyond the marina floating red and white balls of light mark the edge of the sea and the land, the safe channels through the water.

Jenna is on Tessa's right, on the other side is Tommy, arms folded over his chest. Jenna is bouncing up and down holding a chip dunked in red sauce. Her eyes are bright, her attention switching rapidly between her mum and Tommy as she listens to what they are saying.

There is a fourth person with his back to me. His hair is vole-like, shiny and light brown. At the farm Ronald said he was too busy to stop, yet here he is supping a pint.

Chapter 22

Jenna looks up from her plate and frowns when she sees me.

'Am I going home?'

'Not for a peedie minute,' says Tessa.

'Anyone need a drink?' I say.

Tommy and Tessa shake their heads.

Ronald looks over his shoulder and smiles. The expression sits poorly on his features, it's the sort of grin you might see on a cheap toy clown.

'Pint'll do me, Christine,' he says.

The same as always Edwina serves drinks at that bar. Tonight, with her mallow lips, thick mascara and white-blond hair she looks no more than fifty. When I return, I land Ronald's pint clumsily and it slops onto the table. The creamy bubbles clear, leaving an invisible pool.

There is nowhere else to sit except next to him. The wine in my glass is from a bottle that has been open some time, acidic and very dry. I drink it quickly and my stomach gurgles in response.

Tessa says something to Tommy in a low voice. I can't catch what she says, but Tommy unfolds his arms and smirks. Ronald watches Jenna. She fidgets on her chair and swings another ketchup-loaded mouthful up from her plate.

'Recovered noo?' he says suddenly, turning to me.

'What?'

'Up at the farm,' he says. 'Wandering oot in front of tractors.'

Tessa sits up straighter in the bench and throws me an enquiring glance. It dawns on me that Ronald's changed his clothes and for once doesn't smell of silage.

'I'm fine,' I say.

Ronald sups his drink. He places it back on the table and leans back in his chair.

'You ken that your mum comes over,' he says, 'when bones get ploughed up. Police told Neil he's got to call her if it's human remains. Dad alwis had sacks of bones picked oot fae the fields,

117

used to keep them in the tractor shed. Had to get shot of them too.'

'It's about where things are found, otherwise they're pretty useless.'

'What happens to them afterwards?' says Tommy. 'I mean, you wouldn't like it if it wis your granny dug up and not put back under groond?'

'Be nothing to find if it wis wur granny,' says Ronald. 'Can't believe she ever stayed in the groond.'

'Ronald! You can't say that aboot Granny,' says Tessa.

She's smiling at him.

'Come on, Tess. All those potions for the kye, that uncanny talk aboot the lights on the barriers. Ken she knew what was going to happen to you before you ever did.'

'Well, she got you all wrong,' says Tessa. 'Thowt you'd make something of yoursel.'

Ronald laughs.

'And she kent that you'd be trouble,' he says.

Tessa narrows her eyes, but her expression is tolerant. She looks across at me.

'You were thirsty.'

The glass in my hand is empty.

'No harm in that,' says Tommy. 'Get you another, Christine?'

I nod my head.

'Ronald?'

'Sure, keep you twa company.'

Tommy heads to the bar. To make out she's not been watching our table Edwina refills the pork scratchings and keeps him waiting. Nothing is ever done in a hurry.

Jenna wriggles off her seat and follows the maroon swirls in the carpet. She takes tiny steps, placing the tips of her toes tightly against each other. Tessa watches Tommy; more specifically, her gaze moves over and around the back pockets of his jeans and the smooth muscular lines beneath the worn trousers. It's embarrassing being able to follow her train of thought.

Although both work out of doors Ronald is pale in comparison, less healthy looking.

'Mum, I need the toilet.'

'C'mon. Before Tommy gets back.'

The sound of tapping heels disappears along the corridor. Ronald leans forward, squinting at the reflection of the bar in the bay window. Tommy's fallen into conversation with Edwina who's taking far more time to prepare his drinks than she did mine.

'Seems a long time since the funeral,' he says.

The afternoon in the cathedral does seem a long time ago. The sensation of shock is all I really remember. My senses were blunted, dull. For weeks afterwards it was as if I couldn't taste or smell. I couldn't even feel what my hand rested on, whether it was hot or cold, rough or smooth. Everything was smothered by the overwhelming feeling of loss, a terrible homesick lostness. I dreaded the moments when the grief lifted, little fake moments of normality, because of the pain when it returned again.

'Rob's a fair miss,' says Ronald. He tries to make his voice casual, but there's a deliberateness in the way he delivers the words. 'Whit a shame,' he says. 'Making mistakes wasna him.'

'No,' I say quietly.

The image of the shiny bean-like coffin, surrounded by frothy white flowers comes to mind. I wish Tommy would come back from the bar.

'No under normal conditions.'

Ronald's hand darts under the table and grasps mine. I try and pull away but he keeps hold.

I hiss under my breath, 'Let go.'

He's looking at me fiercely now, his eyes filled with reflections. He squeezes tightly.

'Why'd you come back?' he whispers.

'Let go of my hand.'

He leans over and quickly, roughly, kisses me on the cheek then he releases my hand. Before I can wipe a hand across my cheek Tommy appears back from the bar.

'Christine wis just askin aboot the accident,' says Ronald.

Tommy draws at the froth of his beer.

'That so?'

'No, I wasn't...'

'How wis it in the tank Tom? It's got to be close in there.'

I want to kick him, anything to make him shut up. I don't want to talk about it, I don't want to hear about what happened, yet part of me is so desperate to know that it's always at the back of my mind. My throat tightens, so dry it hurts.

With the red velvet curtains behind him Tommy's face floats like a white sun in a red sky. Tommy draws breath to speak. His words echo around my head like waves glooping under a jetty.

'Pretty much a sub crossed wae a aeroplane,' says Tommy. 'Airtight once you're in, bloody his to be.'

'What exactly do you do in there?'

'No too much, wait for nitrogen to get oot the blood. It's the bubbles coming oot too queek that's the problem.'

'You came up too quickly.'

Without realizing, I say the words out loud. Tommy continues.

'They put you at the depth pressure you were at when you started to surface, then slowly bring you back.'

'How wis it you came up so queek? Did you get the giddies?'

Ronald speaks casually, but his face is excited.

'It's more like pins and needles,' says Tommy, 'little pricks here and there…hard to relate what it's like. The current was fast…and cold…fuckin colder than I've kent it. I thowt we were in trouble…the silt being all stirred up, getting dispersed by the current. It wasna long before I didna ken which way was fuckin up nor doon…'

I try and interrupt, but he keeps talking. The curved surface of my glass stretches the reflections in the bar, everything is distorted, the colours lurid against the black windows.

'…I'd gone too deep…Rob wis even deeper. I kept sight o his air bottles…trusted he kent what he was daen, but he never made to turn roond…I couldna see me hand in front o me face, never mind pick up a scallop you ken? But as long as I kept moving along I felt I'd be alright and we'd get to clear water.'

'What made you come up?' I say.

Tommy takes a drink. His knee is shaking up and down with a compulsive uneven tremor.

'Well it was…I started hearing this voice in me heed telling me to get on with the job…and then I couldna credit the gauge when I saw it. There was no fuckin way we'd been doon so long or gone so deep. I showed him, I showed Rob…but he shook his heed…he wouldna come back…I'd to fuckin pull off his weights…by then I wis in a panic, no thinkin straight, but I kent we had to get up… maybe things were different to what I ken, and maybe I'm no too smart the way I did things, but comin up didno fuckin feel fast at the time. Felt like we wir slow. Like a slow motion picture, you ken?'

'You did your best…' I say.

'Thing is Christine, I kent something wasna right at the jetty…Robbie hardly checked his gear. Didn't even buther rowing with Brian fur buggering aroond with the radio…We've all been doon after a few drinks the night before, I didna see the harm…earning a pound picking up scallops…we'd done it a hundred fuckin times.'

The broken phrases float over the nervous drum beat of Tommy's knee.

'Brian hauled us into the boat, all agitated aboot the time we'd been gone doon. Brian put in a call on channel 16 to be on the safe side, but we thowt we'd gotten away wae it. Had a fuckin laugh aboot Rob's weights gaen to the bottom. But then Rob got kindo groggy…said he'd a headache. We tried to get Rob onto the oxygen, but he kept fuckin flipping off the mask. Then came on me that I felt like I was fuckin made o lead. When we tied up at Houton Rob wisna right. We both had pins and needles up and doon.'

'And Doctor Carnegie was waiting,' says Ronald.

'Aye, he was there. Looked at Robbie then gave me the once uver. When Brian telt him we'd been doon near forty-feet he telt us we'd have to go in the tank for a spell. Rob came roond a bit, started being stupid, fuckin wrestling to get to his feet, near enough walked into the groond…didn't ken what way was up… said he didn't want to go… said he'd to go home. Then he wis haddin his heed saying he was so stupid no one could help him.'

'Carnegie took you,' prompts Ronald.

'Aye, he drove us roond to Stromness and got us in the tank – ambulance was all the way over at the pissing Hope. Sure, it wis a tight squeeze in there wae Rob on a trolley. He settled us in…waited ootside watching for a peedie while, checking the controls and what no. You see there's a time delay before anyone can come in…you can't just open the door. Even if Carnegie'd been right there…ken it wouldna have mad a fuckin difference.'

'That's what the paper said,' says Ronald.

'It was a embolism – bubble in the brain,' says Tommy. His voice loses its rise and fall, becomes quite flat and toneless. 'No one could've done anything.'

His eyes are cloudy, grey like a tranquil sea after a storm has finally worn itself out.

To begin with I think his gaze is simply resting idly on his drink, then I realize he's watching the tiny streams of bubbles rising from the bottom of the glass. The silver spheres spiral upwards through the amber liquid, desperate to break the surface.

'Maybe' says Tommy, 'maybe it was because he was tired oot fae shifting all that shite at The Blackhoose… but Doctor Carnegie said he shouldna have gone doon if he'd had a drink. We'd done it plenty o times before and never had a problem but they say it can catch up with you. Mind on, it was for me and Brian to say if we thowt he wasno fit fur the dive.'

'Passed the police interview, didn't you?' says Ronald.

He's jocular, but there's an edge to his voice.

'Passed? Didn't need to say anything. Dive tanks and computers told the whole fuckin story. Even Brain's GPS was spot on for once.'

Tommy pushes his pint away. His voice is barely more than a whisper.

'Nothing's like being in the tank…that fuckin smell of…hospital…even with the mask on… my eyes shut that's all there is…this smell…Christ, it was…all that sweating and waiting. No, nothing could've been done for him…it was a fluke, fuckin fluke.'

His eyes swim with tears. My head is full of questions. It was all preventable. But how can I be angry with Tommy? It wasn't his fault.

Robbie what were you doing? What where you thinking?

Tommy clears his throat and a little of his normal voice returns.

'Something distracted him. He must have kent he'd gone too far. He saw me signal and fuckin kept going.'

'It was an accident,' I say.

'Like I say, we'd all done a dive after drink before,' says Tommy.

He catches my eye. From across the bar Jenna skips towards us. Tommy pastes a smile across his lips.

'Here y'are, peedie lass. Have a bag of those. Keep you quiet.'

Tommy tosses a packet across the table. Jenna snatches up the crisps then perches next to me. Tessa slots back in next to Tommy.

Thinking no one's watching Tessa reaches over and puts a hand to steady his jigging knee.

'Will you call it a day with the boat?' says Ronald.

'Scallops's good money. But Ah'm no stupid. I need something else to earn a pound. How's you likin teaching, Christine?'

'It'd mean a peedie while retraining,' says Tessa, smiling.

'Piss off,' says Tommy. 'Ken I was never good at anything at school.'

'Hardly knew my way round when I arrived. It's all changed,' I say. 'Moira taking the primary fours, she's been friendly.'

'Moira Gowrie? I didn't think she'd be a teacher,' says Tessa. 'I never heard her say more than twa words.'

I draw breath to say something, but Ronald interrupts me.

'Why did you leave the sooth, Christine?'

The room is suddenly quiet, only the clink of glasses from Edwina idly rearranging the bar.

'I wanted to be back near my family,' I say.

His top lip curls a fraction.

'Lindsay still crazy?'

'She's bipolar,' I say. 'Not bonkers.' I don't want to say any more, but I carry on talking. My voice is high and fast. 'She's on new medication that keeps her more level now without too many side effects. But it's hard for her to get on, to get away from home. You know how prejudiced people can be about mental health issues.'

'You mean like sayin folk are crazy,' says Tessa, throwing Ronald a cool look.

'Keep your hair on,' says Ronald.

Of course they know she's living at home, but I wonder if he knows, if anyone knows about her suicide attempt. Tessa and I still haven't talked about it, not head on, not about why it happened.

Ronald has something else on his mind.

'She was at the funeral,' he says.

There's a moment of silence. Lindsay practically held my hand all day. She can be strong, surprisingly subtle about some things.

'We all miss Rob,' says Tessa.

Her voice is sympathetic, but I think she's missed the point. Ronald's not remembering grief, he's trying to figure something out. Tessa's hand still rests on Tommy's knee. She leans across the table and sneaks a crisp out of her daughter's bag. Jenna scrunches the packet closed and holds it close to her chest.

A group of women enter the bar, they're from the year below us as school. Mary Slater is first through the door, wearing a leopard skin top with tight jeans and exposing her bony shoulders. Ronald puts his empty glass back on the table and pushes back his chair. His face is stony; no clown's smile now. He mutters something under his breath.

'I hope it works out fur the three o you.'

He stands and leaves the bar.

'What was that about?' I say, but when I turn back Tommy has his arm around Tessa's shoulders. No one seems to have heard my question or noticed Ronald's abrupt exit.

'I'm thirsty,' says Jenna.

'Should've shared your crisps,' says Tessa.

'I'll take you home,' I say.

'Thanks Chrissy. I won't be late.'

The generous proportions of the old hotel and smell of wax polish and fried food on the stairs brings to mind a holiday spent in Folkestone. My mother had been working and mostly it had rained. Jenna slides her hand around the banisters and tells me the names of all the boats in the photographs on the walls.

We leave the harbour and take the protected route along Albert Street through town. There is a hard chill in the air and our clothes are riffled by the wind. Jenna does not seem to mind, she skips here and there dodging bollards, flicking up water from puddles.

The deep-set windows of the shops shy away from the wind and show few signs of modification for commercial use. Occasionally, openings have been widened on the ground floors and a handful have lights installed to illuminated displays. It is all so different from the south where everything is exposed and brightly displayed for passers by to inspect, where crowds take pleasure in window shopping.

There's another feature that draws my attention tonight. Either side of every opening whether for a window or door there are penny sized black holes. In daylight it's possible to see screw threads burrowing into the stonework. They hold bolts that secure barriers to prevent damage from the Christmas and New Year Ba – a battle with a ball smuggled through the streets. When we first moved I'd though they were left over from protecting property from bomb blasts during the war. Now I know the game was far older than the war, and that any bomber with fuel and luck enough to get to Orkney would drop its load on the ships sheltering in Scapa Flow. As we walk home the small black eyelets attract my gaze over and over again.

Chapter 23

Tessa returns at eight o' clock. Tommy is with her. He sits watching television in the next room while she goes and kisses Jenna good night. I peer into the fridge, nothing is as tempting as the smell of fish and chips at the hotel. Tessa exchanges a few words with Tommy then looks in my direction. Tommy rises from the sofa and heads to the bathroom.

Dressed in black, Tessa stands in the kitchen doorway. She looks like a dancer preparing to limber up for rehearsals.

'Christine, I've got a favour to ask?'

'Mmm?'

'I'm getting a bite to eat wae Tommy and…'

'I can look in on Jenna,' I say. 'I'm not going anywhere.'

'Thing is…he can't really have another drink then drive back to his place.'

'So?'

'I thowt…can he stay the night?'

'I suppose. The sofa in the end room's large enough to stretch out on, but it'll be cold.'

'Great. I'll fetch you the blankets.'

'What? You're joking.'

'Unless you want three of us in the bed. What d'you think I meant?'

'I don't want him…what about Jenna?'

'She won't ken,' says Tessa. 'He's away at six over to Dounby digging out ditches. Come on, Christine.'

'It's my place. Why should I?'

'It's one night. Why's it a big deal?'

'I'm not sleeping in that freezing room.'

'Oh, at least be honest, Christine.'

'What do you mean?'

Tessa's eyes glitter, jet black, all angles and faces like cut stones they catch the light.

'I don't want to fight,' she says.

'What is it I need to honest about?'

'Robbie's gone and he's no coming back. Not for me, not for Jenna. Not for anybody.'

My heart thumps hard and slow.

'It's too soon,' I say, quickly.

'For who?'

There's a flush from the bathroom. Tommy steps into the corridor and moseys through the living room. He picks up his jacket from the back of a chair and hooks it over his shoulder.

'Want anything, Chrissy?' he says.

'No.'

Tessa lets Tommy walk ahead of her. If he senses the atmosphere has changed, he ignores it convincingly. She pauses before stepping out of the door.

'Can't I move on?' she says.

The tears in her eyes take me by surprise, but it doesn't change my reply.

'No,' I say. 'Not from Robbie.'

The door slam reverberates around the dark kitchen.

A stony feeling grows inside me. I pick up my phone and send Tessa a text, 'The bedroom is yours.' Then I take a bottle of wine from the counter, pick up a glass and head down the corridor.

I switch off the lights. Standing in the dark feels safe, the right place for the self-righteous and self-destructive. My breath calm, I act quite deliberately. Finally, with the door closed behind me I turn on the main light in the end room. The dark shade keeps the ceiling and edges of the room in shadow, only the sofa directly beneath is brightly illuminated. I close the curtains and cosset the room. The piles of letters are waiting for me. I arrange them on the sofa then go back out into the corridor and take a pillow and blankets from the airing cupboard. I wrap a blanket around my shoulders and drain my glass.

The piles have been separated into correspondence between Robbie and Tessa, and other miscellaneous letters. The first pile is more numerous and mostly short messages, the majority written during the weeks Robbie was working on Flotta. They contain pictures from Jenna, one has a caption added by Tessa saying, 'Ducks on the Peedie Sea,' but it could be anything. There are exchanges of factual information about renovating

The Blackhouse, there's the odd piece of gossip from Tessa and occasional reports of technical problems or irritations with colleagues from Robbie. Sometimes there are references to thinking about each other, but there is scant emotional content.

I flip through with no particular interest until a letter dated April fourth.

> ....s*hifting all the cement and sand without a digger takes forever. I'm always here because I'm getting it done. Peedie lass can be up here in the fresh air, she'd like that, but I ken you're not interested until it's finished – it was fair-handed of Neil to let us have the place, but I can't see it's worth carrying on when you spend all the time picking out things that aren't done well enough or we can't afford to have...*

I search but I can't find the rest. As far as I can see it's the last letter he ever wrote to Tessa.

The sound of tapping on the window turns my head. I freeze, listening to the balls of hail rattle around the window nook, plink-plink, they're almost musical as they fall. The thick walls exude a quiet loneliness as if the room resents no longer being the busy heart of the house.

I pull the blankets around my shoulders and turn my attention to the second pile. The letter from Marion that I've already read is on the surface. Beneath, there is a wedge of congratulations-on-the-birth-of-your-baby-girl cards with all pale pink edges, flowers and polkadots.

Then I recognise a new writing style – my own. A scruffier version of what has become a neat teacher's hand, but it is unmistakable none the less. I smooth out the creases and place the page to one side, refill my glass and shuffle through the rest of the pile. I find another letter and place it on top of the first then another and another. In fact there's a whole series of letters that I wrote to Robbie before we left school. It takes a moment before I figure out that of course everything Robbie possessed belongs to Tessa.

It seems so entirely unnecessary to read them since I wrote them, yet I might not ever see them again. I'm curious about who I was. In the first letter I'd written about the options I had for the future; I remember I'd been fishing for Robbie to ask me to stay. I skim through then move on. In the next letter my writing is stretched out, the flicks more pronounced as if the note has been written in a hurry.

Dear Robbie,

Why do you let Tessa hang all over you? You don't have to put up with it. <u>Tell her</u>. She's meant to be going out with Brian – although everyone knows she's only hanging around him because he's passed his driving test and can pick her up in that deathtrap machine that he thinks is so amazing. Tessa's dad hates him - mind you, her dad hates most people. She ended up at mine on Saturday night again because they'd had such a row. She'd walked most of the way then someone picked her up and gave her a lift over the last barrier. She's being a bit weird at the moment, kind of given up about exams. I don't know why. She says she's going to fail them all.
Don't say anything to her about us <u>at the moment</u>. Okay?

Love Christine

There's half a page of torn filing paper.

Dear Robbie,

I wanted to explain about last night – I wasn't really cross with you, I know it made me look bad the way I reacted, but Lyndsay'd been on at me all day. And I'm sorry about her flirting, she'll do it to anyone. She's completely unpredictable at the moment. Most of the time she's not taking her pills – Mum and Dad have no idea half the stuff she gets up to.

Did Tommy get home without being sick again? (Remember when he puked in Tessa's shoes at the beach?) I'm not too bad, bit slow and fuzzy headed. I was worse after the Christmas party when Tessa had that bottle of rum.

Mum and Dad keep talking to me about university. They say I should get off Orkney and do my own thing but at the same time don't trust me enough to have a party in the gallery. I'm sick of never doing anything exciting.

I want to go out – or could you come over here? Mum's got another conference and Dad's going this time for a change. We don't have to tell anyone you're coming over, especially not Tessa, you know she can't keep secrets.

Love Christine.

It had been big deal to write 'Love' on the end of the letter. Robbie knew Lindsay would be there, and that she'd be a bitch and tell everyone.

Dear Robbie,

I guess it's not your fault your cousin was visiting while Mum and Dad were away. Lindsay had two blokes from Electrorkney and Neil over playing poker until four in the morning.

At least they didn't break anything. I suppose it was an okay night, but it would have been better if you'd been here. I'm going to be helping out at the gallery once school

finishes. Might get enough money to go south
for a trip. What do you think? Could go to 'T
in the Park'? See you at the party.

Love Christine.

The next letter is dated the night of Tessa's party. It was written in the early hours of the morning. There was no mobile signal up at the farm back then and anyway I didn't want to send some lame text that might not arrive for hours. I never knew who'd pick up the phone if I tried to call him at home.

The risen sun had burst between two shifting towers of cumulonimbus as I went out to post the letter. I was still wearing my black dress, woozy from lack of sleep and drinking.

Dear Robbie,

Forget everything I said. It was the wind
driving me crazy – and too many cocktails.
The party's still going on and I'm at home and
all I can think about is you.
    Come over soon, really soon. I'm at the
gallery all weekend. There's no reason not to
tell Tessa about us now. I LOVE YOU and
I'm sorry.
    Come over soon,

Christine.

PS Maybe we can pick up where we left off?

The sun withdrew leaving a pearl-grey sky with tumbling boulders of clouds as I pushed the envelope into the postbox by the gallery turning. The wind stole the air from my nostrils, flushing out the warm alcoholic vapours. I wanted Robbie to know wherever he was I loved him, that I would always love him and nobody else could take his place.

The writing on the next letter is ragged, full of untidy flourishes. Words are crossed out, re-written heavily then underlined. There's no signature, no 'Dear Robbie' at the beginning.

Why did he keep it? Did he never have a clear out? Surely that's what people do when they get married.

Robbie you knew I was angry when I said those things. You knew I wasn't serious. Do you think I wanted to go home? It's ridiculous. Were you trying to be stupid?

How could you do this to me? Tessa's my best friend. Do you have any idea what it feels like?

When you realise what you've done I hope it hurts like hell.

I don't want to see either of you ever again. I can't even think about you. You and Tessa can do whatever you like.

I'm leaving.

Christine.

I didn't write to him again. We didn't communicate. Nothing except the invitation to the wedding two years later. They knew I wouldn't go.

I expect nobody thought I would go to Anne and Brian's wedding either.

Chapter 24

The crumpled letter is clenched in my hand when I wake. My cheeks are tight from dried tears. Something has woken me, a creaking sound, the sound of something moving in the darkness. I cock my ear and listen. The wind is soft and low outside then the sound comes again, a restless rustling, shifting. There's a short muffled exhalation, a release of breath. A moment later there's the mutter of a male voice followed by a female murmur.

I pull the blanket high over my ears and curl up tightly in a ball.

I remember the monotonous grey-white summer days waiting to leave Orkney, walking past the post and wire fences to the beach, staring at the grey and blue horizon when it appeared out of the haar.

I craved privacy somewhere it was impossible. At school always the first items for dissection in the common room on Monday morning had been who had done what over the weekend. We perched like cormorants on the arms of the battered chairs or leaned on the scratched study booths. Whispered details became more and more intimate as rumours circulated, laughter was loud and sudden. Had so and so done it yet? Had they done it more than once? Had they done it properly? Did they even know how to do it properly? Would they get caught?

Mostly Tessa had brazened things out, boasting and exaggerating to throw people off the scent of what she'd really been doing. She enjoyed it. It was all a game.

Questions pound inside my head, the same ones I had at the time, over and over again. A strange feeling of nausea rises from the intensity of memory, my anger feels fresh.

The shadows in the room don't make sense any more. The texture of the darkness doesn't correspond with the shapes I know are there. I close my eyes and let the letter fall. It grazes the blanket and glides to the floor. I press my fingers against my lips and stay still while a flush passes over me then rest against the cushions. My muscles soften, relaxing against the cool leather, my body curled in the mess of blankets. It's not the same as being held; it's a lonely empty place to search for comfort.

I've spent weeks forbearing, weeks smothering grief, weeks surviving the broken-hearted wretched loss while life continues around me.

I'm thirsty, but I don't want to move out of my coil of blankets. A bitter taste grows in my mouth. At times, I wonder whether things were the way I remember them. Everything seems foolhardy, inconsequential.

I want to believe it impossible for feelings to be conjured out of nothing. I want to believe that the sharp thrill when our eyes first met at Anne and Brian's wedding was reciprocated.

What right do you have to be so hard on Tessa?

I let the blankets slip. I stay still, feeling the small sharp sting of the cold. My skin goosepimples. My stomach is tight like a knotted chain.

I picture Tessa and Tommy curled up next to each other. Perhaps they are still moving, performing some afterthought act. Perhaps, not long from now, Tessa will think Tommy takes up too much space in the bed and breathes too heavily. Perhaps, she'll think she's better off sharing with me.

Maybe she's making other comparisons.

I'm alone, toes aching with cold, feeling slightly sick again. I cover-up, pushing into the small warm hollow my body has made.

There's a satisfying splash of paper as the letters are knocked overboard.

Tessa has never mentioned having the letters I wrote to Robbie. Really, they should belong to me – she can't be vexed about me reading them.

As I drift to sleep my thoughts wander back to a memory. It is not accurate. The passers-by in the street are people who could not possibly have been in Orkney; my grandmother, a girl called Maya who I kissed during fresher's week. She holds a door open and smiles at me as I walk into the shop where Tessa worked.

Inside, I stroll past the displays of cotton dresses. Tessa is folding piles of white cloths. She's wearing the same dress she wore for the party.

'Whit like?' she says.

'No bad,' I say.

'Get home all right?'

'Did I miss anything?'

'No much,' she says.

She folds another cloth, pinching the corners with sharp red nails.

'I didn't want to leave,' I say. 'Do you think Robbie was upset?'

'Upset? Why should he be?'

'Because I went early' I say.

'I didn't notice.'

There's a loud slam somewhere out of sight. I'm distracted for a moment and when I turn back Tessa has moved. She's standing at the edge of the children's clothing. Munchkin-sized outfits hang in tiers along the walls.

'What happened?' I ask.

Tessa smiles at me, teeth shiny and white. A surge of love sweeps through me. I picture us rolled up in our towels after swimming with our heads poking out and waddling around the changing room.

God, how I loved her.

There's another slam. Rain begins to drum on the skylight.

'Nothing,' she says. 'Nothing happened.'

She had a chance and she didn't tell me.

Chapter 25

When she finally told me, the day and night were beginning to make sense again. The weather was mild and there was a rare humidity in the air that exacerbated the feeling of calm.

I was driving Tessa home from work – after the party, Dad had started taking me out daily for drives, it didn't take long to reach the standard needed to pass on the island roads. She sat leaning forward a little in the passenger seat, eyes on the road ahead. The car quickly began to feel warm.

Hay crops were being mown and around the horizon tractors worked in pairs mowing and hauling grass for winter fodder. Round bales studded the fields like peppercorns on ham.

I'd been working in the gallery and Tessa in the shop. Robbie was busy working for his father. Despite what had nearly happened at the party one way or another we'd hardly seen each other, we certainly hadn't taken up where we left off. If I came into Kirkwall for shopping I'd pick Tessa up then drive her back to the farm to save her the long slow bus journey.

The distant hills were lilac. There was a gentle merging of sky and sea, nothing to indicate the true position of the horizon. It was impossible to tell if the catamaran sliding towards St Margaret's Hope was in the air or on water.

Tessa had started telling me about her new uniform.

'I've to choose a suit or dress. I've gone for the dress…Mum'll adjust it. Val said I get twenty percent off new stock when it comes in, which is handy. I'm on the till tomorrow on my own.'

'There's a cruise ship,' I said.

'Val said they want new trainee managers. And at Christmas there's a special preview evening. Last year they got a bonus in January, but…'

'Doesn't it look weird,' I said, 'like the islands are floating.'

'Kind of, but I'm no thinking that far aheed…'

'You can't even see the chimney for the flare on Flotta.'

'I suppose.'

At the second barrier the sea was flat and granite-grey on one side, green and rippled on the other. The road swung rollercoaster up the hill and then down beside the beach. On the ragged shore sheep wandered and grazed the coarse grass and seaweed.

A few sharp turns took us to the next barrier. Shipwrecks jutted out of the water on either side, grey and white water frothing around the rust-wrecked decks; bright pink buoys were tied at intervals around their decks to lobster creels and shone out in the soft air. Tommy and Robbie had already started making the odd dive. Brian had heard of a boat they could use from someone on Westray and they'd plans to make money collecting scallops for hotels during the summer season.

'How's the shop going?' I said.

'It's all right.'

Tessa looked out of the window. Her face was very pale. It looked like she was spending too much time indoors.

The road continued to wind around the fields. Cows rested like upturned yoles after a day grazing and chewing the cud. Black backed gulls skimmed over the low cliffs sending arctic terns boomeranging into the sky to protect their young.

A tractor and trailer had stopped by the turning to the farm. Neil was yawning in his cab while grass tipped from his trailer into the winter silage store.

I turned up the lane into the steading. Splatters of muck indicated the recent passage of cows through the yard. At the side of The Byre I turned off the engine and firmly pulled on the handbrake. Tessa's face showed no interest in our arrival and she remained posed as she had throughout the drive. I wobbled the gearstick too and fro to make sure it was in neutral. The action caught Tessa's attention, shaking her out of her reverie.

'I should learn to drive, now I've a few quid,' she said. 'But there're other things I want.'

She still made no effort to leave the car, her legs swept backwards almost gripping the seat, her hands pressed against her thighs.

There wasn't room to face each other and talk properly. The dull sun pressed against the glass, even more oppressive now the car was stationary. I could feel warmth through my clothes and on the side of my face. My hands were clammy where they rested on the wheel. I wondered why she didn't invite me inside.

'Christine?'

'Yes.'

'I want to tell you something. I've wanted to tell you for weeks.'

I had no idea what she was about to say, yet my heart started to beat more quickly.

'I'd have done it sooner… but I can't stand what you'll think…and I can't keep seeing you and not say anything. I've got to tell you, but it's no easy. I've tried to make a start, but you…there was always something else we ended up speaking aboot.'

She had a sort of animal look beneath her make-up, her eyelashes, rich black as ever, her skin powdered, but there were grey patches under her eyes, tiny red capillaries stretched across the whites.

Her lips came together and set themselves into a serious straight line, then she began again.

'I don't know if I can do it….then I can't not do it. Noo I've started at least, so I'll have to go on.' She gave a short laugh, 'And…even if this is the last moment you're my friend I'll always be yours. Whatever happens.'

'Tessa, whatever it is you can tell me.'

'I'm pregnant.'

'Pregnant?'

'Only by a few weeks. I hardly needed to do a test. I'm no like you with months in between. I did buy one though and there it was – two blue lines. I've not told anyone else.'

'What're you going to do?'

'I can't seem to think…The days go by and I ken I need to do somethin…I can't keep it secret forever….it's all so crazy…I never thought it'd happen to me.'

I leaned over and put my arm around her shoulder. She leaned towards me and rested her head.

'It'll be okay,' I said. 'I'm here. We'll figure it out.'

'No,' she said. 'Can't you see? It's not okay. I've been so stupid, Chrissy.'

I squeezed her shoulders and tried to think of something more reassuring to say; something that didn't sound untrue. We both knew Alfred would go ballistic.

'I ken what I could do,' she said, drawing away from me.

She began to rub the dashboard in front of her, making small disturbances in the dust.

'An abortion?'

'It's early enough,' she said. 'But it's no...I don't think I could do it. Not because ...'

'What?'

'Do you think you could keep it secret? Living here? But it's no just that. It's... '

'You can talk to someone,' I said. 'I'd go with you.'

'It's who the father is,' she said.

'You don't have to tell anyone.'

'I've thought about that. I think about it a lot, but...it's the same reason I couldn't not tell you. Once you know, Chrissy... and you see I've got to tell you then...'

'What?'

'...it was at the party...efter you went,' she said. 'I suppose we were both a bit blootered and we both needed someone.' She pauses. 'Robbie was there.'

My hands slip from the wheel. Her words tumble, roll against each other, dislodge the sense of what she is saying.

'It wis once.'

'It's not true,' I said. 'Not...true.'

'It is.'

'You wouldn't. He wouldn't. You were never even interested in him. You said you were pals, you'd never think of him as anything else.'

'You never said anything to me about how you felt about him. Even though anyone could see you couldn't keep your eyes off him when you were in the same room. God, you're so wrapped up in yoursel.'

'I'm not the one...Tessa, even if I didn't say anything you knew how I felt.'

'I wanted to tell you,' she said. 'And I've told you noo.'

'What do you want me to say, Tessa?'

'I wanted you to understand,' she said.

I turned the key in the ignition.

'Don't go. Please. Let me explain.'

'Are you going to tell him?'

I put the gears into reverse.

'I told him I was on the pill. That it'd be fine.'

It was as if concrete had been poured inside me, filling me up, setting hard.

'Get out of the car. I want to go.'

'Christine, can't you stay? Come inside, please. I don't know what to do.'

'I'm going.'

Tessa fumbled for the door handle and half-tumbled out of the car. She stood hugging herself watching me reverse, a wild pathetic hope in her eyes that I might change my mind.

I turned the wheel full lock and spun the car backwards. I swerved away between the barns narrowly missing the tractor and trailer coming up in the opposite direction.

The landscape disappeared around me. A place to inhabit and nothing more, nothing more. It was a place that could be left behind.

Lindsay did not want me to go. The week before I was due to leave she'd threatened to take an overdose of some painkillers she'd been prescribed for her broken toe. Dad had called Doctor Carnegie to the house. I don't know what they talked about, but afterwards she apologized, said she was bluffing, and handed over the pills.

There had been a period of calm, of apologetic politeness that lasted until I went away.

Doctor Carnegie had said her suicide threats were simply threats – not a central part of her illness, it was a way of expressing how low she felt. Her new medication is Zyprexia, two small white pills to be taken every breakfast time. She complains about the side effects, putting on weight and feeling dizzy. If it were me I'd take them. I'd want to be normal.

I don't know how Robbie found out Tessa was pregnant; perhaps she told him straight off, but whatever happened he didn't try to contact me afterwards. Tessa is not good at keeping secrets. She tells people, hoping they will keep them for her.

Chapter 26

The wind has died completely by dawn and the dull light of autumn is smudged around the curtain poles when I wake. The sound of water comes from somewhere, an uneven splattering noise. A bus rumbles past. I pull my crumpled shirt over my exposed stomach, resentful of a poor and uncomfortable night's sleep.

I gather the letters and replace them on the bureau in a single messy pile. Being upright awakens pressure on my bladder. I swing open the bathroom door while unzipping my trousers.

'Steady-on, Christine.'

'Jesus, Tommy. What are you doing?'

'Getting a shave. Got to get to work.'

He puts a pink razor on the side of the basin and splashes water on his face. Droplets fleck the mirror. My expression reflects back at me, frown lines, pursed lips. Tommy flashes a relaxed smile.

'That's my razor,' I say.

'No bad, funny lass's handle, mind.'

He winks at me in the mirror, pats his face with a towel then leaves. I close the door quickly and slide the lock then sit on the toilet with my head in my hands. I stand under the hot water of the shower for a long time. Even after I brush my teeth a bitter metallic taste lingers in my mouth.

There's no sign of Tommy when I come out. The bedroom door is open, but it's still dark inside. Tessa's body twitches when I switch on the overhead light. The room smells musky, breathed out alcohol mixed with male deodorant and cigarettes. I catch the scent of Tessa's sweat, peppery and sweet. Her clothes are everywhere, her yellow dressing gown lying in a silk pile at the foot of the bed. I try not to look closely, but can't help imagining creamy inkblots in the creases of the bedlinen.

Tessa stays beneath whirls of duvet, in space warmed with someone else.

Part of me wants to sit on the side of the bed and talk. Part of me wants to be honest and share everything with her, but I pull a sweater over my wet hair, turn off the light and close the door.

I drink tea, eat toast and mark exercise books. Before leaving I knock on Jenna's door and tell her it's time to get up. I don't go back to Tessa.

Outside, the air is damp. Water stains the edges of buildings and walls, forms rings around discarded gum and cigarette butts.

For the first time I wish I'd never come back. You see, I'd adjusted to the south. I'd made friends. I was beginning to know the town and navigate its one-way system without panic. I'd stopped feeling daunted when surrounded by people I didn't know. I'd become accustomed to being unrecognised. There was nothing in the south that evoked memories of the past, nothing that connected me to anyone. I could have been altogether a different person. Physically I was the same, but I could make myself up as I went along. In Orkney I'm embedded in everything, part of history.

For example, this morning on Main Street, I know Mattieus Stollen who is driving the street cleaning machine. The furry ear flaps of his hat bounce up and down like cocker spaniel ears when the buggy jerks. He's banned by all four pharmacies on mainland Orkney from buying certain cough medicines. Several older cashiers who're partial to a drop of something themselves still sell him a bottle. There can't be too much harm in it, assuming his vehicle is speed-limited and that the rotating brushes would cushion any accidental impact. And I know he's got one tooth left at the front and pretends to be deaf. He looks seventy, but is in fact fifty-eight.

I know all this about the road sweeper – someone I've never even spoken with.

The vehicle scuttles along the street, bouncing over the stone slabs, cigarette smoke leaking from its cab. I turn away from the cloying burnt treacle fumes.

In the newsagent window there are three black-edged funeral announcements. Two of the names are familiar and the third rings a bell. My family has only lived on the island for twenty-years so I can't be expected to know everyone yet.

In the south, where mazes of red brick terraces surround multi-story car-parks and churches have security keypads, I often thought about Orkney. I thought about Robbie a lot. I imagined his life with Tessa and I thought how I must be fading in his memory, how her face would be always before him, her body beside him. And they had a baby. That changed everything.

Chapter 27

There are already lights on in the pharmacy. Mrs Garriock is behind the counter sticking tickets on white paper bags. I turn up the road past the cathedral. Inside the iron railings the lichen stained graves are sheltered beneath the red walls. This ancient kirkyard is long since full; fresh graves are dug in St Olaf's cemetery, where I have still not visited.

News that Robbie and Tommy were in trouble was out quickly; every moment was seen by somebody. The events mixed like a drop of dye through water into community gossip, swiftly imprinted into the pavement then trodden underfoot. Of course, I wasn't on a list of anyone who should be informed; that was Tessa.

But the car journey from the jetty to Stromness was seen and noted by Mrs Dunnet who worked at the Bath and Tile shop, who was on the phone to her cousin Mrs Sutherland. Mrs Sutherland herself was on her way out with a delivery from the bakery for my mother's evening class – that was how my father found out. He understood that I'd want to know.

The playground is empty when I arrive. There's no one waiting for me, no one in the street. I have to wait for Bruce Jones the janitor to unlock the main entrance. Grey-haired and blue-eyed he has an Irish twist to his accent that places him on the Western Isles. He is nearly seventy; but for the white hairs growing from his ears and nose, you would put him as twenty years younger. His uncanny appearances at playground spats keep the children in awe of him and he can fix anything from a basketball hoop to a finger.

The day passes without excitement. It is five o' clock before I leave. I've had no communication with Tessa all day, although I can guess what she's been thinking.

A sort of telepathy used to exist between us. We'd sit watching people without saying anything, then a glance, a nudge, a sigh or quite often not even that and we'd understand exactly what the other had been thinking. We could mutually exclude people from our conversations with ease, sectioning off our own private space.

I thought it was exceptional at the time, but I perceive it between my pupils, this secret sensitive mind reading. I also thought – I don't know why – that we would grow out of it as we became older.

Even after everything that's happened it remains surprisingly intact. It is not something that *can* be got rid of.

There are times when I want to forget her. I want there to be less in common between us. I want our experiences to be separate. For sure, I don't understand how she can have Tommy in our bed, attractive as he might be.

These are my thoughts as I walk home to the cottage. I open the gate and pass the bobbing crocosmia. The curtains are open and the lights are on, but I cannot go inside. Sometimes Tessa and I are like magnets pulling and pushing each other apart. Tonight, I simply can't be near her.

There's a movement by the kitchen window, a lump rises in my throat. I go directly to the car and start the engine. It's time to see Lindsay.

I'm curious about her renovation project. Her plans always suck people in to help, they can't help catching her excitement – especially first time around.

The tidy stone villas with fanlights above their doors give way to scruffier yards with wire fences and communal drying greens. Newer houses have grey harling as protection against the weather. It's not only roofs that have to be watertight in Orkney, walls, windows and doors all have to keep out water jetted by the wind.

The curve runs up-hill past the whisky distillery. Empty hanging basket hooks stick out from the soot-blackened walls. A coach party from a late season cruise ship emerges from the visitor centre wearing an odd mixture of shower proof ponchos and quilted coats that resemble duvets tied up with string.

Afterwards, the country opens up. Stone dykes stretch out in charcoal lines either side of the road, tumbledown in places and backed up with post and wire fences to keep the cows from barging them over.

The car drops into a dip then begins a long shallow climb to the blind summit of the Holm straight. The cloud is breaking open in places to reveal tangerine strips of sky around the horizon.

What the hell happened on the farm?

What was Robbie thinking when he went into the water?

I take the road signposted to Biggins. Beneath it there's another sign in the shape of a swift with the words 'Northshore Gallery' painted in my father's italic script. The road passes through a steading then takes a sharp left turn. George Biggins refuses to have a gallery sign attached to his barn despite tourists pulling up at the farmhouse door every summer.

There was a disagreement between him and my father over a cat. The cat, a feral animal that was familiar from the ditches around the farm, came to have her kittens in the corner of the gallery workshop. Dad made sure they went to good homes then when the kittens were gone he had the cat neutered and brought it back to stay with us.

The animal wandered back to the farm. Biggins noticed the scar on its abdomen and knowing about the kittens at the gallery had come to the house and confronted my father. Dad said he'd done the farmer a favour. Biggins said a cat should always have kittens, that being pregnant and hungry made her a better mouser. He said he always drowned the kittens in a bucket before they opened their eyes, before they'd feel any pain. It was one of the only times I can remember Dad becoming properly angry and my mother having to calm him down.

The cat continued to come and go as she pleased oblivious that she belonged to anyone.

A line of swifts at the entrance of the driveway points the way to the house and gallery. At the back door of the house there is a pile of boxes covered with blue tarpaulin held down by breeze-blocks.

By the converted outhouse door there's a sign saying 'Gallery Open,' swinging gently on its hinges. Along the wall terracotta pots are filled with succulents. There's an old butler's sink filled with miniature plants, some with withered brown stalks left over from summer flowering, others bulging in a single grand rosette with tiny tummy-button centres. In one pot three bright pink pompoms are held an inch aloft from a green tangled mound, the only flowers left this time of year. None of the plants are showy, but they survive. They appear in Dad's photographs and paintings, substitute models when the weather forbids access to the outside.

'Dad?'

There's no reply except the sound of a staple gun firing. I find him stretching canvas over a wood frame. Lengths of wood, graded by size and thickness lean in a rack against the back wall waiting to be cut to size by the band saw.

'Hello, Christine. Lend us a hand and hold onto this. Keep it pulled tight along the edge, that's it.'

He presses the metal edge of the gun firmly against the canvas then fires. He moves and fires again until there is a row of neatly pinned dimples in the cloth.

'Painting?'

'No,' he says. 'No time. Selling too much. There's not many places still open and the coach parties keep coming here.'

'It's good though, isn't it?'

'I haven't had time to do anything this summer. Nothing new.'

'The sketches from the brough?'

'Rough drafts. Anyway, they were for your mother. I couldn't sell them.'

'People would buy them.'

'I don't think I'm that desperate,' he replies.

He stacks the finished canvas against the wall and hangs the stapler on a nail. I notice a full cup of tea on the workbench with swirls of congealed milk on the surface. There's another half full cup by the printing screen.

Above the workbench there are three shelves. On the lowest are paints. These are in no particular order and have the appearance of toothpaste tubes, wantonly squeezed in the centre. Globules of paint sneak out from beneath the octagonal screw caps. On the centre shelf there are jam jars filled with pins and nails and picture hanging hooks. Bottles of glues, fixatives and cleaning fluid are arranged on the top shelf. They're orderly, recently sorted out; many have been discarded.

He stands for a moment lost in thought, the glow from the skylight highlighting the grey in his hair and beard.

'Is it Lindsay?' I say.

'What?'

'That's bothering you.'

He takes off his glasses and rubs at the dust on the lenses with the tail end of his shirt.

'Is it that obvious? She doesn't show any sign of letting up.'

'So?'

'I know it's a rebound from being so low. Don't get me wrong… it's better…she's happy and full of plans for the future. But she remembers as well as anyone what's happened in the past. It never stops her from being enthusiastic though. I suppose I admire her.' He pauses. 'But there are times it becomes a bit desperate, her certainty that everything is going to work out. She really wants to show you that she's well. That what happened was more of an accident.'

'She doesn't have to show me anything…'

'It was very hard for her when you were away studying and when you got a job in the south…she felt she'd lost you. Now, she's on a high and of course I'm happy. But …I needed to spend some time out of the house. I've been putting it off… every time I look around…'

From speaking quickly and evenly he flounders abruptly. His lips start to tremble.

'Dad?'

'I see her…how I found her. She was there…lying there.'

He raises a hand and makes a gentle motioning gesture from side-to-side. He looks desolate, lost.

I step past the canvas and give him a hug. His hand presses the back of my head. The fibres of his jacket smell of wood glue. He releases me and I step backwards.

'You know she'd stayed up late waiting for you…thinking you'd come. I went to bed and she was just watching television. When I didn't see her at breakfast I assumed she was having a lie-in. But she must have got up early…or maybe she didn't go to bed.

'When I came across everything was quiet, but the workshop door was open – not how it should be. And somehow I knew she'd be here. There was this huge sense of disorder, not violent– it was like she'd been muddling everything… making it how she needed to it to be.'

He wipes his eyes, dislodging his spectacles. Then he takes a step back and rests his hand on the workbench.

'It must have been awful, Dad.'

'I saw her lying there … and my first thought was, she's done it. She's succeeded…and this wave of selfishness swept through me. How could she? I thought it over and over again. How could she? How could she do this to me? To your mother? To you? It was all about me –not her.'

'You're the most patient, the most…'

'I'm not. I try, but I'm not….and I didn't have any feeling for her. No sympathy. I couldn't think about what she'd wanted, that to her it was success. I wanted her so badly to have failed.'

'It's only natural,' I say.

'Is it? When she was at her very worst, in those terrible…it was…that there was a way out gave her hope. That there was a way of stopping it all. She said the thought of suicide stopped her going out of her mind.'

'She didn't mea–'

'She's not crazy, Christine. She a wonderful, loving, talented…. much more artistic than I'll ever be and…she has to fight this battle day after day.'

His eyes brim with tears.

'She's a strong person,' I say.

'Determined,' he says. He laughs weakly and wipes his eyes. 'Like your mother.'

I stare at the surface of the cold tea. I'm being guarded when he needs me to be open. It's the first time we've talked about what happened. I don't know what to say. I don't know how to say I'm sorry and I don't want to lie.

He looks at the shelves, his gaze running along the glues and fixatives.

The band saw guard is flicked up, exposing the saw toothed cutting strip that disappears into the metal plate.

'I knew,' he says, 'when I saw the aerosol can. I knew when the seed had been sown. Years ago there was a report from the Sheriff's Court in the paper about a boy. He'd tried glue sniffing. He wasn't really a bad boy. He'd been rushed to the Balfour by his brother. They couldn't revive him.

'At the time she'd asked me about the types of aerosols I used in the gallery. She'd said she was worried about the fumes. I told her that there were enough draughts and cracks in the windows to kept me well ventilated. She needn't worry.' He pauses.

'I should have made a cabinet when you were younger. You were always playing among the paint and pots. It should have been the first thing I did.'

For a moment his voice is angry, self-reproachful.

'You were always there,' I say.

'You were good girls,' he says.

His voice is absentminded, a period of silence follows.

'Your mum will be pleased to see you. She's only been back since lunchtime, there was some delay with the flight. She'll be catching-up with everything.' He smiles at me then says, 'She works very hard. There's not many people like her.'

It's true, and today I want to see her.

'I'll leave you to your canvas. Unless you need any more help?'

'No. I suppose at least if I'm moved to paint they're waiting for me. A cup of tea would be nice.'

I take the other cups and go back through the gallery then across the courtyard over to the house. In my mind's eye I picture Tessa and I on the back step sucking ice-pops, waggling the plastic tubes full of bright fruit flavoured slush. The memory is sharp with happiness.

Lindsay meets me in the corridor. She's carrying a cardboard box jammed with lengths of broken skirting board.

'Hi, Linds–'

'Christine. I've something I must show you. Let me chuck all this down. You really should have come sooner – then you could have told me what you thought but it's too late now, I'm too far along and you won't believe how expensive paint is to buy. Mum's being tight about the shelving I want, I'd have a go at doing it myself but she says it needs a proper joiner. Anyway, I'm still going to have a go at making the window seat. It can't be that tricky, funny shaped box with a padded lid really. I've been researching on-line, there's loads of videos. I could easily make it in the workshop – if Dad ever lets me in there.'

I walk ahead of her into the kitchen.

'Where's Mum?'

'Are you making tea? I'll have a cup. I've been up since six.

It's an Edwardian theme by the way.'

'Edwardian?'

'It doesn't matter about the rest of the house matching. There's so much that needs doing. Micky Scott'll make any shape you want for stained glass. I was thinking flowers, roses probably but then I thought, what about the sand dunes and the sun coming up and all different yellows and blues or it could be seashells, something with waves coming over. You'll have to see the designs – I'll get my sketch book so you can see…'

'Is she in the study? God, I can't believe it's almost dark already.'

'I took out some books from the library, but they didn't really have what I wanted so I've been making up my own designs. How much detail do you think I need to add? Hard to know what the glass will look like.'

'Sounds great, Lindsay. Let me speak to Mum before I come up.'

'Sure. You will look though? You won't recognize your room. The carpet's gone and I've stripped the floor. I started taking off that horrible woodchip wallpaper but Dad said to leave it because the plaster was no good underneath. I'll get the uneven bits all patched up when I've done other things.'

'Why are you doing my room?'

'You're not here. I mean, you are, but you're not staying, are you? You're staying with Tessa, or I suppose she's staying with you. God, I heard about what happened to Jenna. I would *not* have coped. I hate injuries, can't bear them. Don't tell Dad, but my eventual plan is to do the whole house to get proper experience of different techniques. You never know, it might be so good that you want to come back.'

'You shouldn't…'

'Don't worry, I'm not serious. God, the look on your face. I'm going to put together a portfolio, start showing people what I've done.'

'Can you take this over to Dad? I'll be up in a minute.'

'Okay. But I already took him two cups. He said he didn't want to be disturbed. He said he's rushed off his feet. Oh, could you get Mum a bit more on my side? I know she's thinking I'm wrecking the place. Tell her…I'm adding value to the house.

Nobody's paying me to do all this. Free labour, you see.'

'All right. See you in a minute.'

Lindsay takes the cup. She walks away with swinging steps; her whole body fizzes with energy. I stir sugar into a black coffee and head across the sitting room towards the narrow door that leads into where the animals would have been kept.

'Coffee?'

'Christine, how nice. Thank you. How are you? How's Jenna?'

'Pretty much her usual self.'

'Good. Did Tessa take her back to the doctors?'

'No. She seems fine, really.'

'And Tessa?'

'Fine.'

My mother's eyes are unblinking, completely focused in my direction. I blow on my tea and glance away out of the window. The thick-walled room is insulated from the sounds outside. Dad calls it her 'Still, small place of calm.' Outside, the sky is very dark blue, the stone walls stand out blackly on the hillside. Out of the corner of my eye I see Lindsay closing the door of the gallery behind her. Her shoulders are relaxed, her stride purposeful. I can almost hear her humming.

'I saw Alfred,' I say.

'Alfred? Why?'

'He wanted to talk to me. He wants to see Tessa more. He says he wants to get to know Jenna.'

'This is new. Why do you think he wants that? Is it because Robbie died?'

'I don't know.'

She looks back to her desk. Photographs of a low cliff are placed side by side in a horizontal line. In each shot there is a pole with red and white markings for scale. Nothing about the orange clay or grey boulders looks remarkable, yet she says that the site of the ruined chapel at the brough is unique in Iron Age archaeology. There is urgent need to preserve and record the site before the winter storms. She has been petitioning funding organisations for money to finance a breakwater that would protect the cliff from further erosion and save the burials for future research.

'It was almost as if he wanted my advice,' I say. 'I don't know what I can do.'

'He wants your help. You should tell Tessa you spoke to him. It's her decision.'

'She's as stubborn as he is. Anyway, she told me how he chucked her out. He said he never wanted to see her again.'

'Do you think he's changed?' she says.

'No.'

'What about Tessa?'

I can't help but laugh.

'She's just the same.'

'Are you sure, Christine?'

A queer silence suddenly grows in the room. Then the two-toned whistle of an oystercatcher passing over the courtyard somehow penetrates the walls and cuts through the silence. It fades quickly and is replaced by nothing.

My mother reaches for a sketch of a tomb. It's labeled with arrows and letters, a scale bar carefully drawn at the side. I recognize the outline of the broken mediaeval chapel walls.

'Did you have any success?' I ask.

'What?'

'With funding.'

'Some. More of the graveyard will be lost this winter and it won't be long before the sea destabilises the chapel walls. At minimum I need a team of four to record the site. It's a catch-22, the more finds are exposed and washed away the more interest there will be, but then the material is already lost, no in situ data, no topographic record. A large collapse, as happened further up the coast last year, and much of what's valuable will be lost. There are already issues about safe access, moving vehicles and equipment. The path is a death trap from the farm.'

'I bet getting permission is a bundle of laughs.'

'Actually, I've been surprised. Was it Neil or Ronald that was in Lindsay's year?'

'Neil.'

'He's quite reasonable. Obviously, he doesn't see the significance of what's there – they've been filling in holes all over the farm for generations, levelling them over. Half of them are forgotten now. Who knows what's been lost?'

'Well, what do you expect?'

'If I'm right, the close association of the chapel with traditional Norse burials could be unique to Orkney. Zones one, two and three have significant numbers of burials. Dating puts the site at Iron and Bronze Age with significant continuity of occupation back to the original Brough. From what we've found so far there's a significant number of children among the burials. We're only on the edge of what could be discovered here. The distribution could be very interesting. It might even be unique to anywhere. It needs to be preserved and then made publicly available.'

I wonder if she realises that sometimes she sounds like a textbook.

'No chance. It won't happen,' I say.

The vertical lines deepen between her eyebrows. She tucks her hair behind her ear and lifts the drawing to see it more closely. The precisely drawn lines resemble a contour map; to her it's alive with meaning.

'I'd better go and talk to Lindsay,' I say.

'She's driving your father mad, and that's saying something,' she says.

'It's because he knows he'll have to fix it all up again when she's finished.'

'Undoubtedly.'

Night has fallen, the pool of lamp light is bright on her desk. The walls of the study are lined with photographs of stained skeletons emerging from the clay. They have always been present in one way or another during my life. Tonight the skeletons, which have never really bothered me before, have a sense of foreboding. My eyes are drawn irresistibly into the curves and shadows of the emerging bones.

She adds some shading to her diagram then says, 'I might see if I can get her outside, put her talents and current energy to use taking some photographs.'

'At least the sea's doing all the hard work. You won't have much digging to do.'

'Hmm?'

She is absorbed again in her work.

I leave her and go upstairs. When I walk in Lindsay gestures gleefully at the bare floor and walls. Plaster peels away in places where the wallpaper has been stripped away. There are uneven slits where the unpromising floorboards meet the wall. Splinters stick in my socks as I walk over to the window. Another part of my past has been erased, ransacked.

Lindsay flips open her sketchpad. Ink drawings of landscapes flick past as she turns the pages. The intricate cross hatching creates a sense of great depth and scale; in the margins drawings capture minute details of plants and birds. Colour floods the end pages; one is full of daffodil yellows, another crimson, a third every shade of green. It's mesmerising, amazing to think she has done all this. It's impossible to pick out anything solid in the splurges of colour and spiralling designs.

'Maybe I should be more bold,' she says. 'Do you think I should go for something completely modern or clash things a bit? What do you think?'

'This is nice,' I say, pointing at a smudge of deep blue.

I know my response is inadequate, pathetic.

'Do you really think so?' says Lindsay.

Her expression is open, childlike, desperate to please. The wave of affection that grips me as I look at her is so strong it's unsteadying. I brace myself against it and the memory of the hurt I've caused.

Chapter 28

When I return to the cottage it is late. Everything is orderly, there's no smell of pub or cigarettes, no male clothing. Driving back, I'd considered that Tommy might be putting in a repeat performance. and it's a relief to find Tessa alone and already asleep.

Quietly, so as not to wake her, I change clothes and slip under the duvet. The night passes in a blink.

'Christine?'

'Hmm…what?'

Tessa's voice is muffled.

'I've got you some tea,' she says.

'What time is it?'

'Eight-thirty. I've got to go.'

There is the knock and shuffle of shoes being searched through in the bottom of our wardrobe. A shadow moves across the light, there's a hand on my shoulder. Green and red shapes dance on my eyelids.

'Sorry, I should've asked about Tommy sooner,' she says close to my ear. 'I didn't ken you'd be surprised. He's decent. A bit…well, you know.'

Her hesitation piques my curiosity and I open my eyes.

'A bit what?'

'Nothing. Don't worry about it. Jenna's in bed drawing. I've told her not to come through until she hears you get up. She's had breakfast. I'll be back aroond six if everyone's on time.'

Tessa fiddles with a zip on her boot then heads to the doorway.

'Is it serious?' I say.

'With Tommy? He's no a serious type of person, but I like him fair enough and he's keen. Can you give him a break?'

'He could at least wear a towel.'

Tessa's top lip curls into a smile.

'I'll tell him,' she says. 'You remember, Robbie's mum's busy so she can't take Jenna this afternoon?'

I nod.

She calls goodbye to Jenna then gives the back door a generous slam. I put my head back under the covers. From Jenna's bedroom comes the rhythmic whumph of bed acrobatics.

Robbie's mum usually takes Jenna on Saturday afternoons when Tessa's working, but today she is busy because the Hallowe'en window is being put up in the shop. It's grown more elaborate over time; Robbie used to delight in it when we were younger. There's a skeletal hand that hovers above a bowl of sweeties on the counter. Tempted customers trigger its grab reflex. It's made me jump for years.

I've walked Jenna over a couple of times before. The exchange is awkward, the small talk disjointed. I've no idea if Robbie said anything to them about our relationship.

In primary school I was invited to his party with Tessa and other girls. His birthday was on the third of November. When we were teenagers it was usually celebrated by getting soaked and freezing cold at the bonfire down at the Peedie Sea. The pipe band plays and the fire is lit almost regardless of risk. The wind-swept flames roar out to the leeward side like some crazy jet engine.

The bonfire was when summer was finally packaged away in memory, even though the fields could still be busy with the last of the harvest and the sun high at midday.

One year, when Lindsay and I were quite young, the night was very calm. We stood on the shore of the boating lake, glow rings around our heads like miniature fluorescent halos, and watched the fire. It burned slowly, the flames casting a true reflection rather than a bright blur onto the water. There was a pair of white swans that came gliding across the orange and black ripples. Even with the noise of the pipes and fireworks they didn't take flight.

Tessa had been taken by Alfred and Marion. She'd been given a sparkler and made mad electric tails in the air. Robbie would have been there somewhere, so would Brian and Anne, so would Tommy, Ronald and Neil. They would have all been there somewhere.

I've seen newlyweds Brian and Anne walking around town together on Saturdays, her spray tan completely faded from the big day. Tessa did Anne's hair for the wedding of course. She told me that Anne insisted Tessa fix a hairpiece for her. Anne thought it would look elegant with her low backed dress. Later, Robbie commented that her hair resembled a horse's tail – Brian said she looked amazing.

When I'd stepped off the plane on the day of the wedding I might as well have worn a sign saying, 'From The Sooth.' I'd cursed the humid afternoon in Guildford when I'd been tempted to choose one of the newly arrived floaty dresses at the department store. I'd even bought open toed shoes and a matching handbag. Perfect for an afternoon by the languid river – but no barrier to the fresh breeze off the Pentland Firth.

Typically, my flight had been delayed and I arrived at the cathedral after Anne's grand entrance. I sat at the back, my eyes down. My heart beat rapidly at the excitement of being back, of the transgression and unexpected return.

After the service everyone crossed the road away from the cathedral and gathered together on the lawn in front of the Earl's Palace. The tumble down monument to previous centuries of power and greed is a traditional place for wedding photographs.

Compared to other folk, who should have known better having never left Orkney, I was actually conservatively dressed for the event. Tessa was wearing a fire-engine red jersey dress tailored to finish a fraction below her bottom. She had the same slightly artificial skin colour as the bride but it suited Tessa better. The close fitting curves of her dress revealed her body, which seemed totally unchanged by childbearing. She had no accessories but wore perfectly matched high-heeled shoes. Jenna was dressed in a bright red cotton dress with bands of white stripes. It was the sort of dress that is impossible for a girl to wear without twirling around.

It wasn't long after I had crossed the road to the Earl's Palace and stood to watch the photographs being taken that Tessa teetered towards me. Jenna skipped behind her, one hand fluttering the edge of her skirt.

Her eyes had sparkled in the dappled shade. She embraced me tightly, introduced me to Jenna then proceeded to fill me in on the relationship comings and goings I needed to be aware of before speaking to anyone at the reception. It was like the last six years had never happened.

A constant effort was needed to resist looking for Robbie. If I relaxed for a moment my eyes began to search for the curve of his shoulders, the tilt of his head in the assembled crowd.

When my wayward gaze finally found him, he looked straight at me. The waiting was over. My anger disappeared. It was like the first breath I'd taken since leaving, the first sweetness. A wave of relief swept over me that threatened to build into a flood of tears. For the rest of the afternoon, a sensation of nakedness stayed with me wherever I went.

A coach had been arranged to take us to the East Mainland community hall. I sat next to Mr Foulis who brought me up to date with how poor the spring weather had been and how late the kye had been put out of the barns.

Inside the hall pearlised white balloons looped with streamers were hung to cheer the plain windowless walls. The weather was improving and the fire exit doors were pushed open to let in light and the fresh breeze.

Tessa flitted past carrying a champagne flute and seemed always to be trying to find Jenna. Everyone I spoke to listened politely to my descriptions of the south. It was as if I'd simply been away for a long weekend before seeing sense and coming back home.

About ten o' clock Jenna was sick from eating too much Death-by-Chocolate cake and Tessa called a taxi to take them home. She waved to me from the door and ushered Jenna, now wrapped in a cardigan, outside.

Robbie and I ended up standing next to each other at the bar. It would have been too obvious for either of us to turn around and walk away without saying something to each other. The small place where our elbows met was sore with pleasure.

'Do you want a drink?' he asked.

I nodded.

'Pint of Tennant's, and a whisky and coke.'

We took the plastic cups from the hatch and sat at an empty table a little apart from the others. The band was setting up, fiddler, guitarist, drummer, there was a squeeze-box tucked in behind the red curtain. They were well loosened-up from the food and drink with shiny red cheeks.

Guests settled into a rhythm of drinking, fetching and carrying. Children had long since escaped outside and along with the smell of cigarettes the scent of the fresh cut grass drifted in through the open doors.

Robbie sat half-smiling, watching the room, creases around his eyes. His hair had grown and curled into a sort of wave that tucked back over his ears. He had an old fashioned sort of face, like you might see in a black and white photograph. I studied his expression, wondering if his feelings could possibly mirror my own.

A sound from the next room brings me back to present. There's another, louder this time. Thump! Thump! There's the sound of Jenna crying. Robbie's image disappears.

I throw away the duvet and jog along the corridor.

'Oh, Jenna. What've you done?'

'I banged my head.'

'Again? Where? Let me have a look.'

She rubs a spot above her ear.

'A peedie red mark. Come on, let's get something to eat.'

The time passes slowly for what's left of the morning. Jenna seems content to fuss around the house or play in her room. I get on with marking and preparation for parents' evening. It's meant to be an informal event but I don't want an evening of small talk. I sit at the kitchen table, listening to Jenna play and the clock tick.

'Canna ring Mum?' says Jenna.

'She's working. What do you want to do after lunch?'

'I don't know. I want to speak to Mum. Ple-ase, Christine?'

I give her my mobile. She speaks to Tessa for a few minutes about nothing in particular then hangs up.

After lunch I offer to draw Jenna some pictures. She isn't really interested and scribbles rainbows one after the other hardly looking at what I am doing. I don't blame her; my father has passed nothing of his creative ability to me.

'I used to send pictures to Dad,' she says.

'Oh.'

'So he could decorate his room in Flotta.'

She pauses briefly, casting a critical eye over an arc of tangled yellow crayon before taking up the job with orange.

'He wis a fireman,' she adds, casually. 'But he never put oot any fires.'

The rainbows spread over the floor of the dull room. I watch her diligence, the rhythm of her hand as she covers the paper. Part of me wishes that I had the house to myself.

Later, I find a treasury of princess stories left by a previous tenant and persuade Jenna that we read them in her room. She lets me choose the story and we lean together on the pillows. Afterwards, she begins a picture of the Beast handing Beauty a rose. When I return five minutes later she's asleep, the rose a blot of bright red. I leave her and wander back to the living room.

There is a nothingness to the afternoon. It is neither bright nor dull outside. A slow wind nudges the tattered leaves on the shrubs. Fatigued from the week my mind feels slack. Sleep seems a good way to pass the time. I slouch against the doorframe staring at the gaps and imperfections of the garden wall. Then I turn, head into the bedroom and lie down on the duvet. The temporary chill of the cover is soon replaced by the warmth of my body and I drift to sleep.

A buzzing sound intrudes my doze. Groggily, I squint at the clock and reach for my mobile. It says three fifty-eight in the afternoon.

'Hello.'

'Whit like, Christine.?'

'Ronald? How did you get this number?'

'What are you doing later?'

'Later? I don't know. I've just… I've no plans.'

'Ah'll take you to the Chinese.'

'I don't think so.'

'You said you didn't have any plans.'

'I mean…actually, I'm not feeling…'

'Don't you like Chinese?'

'I'm looking after Jenna whilst Tessa's working. I don't want to go out, Ronald.'

'Is that with anyone or just me?'

There is a short dry laugh at the end of the line.

'I'm tired. That's all it is. I'll see you around.'

'Another time?'

'Bye, Ronald.'

I end the call. Part of me wants to return to bed, even though it's ridiculous to spend Saturday afternoon asleep, another part of me feels nervously energetic after the phone call. I know I will not be able to go back to sleep.

Outside the sky is unchanged, as if no time has passed. I go and check on Jenna.

I remove a felt tip from near her ear and turn the duvet down so she will cool and wake. Her face is pale against her blond hair, the bump on her forehead a distinct khaki oval. Without animation Jenna looks quite plain. Even in her sleep Tessa's features are beautiful, there's something about her.

At five o' clock I go into Jenna's room and turn on the light to dispel the gloom. She shifts in bed and sighs loudly.

'Your mum'll be home soon.'

She pushes up on her elbows as Tessa would.

'I don't want to get up.'

'Let's see what's on the telly. Might be a film.'

The noise lures Jenna through. Once she's curled on the sofa I shower and change to try and dispel the lethargy of the afternoon. I take care choosing my clothes then come back through to the lounge.

'I wish Dad was here,' says Jenna out of the blue.

I don't reply.

'He'd take me to the park,' she adds, staring at the screen.

'I could take you to the park,' I say. 'If you want.'

'No.' She sighs. 'It's getting dark. I don't want to. Canna have some crisps?'

Her attention stays on the television screen. This one mention of her father, in front of some messy game show, seems deliberately designed to put me in my place, a counterbalance to our day together.

There isn't anything from teaching that seems relevant to my relationship with Jenna. Above all else, she's Tessa and Robbie's daughter. I get her a packet from the cupboard then go and blow-dry my hair.

My hair is curlier, thicker than I've known it before. When I was in the south a student hairdresser used a razor comb in an effort to take out some of the weight. It was my first haircut not done by my mother, Lindsay or Tessa. Although Lindsay's efforts when I was eight had unequivocally had the most madcap results, the razor 'thinning-out' left me looking almost equally as strange.

Tessa has always experimented with her hair. After Grease was finished her attempt to tone down her lurid yellow hair colour to a more natural shade turned her hair a strange grey-green. Six months later she had all the damaged hair shorn off. Her face suited the boyish cut. Even my mother had remarked that she'd looked cute.

The effort with brush and dryer results in the smell of burning hair caught in the motor and more rather than less frizz. I don't know why I'm in the mood to persevere. I'm possessed by determination to make my hair flat, sleek and soft.

Searching for hair-straighteners I pull open Tessa's top drawer. It's filled with brightly coloured underwear. There are animal prints, stripes, polkadots, some trimmed with ribbons and some unlikely all in one outfits.

Robbie would have seen them all – touched them all. There's an open box of condoms and a shiny pink canister of some sort of gel.

I close the drawer, pull out the next and find what I'm looking for and a tube of miracle anti–frizz hair gunk.

'Everything all right, Jenna?' I call.

'I've finished my crisps.'

There have been times Tessa and I could easily swap clothes. Not at the moment. The cold weather has increased my appetite for sweet things, fudge-topped doughnuts in particular.

Most of my clothes for student nights out could be donated to the local charity shop for all the likelihood that I will wear them again. I pull out a black top gathered under the bust and a pair of wide trousers. Being here means an end to flirting with people you are never going to see again; people know what you wore last week, they know what you did.

I'm finally satisfied with my reflection.

'This is boring,' says Jenna when I come into the living room.

'Change it. Do you want some tea?'

'No.' Jenna looks at me. 'Are you goin oot? Mum always looks nice when she goes oot.'

'I just wanted to get changed.'

'Why don't you go on a date?'

'Nobody's asked me,' I reply. 'I like staying in anyway.'

'It's because you've got no friends anymore. Because you went away. Why did you go? Mum said it wis because you wanted new friends, that it's too cold and windy fur you here.'

'I like it here.'

'Are you goin to go again?'

'I'm a teacher at St Olaf's now.'

'I know. You're Miss Marner. But you could go if you wanted.'

'I could,' I say.

'Could we still live in the cottage?' she says.

'It would depend. What do you want for tea?'

'I'm no hungry. Canna have another packet of crisps?'

I shake my head.

The sound of laughter draws my attention. A moment later the backdoor opens and Tessa steps into the kitchen. She's followed closely by Tommy and Neil. The smell of beer and fried food floats ahead of them on the cool air.

'Sorry I'm late, Christine. Are you goin oot?'

'No.'

'Mrs Brodie needed a wash and set for some recital she was giving. Helga refused to do it efter the stink she kicked up last time. I tried to make her look a bit more modern, less of a helmet heed anyway. She gave me a tip.'

'Whit like, Christine?' says Neil.

'No bad.'

Tessa lays her hand on Tommy's shoulder.

He grins at her.

'Go in,' she says. 'I'll get a cuppa on.'

Tommy stays in the doorway to the kitchen where he can see Tessa. Neil ambles into the sitting room.

'Move up, nipper,' he says to Jenna, scrunching in next to her on the sofa. 'What've you done to your heed?'

'Ran into the gate.'

'It's a fine bump.'

I sit on the floor near the television.

'Anything come o visiting the farm?' Neil asks.

There's a pause before I realize he's talking to me.

'No,' I say.

He leans forward, rests his elbows on his knees and spends some time examining his hands. He turns his face towards me, his eyes are lighter than Ronald's, kelp-coloured.

'He wants to see more o the peedie lass,' he says in a low voice, tilting his head very slightly towards Jenna.

I glance at Tommy. He doesn't seem to be listening, more intent on watching Tessa in the kitchen.

I shake my head at Neil. He shrugs and leans back on the sofa.

Tessa returns with a tray of tea and caramel wafer bars for everyone. She and Tommy sit on the floor, backs against the sofa. We watch as people come on stage to compete in the show. The lights dip, piano notes break the the silence and a sweet untrained voice begins to sing. The tune develops and becomes more complex, rising and falling. A particular chord, held imperfectly, that makes me remember Robbie is gone.

The last refrain drifts into soft repetition of the original tune. In the quiet before the audience begins to applaud, Jenna speaks.

'Christine's really nice. Uncle Neil, you can be her boyfriend.'

She smiles at me and nods her head.

'I don't know,' he says putting down his cup. 'I don't think she'd like the farm. Too many tractors racing aboot. An' some days it doesn't smell so guid.'

'Oh,' says Jenna. 'But you could ask her. She's had a shower and specially done her hair even though she's just stayin in wae me.'

'Well, would you like to come fur a drink, Christine?' says Neil. His eyes are serious, the tone of his voice serious too.

'I…'

Tessa is running her fingers over Tommy's hair, her eyes mischievous.

'You need a haircut,' she says.

'Get off,' he tells her. 'Go get me another biscuit, woman.'

She giggles and shakes her head.

Only Jenna is really paying attention to Neil and I. Her head turns from me to Neil and back again.

'Okay,' I say to Neil. 'It'd be good to get out.'

Chapter 29

The tractor cab overlooks the cottage wall, its bright yellow paint clashes with the glow of the streetlights. Although he's not in overalls the scent of harvest seems to fall from Neil's clothes. Once we're through the gate he shortens his stride so as not to pull ahead. We pass the wood shingled houses on Junction Road, their gardens a mosaic of wilting summer flowers, broken delphiniums criss-crossing in the darkness.

'How long will you stay?' he says. 'Before going back sooth.'

'Why does everyone keep asking me when I'm leaving? I work at St Olaf's.'

'I ken, but, you'll no be stopping in Kirkwall, will you?'

'What do you mean?'

He says, 'You'll go again,' in such a matter of fact way that it makes me angry. I draw breath to reply but his attention is distracted by someone smoking in the recessed doorway of the furniture shop.

'Whit like, Sigurd?' says Neil

'No bad,' he says.

He nods at me and we pass by. We follow the curve of the road that leads to the harbour. Silence falls between us. When we reach the pedestrian crossing outside the library we cross together and leave the main road. Even though I don't owe Neil anything it's important to me that he understands why I came back.

'I like seeing more of Lindsay,' I say, lightly. 'She missed me when I was away.'

'Didn't you miss her?'

'I suppose I was busy,' I say.

'Being a student?'

'No. I mean…yes.'

Blood rises to my cheeks.

'It's different. When you're away…there's all these things going on…'

'And you didno think too much o home,' he says.

I want to tell him that I did think of everyone. I wondered what they were doing. I wondered if the tide was low and if the wind was strong enough to rattle the roof tiles or simply a bog-standard gale. I want to say all this, but a small almost undetectable sigh escapes Neil's lips and stops me speaking. A short stab of guilt finds its target in the solar plexus.

I can't let the conversation finish here.

'You know Lindsay's renovating the house now,' I say.

'I ken, I've been takin awey the bruck.'

'Oh?'

'It's no bother.'

'She gets a bit carried away with her projects. Anyone would think she's totally single-minded all the time, but she needs support. She doesn't have it easy.'

'She seems all right just noo,' he says. 'Better.'

The word hangs in the air.

Briefly, our eyes meet and I realise he knows. It's a relief not to have to tell him. Neil seems tense for a moment then his hand brushes mine and he relaxes. We walk on together.

The imposing front of the Masonic Hall draws near on our right, the lettering glinting dimly over the doorway. Above, carved in sandstone, are the outlines of the Masonic signs – the compasses, the star and the eye. Cracks of yellow light escape between the closed shutters behind the high windows.

Ahead, on the other side of the junction, the The Catcher is more welcoming. Light shines out through the uncurtained windows, half covered in condensation and promising warmth. There's the sound of a fiddle, but no stomping or calling to suggest it is a live performance or dance. We're long past festival season.

Neil holds the door open. Briefly, I hesitate, remembering the last time I was here. I make an effort to smile. It's hard to understand how the time has passed, but it has, second by second, bringing me here.

A painted cartoon of the bass and treble clef dance a jig together on the door. In the short passageway that leads from the main door there are signed pictures of local bands. Inside, the chairs and tables are darkly varnished and suited to a croft kitchen. The walls are wooden panelled up to shoulder height and add to the sense of homeliness.

Old cabinets with glass-fronted doors lean against the back wall. There is a motley collection of instruments within each. A couple of chanters are marooned on the top shelf. The fiddles are numerous; glossy maple curves cut across with brassy strings and smooth fingerboards. There's rosin dust under the bridges and the tacky residue lies on the shelves. Some of the violins are more dignified than others, some are wretched unusable things that no one has thought to throw away. In the left hand cabinet some of the instruments have handwritten price tags tied to their necks and notices of musicians offering lessons with the dates and times when grade examiners will be visiting the island.

The humid air tells of a busy Saturday afternoon and the two staff behind the counter are concerned with tidying round, reorganising leftover food rather than serving drinks.

'Lindsay should look in here for ideas,' I say. 'She's working on an Edwardian style. '

'This Edwardian?' he says.

'More Edwardian than our house.'

'You shouldna be so hard on her Christine. It's no a bad project, and she's always been artistic.'

We take our drinks to a table by the window. Here we can see into the street. No one enters or leaves the Masonic Hall. Occasionally, someone walks towards the cathedral folding notes into their wallet after visiting the cash machine.

'How's the farm?' I say.

'Bailing for Stocken today,' he says. 'Waste of space that he is.'

'Why d'you go all the way over there?'

'Paying bills.'

By the fire someone knocks their table, the glasses jostle each other, but nothing falls. From the accent and rhythm of their speech you could mistake the group for being local, but I can't understand what they're saying and realise they're Norwegian visitors. Neil looks over and steadily takes in the tourists.

There is a subtle tension in Neil's movements as he turns back to face me.

'What aboot Uncle Albert?' he says. 'You were spaekin to him. Do you think Tessa will come back to the farm.'

'He threw her out.'

168

'Aye. You ken she had it coming.'

There is a pause in our conversation. I wish for a fresh breeze, something to blow away the heavy rebreathed air.

'He should speak to Tessa himself,' I say.

'Alfred make first move? You're kidding.'

'She wouldn't listen even if he did. God, I used to hate him when we were younger. It was terrifying sometimes, the rows he'd give her over nothing. He was so hard on her.'

'He's changed, Christine. He's no the same man.'

'I can't change her mind, Neil.'

'Did Alfred spaek aboot anything else?'

'Like what?'

Neil shrugs his shoulders. He sips his beer then changes the subject.

'See me in that photo,' he says, nodding at a picture on the wall. 'That week's the best I ever got with the fiddle.'

'I didn't remember you played.'

'I didno really. Nothing like as good as Tessa. She fair blew folk away. Mind on, they're no musicians hands are they?'

He sets his hands on the table. There's a fresh tear across one knuckle, the exposed layers of skin raw and pink. There are scars from dozens of other scratches and one of the nails is bulbous and blackened.

'It'll fall off soon enough,' he says, noticing my gaze. 'It'll be peedie bit soft until the nail comes back and hardens up again. Cally stepped backwards in the stalls, squashed it between gate and post. He can turn on a sixpence that animal.'

'Cally?'

'Wur prize Charolias.'

'Oh.'

'Sure, he's a big beast,' he says. 'Won best in East Mainland show last year.'

I turn back to the photograph. There are three lines of children all holding fiddles by the neck with their bows grasped alongside. Their faces are open, nervous grins a plenty, gathered from all the schools across the islands for a week of music tuition.

It's easy to spot Neil. He's a head taller than everyone else with a shock of unruly hair. He's always been taller than most, but his hair's kept short now and his forehead's higher and wider.

Even though it's Lindsay's school year my sister is missing. She really wanted to go when the letters were sent out and a place was set aside for her. But the weekend before it was due to start she got cold feet. She didn't want to go into town on the grammar school bus. Even when Dad offered to drive she wasn't persuaded. She'd made up her mind and wouldn't go, she was miserable all week going to school.

Neil remains quiet. It occurs to me that there might be other places he'd rather be on a Saturday night than here with me. Perhaps it was a bad decision to go out with someone at the suggestion of a six year old – even to escape watching Tessa and Tommy mooning over each other.

It doesn't feel right being here. It's too soon.

'Why were you at the school the other day?' I ask.

'Ronald had been going on at me.'

'About what?'

'Doesn't matter, none of my business. It'd been worse for Tessa without you here.'

'She's managing,' I say. 'What do you think of Tommy?'

'He's no bad.'

'It's going to be cramped in the cottage if he's going to stick around,' I say.

Neil doesn't comment.

A group of teenagers come though the door. They drift up to the counter and peer at what's left of the food. They're shy of the woman behind the counter. She stands with arms crossed over her apron, pen and order pad tucked beneath her elbow until a final decision's made. The teenagers take the table in the middle of the room. They sprawl away from each other as if it's the most uncool thing on the planet to sit around a table with friends. My head feels suddenly heavy, the room shifts and stutters. A cold sweat flashes over my skin.

'I'm tired, Neil. I want to go home.'

'I need to get back to the farm anyway,' he says.

'Sorry to spoil your evening.'

'I didn't expect to be oot. Came in to pick up baler twine and met Tommy buying bait.'

'It's not you. I don't feel well.'

He sculls his pint and we make our way out. As we leave the waitress sidesteps past us carrying in the sign from the pavement.

Out of habit we walk close together, nearly rubbing shoulders to reduce exposure to the wind. He offers his arm and I take it, grateful to have something to lean on.

We're back by the Masonic Hall when I see Ronald walking towards us. His head's bent downwards, hands jammed in pockets, oblivious to his surroundings. I think there's a good chance he won't see us and I say nothing even though I know Neil must also have seen him.

He's almost alongside when he looks up. Ronald stops immediately.

'Holy hell, I didn't think I'd see you pair erm in erm. Thowt you'd be at Stocken's. '

'Didn't take long in the end, barley wasn't close to ready. Serve him right no listening to advice. I dropped round to see Tess,' says Neil. 'Bumped into Christine.'

'What's he been tellin you, Christine? If Ah'm not guid enough for you, then he's sure as hell no.'

'Ronald, I didn't think you'd be here…'

'Telt me she was seeknin.'

'It was more to get out of the house than anything else. We just went for a drink,' I say.

'I kent you were a liar, Christine. Didna ken you were a slut as weel.'

Neil slips out his wallet and takes out a ten pound note.

'Quit your pleeping and go get another drink. '

Ronald snatches the money then he presses his fist against his brother's shoulder and whispers something privately into his ear. When he's finished speaking he turns towards me. His eyes shine malevolently.

'The sooner she kens we ken, the sooner she'll be awey,' says Ronald.

He stomps away towards Broad Street.

'Knows what?' I say.

'Nothing,' he says. 'Ah'll walk you home.'

Neil glances after his brother then we set off into the

worsening wind. We walk in silence, still arm in arm until he reaches to open the gate.

'Ah'll say cheerio to Tessa then be awey,' he says. 'Sorry aboot Ronald. Don't worry, Ah'll keep him straight.'

His words are reassuring. Neil doesn't say anything lightly. He's not a light sort of person, not one for chatting and larking about. Too serious, too busy for anything like that.

Chapter 30

In the kitchen, Tommy has his shirt off. He's sitting with one hand resting on Tessa's hip, his face an inch away from her breasts. She leans over him with a pair of scissors, fluffing then snipping at the tufty hair on his crown. There are a couple of open beer bottles on the table. The hair fallen on Tommy's shoulders blends into the body hair on his chest and back.

'Back early,' says Tessa, unstraddling Tommy's thigh. 'Nearly done.'

'Christine's not weel,' says Neil.

The scruffy clumps of hair look like some weird discarded pelt, torn up and scattered over the floor, the thought of the texture, greasiness and smell is repulsive. I lean against the fridge to feel its solid cool smoothness.

'You dina look right,' says Tommy.

'Jenna's not right either,' says Tessa. 'She fell asleep on the sofa.'

'She's been asleep all afternoon,' I say. 'Maybe I'm just tired, I don't know.'

I head through the doorway. The football highlights are on, green light reflects on Jenna's skin, her lips are parted.

'Night, Tess–'

Jenna's body jerks on the sofa. The movement is sudden and rapid, limbs flail randomly this way and that as if she's fighting in her sleep. Her head starts to flick violently from side to side and her back arches away from the cushions.

'Jenna!'

Her eyes are open now, only the whites visible, pupils rolled back under her eyelids. Her teeth champ against each other as her jaw muscles spasm.

I rush towards her.

'Call an ambulance,' I say.

Tommy and Tessa kneel side by side. He holds her legs while Tessa tries to steady her shoulders and soften the movements of her head.

'They could be half way to fuckin Birsay,' Neil says. 'Queeker to carry her over.'

Tessa catches hold of Jenna's hands and holds them still. She absorbs the violence of Jenna's movements, a tight soft cage around her daughter.

'Jenna? Can you hear me? It's Mum.'

Jenna's head strikes against my hand, it feels wooden and hard.

The frequency of her spasms slows then she lies limp, spittle around her lips. Her eyes are sunken like she's been punctured inside somewhere.

'Ah'll tak her,' says Tommy.

He gathers Jenna up in his arms. Tessa grabs his jacket and throws it over her as he strides through the kitchen. Hair wafts to the corners of the room as the back door flies open. I follow behind, in no time we're out of the garden and on the street.

The effort to catch up Tommy and Tessa is making me breathless. Neil jogs ahead through the car park and sets off the automatic door so we can go straight through.

'Left, then right,' he says.

'I ken where to go, beuy,' Tommy flips back.

Jenna's head flops against Tommy's shoulder, her unrestrained arm flails with each step.

The warm anti-septic air of the hospital seems to add more inertia to our movements compared to outside. There's no breeze, no traffic noise, no sound of birds.

Tommy accidentally knocks Jenna's foot against the door to Accident and Emergency, impatient for the automatic mechanism.

'Where's a doctor?'

His voice is loud, not shouting, but urgent.

There's an old man with tissue held up to his eye in the waiting area talking into a mobile phone. He watches us with his good eye as we wait.

A nurse appears from the assessment room and gestures to Tommy to come forward.

'She's had a fit, I think a epileptic fit,' says Tessa.

'How long ago?'

'A few minutes ago, we carried her straight over when it stopped.'

Tommy stands with his arms folded over his bare chest. He looks down at Jenna intently. I've never seen his face so serious. The nurse places two fingers on Jenna's wrist and tips up her pocket watch.

'Has she had one before?'

'No,' says Tessa. 'She had a bump on the head a couple of days ago. But she was fine.'

'Poor peedie lass,' says the nurse. 'Ah'll call the doctor.' She gives Tessa a pen and clipboard. 'Fill in whit you can.'

Tommy rests a hand on Tessa's shoulder. She lets the clipboard flop. He takes it from her and she sits on the bed, cradling her daughter's head, stroking hair away from her face. There are violet patches beneath Jenna's eyes and livid red blotches in the centre of her cheeks. She looks like a worn out doll. I notice a hole in her leggings, it must have been there all day.

The doctor walks through the door. The two buttons on his white coat are under tight strain around his stomach. His moustache is impeccably trimmed and turned up at the ends.

He tuts his tongue softly against his teeth and introduces himself as Dr Copik.

'What has been going on with Jenna?'

Tessa answers his questions.

'Convulsions? You think how long for?' asks the doctor.

'A few minutes. I'm no too sure.'

She looks over to Tommy

'It was over in a blink,' he says.

Doctor Copik looks around at me.

'Yes, yes. Time is hard to manage sometimes.'

He places his hand on Jenna's forehead.

'We had to hold her down,' says Tommy, 'ken she'd have hurt herself.'

'She was watching TV,' says Neil from the doorway.

'I thought she was asleep,' says Tessa.

'Yes, she has fever. Nurse will make better measurement. I listen to her chest. I see from forehead that Jenna is not having lucky week.'

'Is it because she bumped her head? She seemed fine,' says Tessa.

'We didn't wait for a ambulance. I carried her over.'

'Lucky to have muscle man,' he says looking up at Tommy. 'Was also good to be in the cold for her. Fever absolutely was more before you were outside. She is still young enough for good risk of febrile convulsions. I think bump looks okay. Soon she will be back to beautiful self. Most likely fever the bad guy. She is simple unlucky this week.'

Jenna's eyes open. She stares vacantly at Doctor Copik's moustache.

'Sure Doc? It looked like a epileptic fit,' says Tommy.

Doctor Copik pats the side of Jenna's head lightly and observes her features.

'Appears similar, yes. But we don't want coincidence to make us thinking complicated. I think this is not something to worry about.'

He bends low, so his chest is only a few inches from Jenna's face. He shines a light in her eye. Tessa is pale, the tendons in her neck tight beneath the skin.

'This has not happened before?'

Tessa shakes her head.

'Good,' Doctor Copik says, 'then is less likely to happen again. Anything else unusual?'

'She was sick yesterday – I was sure it was too much chocolate. She can't help herself.'

'Ah…too many sweeties. Must always be rationing sweeties with little girls.'

The thought of vomit in the claustrophobic room is overwhelming. The lights begin to weave. There's nothing to lean on, nothing to hold. I watch the floating specks in the vitreous humour of my eyeballs.

I try to gesture to the nurse, but she is busy ticking something on a sheet of paper. I shuffle my feet further apart to balance but the movement has the opposite effect and I feel even more unsteady.

I tilt backwards on my heels and I wonder what Neil was so sorry about then everything spins and turns beige, then grey, and finally black.

'…Neil said she wasn't feeling well.'

'You need a rabbit's foots,' says Doctor Copik. 'Ahh. Christine, you are back to us. Keep feet up. Let blood pressure get back to normal. Maybe coincidence again? Or I think not.'

The hand on my forehead is cool and pillowy.

'I think we must have virus. You have fever too, Christine,' he says. 'Nurse, maybe we take a blood sample for making sure. Yes, yes. One for little Jenna too. Not much fun the needle going into arm, but will rule out some things to keep our minds rested.'

The room is the mirror image of Jenna's assessment room. Posters of human anatomy are pinned on the walls. One is of a skull with lidless eyeballs strapped in place by bands of deep maroon muscle. Next to it there's a giant diagram of the heart crawling with red and blue snakes.

'Never kent you fainting afore?' says Tessa.

'Sorry…you don't need to….you should be with Jenna.'

'Don't worry, she's resting,' says Doctor Copik. 'And has new toy for being brave patient.'

'Can Jenna go home?' Tessa asks.

'After convulsion the body and brain is exhausted. Must be sure her temperature is kept down. You need alarm clock for night, and parcetamol, ibruprofen overlapping. Christine, you will feel better if you copy same,' he says. 'Soon will be all hunky dory. If not seeming better in forty-eight hours go to see your doctor or if worried come back here.'

He brushes his moustache, parting its bristles with finger and thumb.

'Flicker of television can be too much for tired brain. Can act like flash photography, but I think temperature spike is causing convulsions, yes, yes in this case. Plenty rest; keep cold bedroom. But yes, I think she is okay to go.'

'Tommy's with her,' says Tessa. 'Neil's gone to get your car.'

'For Jenna?'

'Both of you.'

'He doesn't need to.'

Doctor Copik bustles to the end of the bed.

'Body has a fight on its hands, you must also rest, Christine.' He pauses, 'One last question.'

'Yes,' says Tessa.

'Why is muscle man having no shirt?'

'He was getting a haircut,' says Tessa.

'Will be nice when finished,' says the doctor.

His eyes glitter with laughter. He leaves the room and Tessa and I are alone.

'He's hilarious.' she says. 'He gave Tommy a hospital gown, he looks like a lunatic with half his hair cut off. Mind on, he's been good with Jenna.' She smiles. 'Whoa there. No hurry for you to go anywhere.'

'I'm feeling better.'

'Weel, you don't look right.'

Tessa puts her hand on my shoulder and gently eases me backwards. She passes me some water. The liquid is chalky, warmish and not at all thirst quenching, but I drink anyway.

'You're not bad at looking after people,' I say.

'No sure Jenna'd agree, ignoring her on the sofa and then wrapping her up in a coat when she was roasting.'

'You're a great mum, you're like a best friend.'

Tessa doesn't comment. She takes the empty plastic cup and puts it on the edge of the trolley by the bed. She glances at a clock on the toothpaste-green wall.

'God, it's so quiet in here,' she says.

It is quite, no echo of wind. It's as if we're in a strange country.

'Thanks for helping.'

'Not much good am I? Tommy was the real hero,' I say. 'Remember we used to call him Captain Underpants?'

A smile flickers on her lips, but she doesn't say anything. A wave of silence wraps around us. A bubble floating back in time.

'It's been a hard summer,' I say.

Under the fluorescent strip light her eyes look black, their centres softly iridescent. She is staring into space then quite unexpectedly she turns to face me and starts to speak. Her voice is measured and calm.

'Christine, do you know what I realize? I don't think I ever loved Robbie.'

Chapter 31

Her voice fills the silence, words sink like stones.

'I don't think I ever did. He loved Jenna. He wanted us to be a family. He *wanted* to get married. I couldn't say no.'

She pauses.

'You went away, Christine – you left when I needed you. What did I ken about having a baby? When you left I'd nobody to speak to. I couldn't speak to Mum. Dad was so angry and ashamed, and…we'd said awful things to each other. It wasn't some row we'd had a hundred times before… it was…God, we said every word that shouldna be said…and couldn't be taken back. I ken he hated Robbie and he'd hate the baby as weel.'

Her eyes are dull disks, caught up in memory.

'How could I be so stupid, like some tink…it wasn't long before everyone kent it had been a one night stand. All I kept thinking was that you were a coward for leaving.'

'Coward? I'm not the one who…God, it's like sometimes you don't remember.'

I feel faint again.

'I *stayed*. I had a baby. I couldna do anything else. Robbie made one bloody mistake.'

'With you. He did it with you. Out of all the girls why was it you?'

'You're looking for a reason when there isn't one. It was a party. He'd drunk a lot. Jesus, I liked him and he liked me. You ken it'd been like that all along.'

'So, it was no one's fault?'

'There's not always a big reason for things,' says Tessa. 'You'd be happier if you stopped asking why all the time. Stop worrying about why other people do things.'

My cheeks burn. Where the fabric of my clothes touches my body it itches like sackcloth.

'It wasn't easy to go,' I say.

'But you did. You went…and I missed you.'

Her eyes brim with tears. She takes my hand, marred as they

are by scars her fingers are still more elegant than mine.

I rest my head on her shoulder. We stay very still, hearts resting close.

'Remember how we planned wur Blackenings?' she says. Her voice is quiet and near my ear. Our foreheads press together. 'The things we promised we'd do?'

We hold each other tighter for a moment then she leans back slightly and giggles. She swipes a tissue from the trolley and dries her eyes.

'Vodka jelly? Super heroes…you wanted to be cat woman,' I say.

'It wasn't the same without you. Tame really.'

I sit forwards. This time the floor stays where it should and my head remains clear.

'Anne's was much better. We'd Tommy's truck for goin round the streets, everyone shoutin and banging the side, all weel coated in molasses by the end o it. Dora got us these peedie red waistcoats, with matching leotards and feather boas so we'd look like cabaret singers.

'There was a bit o a mix-up because Tatty turned up with a load of sombreros and false moustaches that she'd hauled up from London. She put on both costumes – looked like a man in drag. And she had her trumpet, kept playing this Mariachi tune. We looked tarred and feathered by the time we had Anne cling-filmed to the mercat cross in front of St Magnus. Everything fizzled oot a bit efter that – she'd made Dora promise she wouldn't leave her. Me and Tatty ended up at a Karaoke fundraiser at the sailors' club.'

'Bet you boosted takings.'

'We had a certain something.' Tessa slips into, '*You're the one that I want…*' for a few lines. 'No sure we were dressed for it. Robbie said I was mad, couldna believe when I told him I still ken all the words from the show.'

Her eyes glow.

Tears blur my vision from laughing. A feeling of calm gradually settles. It feels that she might be in the mood to listen.

'Can I speak to you about something?'

'What?' she says.

'I went up to the farm yesterday.'

Her face becomes sombre.

'Why?'

'Your dad wants to see you. He wants to see Jenna.'

Tessa leaves her perch on the bed. She goes to the window.

'He seemed sincere,' I say.

She shrugs and leans against the wall, arms folded like a teenager waiting for the bus. She's still wearing her work clothes, all black lycra, wrinkled around her waist and under her bust. Tiny hairs cling to the fabric and catch the light as she moves.

'I didn't know that Freki had died,' I say.

Tessa raises her shoulders slightly then lets them drop again.

'Hips went, arthritis,' she says. 'Bloody dog, remember when he bit Mirabella's arm off? Served him right he choked. God, I don't ken why we ever let him inside.'

There's a moment's silence then Tessa adds, 'Mum told me when the appointment was…stupid dog…didn't know what was going on. It was horrible, the way he went heavy, makin me hold all his weight, like he was squashing me on purpose.'

Her voice is flat, her eyes look fixedly at the floor. I wonder if she's thinking about Robbie.

'You see your Mum,' I say.

'A bit. She doesn't drive too much. Never done much on her own, never felt she belonged here. He's always made the decisions. She doesn't get a say – knocked down her greenhouse, put a boat on her flowerbed and never's put it right. Then she's the one who takes bloody Freki to the vet. There's some folk might think he was right to throw me oot but…most people don't do that sort of thing anymore. He couldn't stand the sight of me, Christine.'

'He wants to say sorry.'

'He's never shown he's a bit sorry.'

'He'd convinced Robbie.'

'Robbie?'

'Your dad said he'd spoken to him.'

'Robbie never went up to the farm, not even when he was workin on The Blackhoose.'

'He said Robbie was going to speak to you, to change your mind.'

Tessa looks across at me. It's strange talking about things that for years have been none of my business.

'Do you think it's true?'

'Honestly Tessa, I never know what your dad's up to. But your mum…it seemed like she was more in control. He listened to her.'

I never thought her life would be my concern again. We'd forfeited the right to be involved in each other's lives, and yet here we are talking about it all, chatting like two old friends.

'Will you think about it?'

Tessa looks straight at me. It's promising that she is not angry.

I love Tessa and Jenna staying with me, but it has never been a solution. When she knows the truth, whether I have the courage to tell her or she finds out from Ronald, she will want a different place to stay. Then she shakes herself slightly, the bangles on her wrist rattling, and the discussion is closed.

'I've got to get back to Jenna. Will you be ready to go when Neil comes back?'

I nod.

When she's gone I listen to the weird holler of the rising wind. I remember details from The Blackhouse; the bubbling trill of curlews as they flew in the dusk; the blue square of light sunk in the thick wall with its view over the dykes and sloping hills. I remember the smooth flagstones, cold under my bare feet and the thrill of the door closing behind me.

The half-light lasted for hours, it was as if the very nightlessness of mid-summer sanctioned our actions. I thought I had everything I wanted.

Chapter 32

The short car journey back to the cottage is exhausting and ridiculous. In the back Tessa holds Jenna on her knee, Tommy sitting next to them in his blue hospital gown. Crammed behind the wheel Neil struggles to find gears in the tiny vehicle. Voices, lights and colours become weirdly intermeshed, the sounds have acidic shades, the colours ring with sharp clanging noises.

The world becomes a mass of garbled sensations, my fever rises. Sometimes weightless, other times immovably heavy, my limbs are disobedient to command. My thoughts wander and tangle, sometimes piercingly clear, sometimes nothing but dull echoes. Whispers in my head transform into urgent, insistent voices. I have delusions…visions of bones being washed out of their graves. The room blurs, refocuses then spins away. Fatigue and fever whirl, trip and carry me through the night.

Overnight, Tessa sleeps in Jenna's room on a blow up mattress Neil brings over. During the day she nurses us checking temperatures and bringing drinks.

Lindsay visits. She sits on the side of the bed holding an old biscuit tin.

'I made it. It won't be very good. There's Cointreau in it, that's why it tastes a bit different…the icing's gone a bit runny, it's made with yoghurt. How do you measure yoghurt anyway? It's so gloopy.'

'It looks…actually I'm a bit…do you mind if you close the lid?'

'You need a spoon to eat it really, more of a pudding than a cake.'

'It's not that, it's the smell…anyway, how's the decorating going?'

'You mean the refurbishing? There's some swatches arrived that I want to show you, not now though. You need to rest. And I've been looking on-line for plans to build a four poster bed.'

'You're going to build it?'

'Why not? Dad's still being a bit of a stickler about the

workshop, but I'm determined to have go. Mum's sidetracking me a bit, she's needs someone to take some photographs of one of her muddy holes.'

'You mean an archaeological site with irreplaceable artefacts that are going to be irrevocably lost and washed into the sea?'

'That sort of thing,' she says. 'There's a heap of stuff I've got for you to sort through: CDs, books, old folders – but you don't need any of that stuff now do you? I brought some over. Mum thought you might want to have a look. Dad says she's sorry for not being around more, but there's a big coastal erosion meeting she *had* to attend. Tessa said to leave it in the kitchen. There's a couple of diaries, don't worry I didn't look at them. And a box of letters. I didn't throw any away but I couldn't help seeing who they were from. Nobody writes to each other now. It's all texts. I'm surprised you bothered. I mean, you saw Robbie all the time.'

She waits, but I don't reply. There's a short silence then Lindsay starts drumming her fingers on the tin. Her eyes roam over the bedside table.

'I like this card. Who's Moira?' she says.

'You know, from Westray.'

'That's good. You're much better at having friends than I am, especially girls. I mean you name one friend I've got who's a girl. You should make new friends.'

'Here?'

'Yes. Here. Why not?'

'I…I don't know.'

It seems a long time since I was in a classroom. Even the idea of being in the school building is overwhelming. The thought of children and noise is too much, everything is too much.

'Christine?'

'What?'

'You, Robbie and Tessa, did you never think…'

'Whatever you're about to say. I don't want to…'

'…let me finish, Christine.' Lindsay takes my hands, moves her face close to mine. 'I wanted to say that I thought for a long time…I thought that you left Orkney because of me. When you didn't come to the house like you said you would, after being away all those years, I thought it was because you couldn't face seeing me. That you didn't ever want to see me again.'

'Why would you think that?'

'Mind on, Ah'm no a guid sister,' she says in her best Orcadian.

Her eyes glitter.

'It was nothing to do with you,' I say.

'I wrecked things all the time, Chrissy. I fucked about. Christ, I gave up trying to stop myself. I didn't know if I could half the time, and it was too much risk to even try.'

'You were ill.'

'Do you think I've forgotten it all? Do you know how humiliating it is to remember everything? But it's part of me. It always will be. I've accepted that.'

'You're better now though, aren't you?' I say.

'It's me,' she says. 'Not part of me, or an illness. It *is* me.'

She stops talking. Her shoulders and arms rest easily. Her features are relaxed and calm, as if she were never anything else. I look into her green-grey eyes with their tight black dot of pupil.

'You're stronger,' I say. 'I can see that much.'

'What about you?'

'Feeling better. October break, so there's no rush to get back to school.'

'I wasn't talking about that. Since the funeral you've not said a word about what happened with Robbie. You can talk to me. People care about you.'

'I'm okay. I'm managing.'

'Don't be such a fucking island all the time.'

'What? I'm not ready. I can't...'

'You can, but you don't,' she says. 'It doesn't matter now...and I don't hold it against you...but I knew you always loved Tessa more than me, even though I'm your sister. No matter what I did, whether it was good or bad, it hurt that I was never as important to you as she was.'

'That's not true.'

'Mum and Dad knew as well. It wasn't easy and now...I want...can't you see, don't you remember you used to be my baby, my dolly, my companion? Whatever was going on you were by my side and I loved having you there and you used to love me too. But when we moved here it was as if you wiped all of that from your memory.'

'I didn't...'

But there's truth in what she says.

'Maybe there were other things you were trying to forget...but they're okay to talk about now. I remember the things Mum did. I remember more because I was older. The scenes in shops, Dad trying to cover up when she didn't come home. I was there. It's as if everything good we've ever done together didn't happen because you've blocked it all out.'

Her eyes twinkle and she says, 'Remember the poker night? Don't roll your eyes, Chrissy. We had a fantastic evening, both of us. We had a great time, why not admit it?'

'I can't believe how bad we were,' I say. 'It was like you were losing on purpose.'

'I was not...not really,' she says.

'God, what was his name?'

'Wriggles...'

'Very appropriate...'

'I don't want to know...'

I picture Wriggles talking to my father in the kitchen in his boiler suit. We both burst into giggles.

'It's good to see you laugh,' she says.

'You have horrendous taste in men,' I say. 'More success, but honestly...

She smiles at me, a faint blush on her cheeks.

I'm happy that she's with me.

'I know you'd listen. I do,' I say. 'But it doesn't have to be now, does it? When I'm ready I will. It's complicated with Tessa.'

'I suppose that's a start.'

She sweeps her gaze around the room.

'This place needs some work.'

'Lindsay...'

'Okay, okay. Don't worry. Even I wouldn't start wrecking someone else's house. At least you could hang a picture though. Do you want me to bring one of the boxes in?'

I nod. She picks up the cake tin from the floor.

'I'll put this back in the kitchen, you can get some later...' She keeps talking as she walks out of the door. '...Tessa said I should leave everything in the kitchen, but I'll bring one in.'

When Lindsay comes back she deposits an old banana box on

the floor beneath the window. There is a spray of pink carnations on top.

'I'd better go. Neil's waiting outside.'

'All this time?'

'Oh, he doesn't mind. I'm giving him a hand with something. By the way, the flowers are from him. And don't feel you have to eat the cake, probably best to ignore for a week and then scrape into the bin.' She bends and kisses my forehead. 'Dad sent soup, he'll be over tomorrow. Mum's in Zurich until the weekend, she sends her love and said you must rest. I'll be back soon.'

Later, I pull the box up on the bed. There isn't anything of value inside, a necklace Robbie gave me in fourth year, a whale fluke on a leather thong. He'd been away to Inverness visiting a wholesaler with his dad and brought back loads of test products they were going to sell in the shop. There's a couple of CDs whose bands have long since split.

Buried at the very back of my mind there was always a suspicion that Tessa had the same feelings for Robbie as I did. Speaking about it would have broken the magic between the three of us. In my heart I knew why it was her. I saw what he saw.

I push the box away and stretch my limbs. Outside, bright orange-throated flowers wave in the breeze. A starling alights on the wall, it's beady eye blinks once then it flies away.

An ache grows in my chest, it runs through my limbs. My ankles, knees, elbows and wrists feel swollen and tender. The inflammation sends pulses of pain along my nerves, as if they are being washed in saltwater.

Chapter 33

The next morning Jenna has a rash over her arms and legs and bright red cheeks. Tessa takes her back in to Accident and Emergency. She tells me afterwards how Doctor Copik had frowned and pronounced that Jenna had 'slapped cheeks' when he saw her. Tessa had insisted no one had touched Jenna, certainly not slapped her, at which point Doctor Copik had apologised. He'd told her that it was another name for parvovirus B19, common and generally harmless once the fever has lifted.

Over the next twenty-four hours my fever also breaks, but my aching joints keep me in bed; it's as if my body is unwilling to become well again. A week later Jenna is recovered and restless, although the rash remains.

Tessa is starting to go stir crazy. I'm dozing when her excited face appears around the door.

'Come for a peep at the farm annex?'

'The annex?'

'Neil says we can have it. He's told Ronald to shift out, says he can stay in the barn for all he cares. Tommy's going to meet us there.'

'I didn't think you wanted to live over there. What about the barriers? What did Ronald do?'

'God, I don't know. He's always doin something. Come on.'

'I know what the annex looks like.'

'Don't be like that, fresh air'll do you good. Lindsay's been helping Neil with the painting. It'll be a trip oot at least.'

'What about your dad?'

'If I see him, I see him,' she says and pulls back the curtains. 'Lindsay's pickin us up in half a hour so you don't even have to drive.'

I don't have the strength to do anything except comply with her wishes. Dressed in old, warm clothes I find myself sitting in the front passenger seat as Lindsay pulls away from the cottage. Memories of Tessa's birthday party flash past with the lichensplotched dykes.

In such a treeless place it is the dykes that give texture and rhythm to the land. I'm struck by a feeling of smallness, of inconsequence, that nothing I do is of any importance. Elongated drops of rain split across the front windscreen. There's a strong east wind, but the tide is low and the roads across the barriers only dampened by salt spray in places. An occasional spume of froth shoots up against the sea wall and then flops back onto the cubes of concrete beneath.

'Finally started painting your room,' says Lindsay. 'The walls are going to be deep yellow, a sort of dark mustardy colour. It doesn't sound very nice, you have to see it to know what I mean. The wallpaper has this geometric pattern, it's very trendy, cost a fortune and then I had to pay extra to get it delivered.'

'Doesn't sound very Edwardian,' I say.

'Oh, who wants to follow a theme? Anyway, I think it's going to be amazing.'

Lindsay turns to talk over her shoulder to Tessa, one eye on the road.

'I've hired a machine to sand the floors. Much cheaper than getting someone in, and who wants someone else to do it for you, can't be that hard. All right in the back?'

'I want a car like this one,' says Jenna.

'It's quite sporty. Ever driven it, Christine?' says Lindsay. 'I try and get my hands on it whenever Mum's away.'

'Do you mind slowing down? I'm still not feeling great.'

'Can't think she ever gives it a proper run,' she says dropping down a gear. 'Corners like a dream.'

'We're not in a hurry,' I say.

'Dad had a red car,' says Jenna. 'I want a red car when I grow up.'

Lindsay turns full around, taking her attention from the road ahead.

'Yes, he did, didn't he?' says Lindsay. 'Wasn't it a…?'

'Jesus, pay attention,' I say.

An old man and his dogs do not so much as flinch as the car shaves past them.

After a short pause and no reduction in speed Lindsay launches into describing her plans for staining floorboards.

The car sweeps around the curve to the next barrier, dipping down the slope by the old water-filled abandoned quarry. Waves lap against a sunken ship clustered around with bobbing, luminous pink buoys. Then we head away from the water, a sharp right hand turn and there's the sign for the farm, the bull's horns pointing the way up the track. The sign has the same permanence as the dykes and fields themselves.

Without indicating Lindsay brakes hard and turns the car into the steep gravel lane up to the farmyard. An orange highway maintenance truck is outside the barn doors, the flatbed loaded with cones and concrete mixer. Tommy's in matching bright orange overalls, leaning against the truck talking to Neil, cigarette cupped in his hand to keep it alight in the wind. A sense of uneasiness grips me about being here.

Lindsay turns the car in the yard before she stops outside The Byre, leaving the engine running. As Neil strolls over she opens the window. He bends and looks inside the car.

'You're lookin better,' he says to Jenna. She grins and scoots out behind Tessa into the blustery fresh air. 'Aye-aye, Christine.'

'Hi Neil,' says Lindsay. 'Told you I'd bring her. I'm going to push off now. Mum's worried about the tide, I'll drop by later. Hope they like the colours.'

'Dead right,' he says. 'I'll get the key.'

I'm half out of the car when Lindsay leans across and grabs my arm. Her words jumble into each other and I can't make out what she's telling me. Her eyes sparkle as she speaks, it seems it must be especially good news, but more than likely it's nothing except plans for new curtains. I shake my head.

'Tell me later,' I say.

Tessa, Jenna and I huddle together in the lee of The Byre. The wind flips our hair upwards as it spirals into the protected nook. Jenna happily pokes about in the containers where Marion grows cuttings. She squeaks in delight at the discovery of a kitten hiding inside a tangle of ancient honeysuckle. The smokey-coloured animal is coaxed and teased out from the twisted stems. Delightedly, Jenna cradles the mewing animal in her arms like a baby.

Cigarette finished, Tommy comes over to join us. He leans next to Tessa and watches Jenna stroking the kitten's belly.

Tessa's gaze shifts from Jenna to Tommy in a regular, methodical way. She doesn't notice the door inside the porch open.

Even though it is almost noon, Alfred's wearing striped cotton pyjamas. His face and hands stick out from the collar and cuffs, scrawny and thin. Of course, I've never seen him like this. He was always dressed and out to work before Tessa and I got out of bed when we were girls.

'Whit do y' want?' he calls, pointing at me.

Tessa turns. His tone is short and aggressive, as if he's warding off strangers.

'Neil's getting the key for the annex,' I say.

'Whit do you mean, key? Whit you spaekin aboot?'

'It's Christine,' I say.

'Marion, Tessa's home,' Alfred calls into the house. 'Told you she wouldna be much longer.'

Marion's voice replies from inside.

'Close the door, man. It's cawld. You shouldna be oot o bed. Let me by and shut the door.'

Tessa is closely inspecting her father.

His muscles have withered. He looks as if he's escaped from somewhere then found he has nowhere to go, and that he has forgotten what he was escaping from.

'Thur's folk here, woman,' he says, 'at the door.'

'No one comes up here, Alfred. Come away noo.'

Marion begins to turn Alfred away, but he pushes against her arm. She makes another attempt before finally glancing outside the door. Gladness flashes over her face.

'I kent Christine'd do it. Didn't I say, Alfred? she says. 'Weel, whit are you staying ootside fur?'

She opens the porch door.

Tessa steps up still observing her father. Everything in the porch has grown small, Alfred and Marion strangely old since I visited last.

'Why's he wearing pyjamas?' says Tessa.

'Latterly, he's not been keeping weel...and he won't bide upstairs, will you?'

Alfred gestures towards Jenna. She is tickling the kitten's nose with a bit of straw, holding out her hand to receive light pats from its paw.

'Peedie lass. Ah'd have kent her anywhere. Poor peedie lass with no fither.'

Alfred shuffles into the porch. Marion holds his arm, navigating him through the boots and junk on the floor.

'Tell her to come in and see her granddad. She'll fairly blow away oot there.'

Alfred raises a hand, his fingers tremor.

'Mum?'

'Doctor's no got to the bottom of it, some days he's all wandering aboot the hoose. Some days he'll sit and sit, and Ah've no idea whit's going on in his heed. It comes and it goes. Mind, we can manage if he doesna mak too much fuss.'

Marion turns to Alfred, more determined.

'Noo, you're coming in wae me,' she says. 'Back upstairs.'

Alfred doesn't stir. The soft hiss of the rain on the corrugated plastic roof fills the small structure. It is stuffy and warm compared with outside.

'You wanted to see me,' says Tessa.

Alfred turns and squints at her.

'How's that baby of yours?'

'What's he playing at, Mum?'

'Don't mind him,' says Marion. 'Can't get him to spek sense th'day.'

'What did you want?' says Tessa. 'Christine said you wanted to see me.'

'An that Robbie, where did he go?' he says. 'Awey t' work?'

'You threw me out. Don't you even remember?'

Tessa's face takes on a petulant childish look – hurt and upset. Outside, a quad bike skitters into the yard and pulls up in front of Tommy's truck. Ronald turns off the engine and tramps into the farmhouse.

'Why don't you come back, Tessa? Ah'd keep the dog oot o the bairn's way.'

'You don't ken what your spaekin aboot,' says Marion.

'You don't ken even what happened to your own dog?' says Tessa.

'Ah'd get to know the baby. We'd be more friendly.'

'It's been too long, Dad.'

192

'But where do you stay noo? No in the toon, you're a country lass.'

'I stay with Christine.'

'Come back an stay with us, Tessa.'

'You never could say sorry. You still can't bring yourself…'

'Weel, I thowt you were a fool…getting caught oot. I stand by that… I was ashamed of you…..Ah'm working aal hours, hardly seeing your mither and that's how you behave. Same wae your fiddle, couldna stick at anything.'

'All you did was work,' says Tessa. 'You never came to see anything I did. You never wanted me to do anything.'

'Can't you see you were mine?' he growls. 'You didna listen to me!'

His eyes are wide, lines of strain stand out on his forehead. Marion takes Alfred firmly by the arm.

'It's no need getting upset. Tessa can come another day when you're feeling more yoursel.'

'I want for you to bide at home where you belong,' says Alfred. 'An I told Robbie it wis best to have everything oot in the open. He's not a bad beuy, but off he goes cheust the same, and worse for drink. It wasna my fault.'

'What do you mean?' says Tessa.

'He'd been arguing with Ronald again afore he came in. It wis the only time he ever took a drink wae me, an man he wis thirsty. I said you'd be pleased Christine was moving back, that you'd aal be friends afore long. I told him I want things better between the family. I ken if anyone'd persuade you it'd be Robbie, or Christine.'

The muscles around my belly tighten, my breathing is shallow. The effort of standing is sapping all my energy. I stare at the scratched wallpaper inside the doorframe while memories of midsummer collide with images of swirling sediment and freezing water.

'He agreed?' says Tessa.

'He kent family wis important.'

'Alfred, come on noo,' says Marion, taking his arm.

'What is it woman? Where am I going in such a rush?' He looks back over to Jenna. 'Seems a blink ago it wis you and Christine pinching oot the flooers like that peedie wife. I always liked seein you while I wis gan to and fro. Why are you here, Tessa? Is The Blackhoose finished?'

'It'll no be finished,' says Tessa, flatly. 'What were you sayin aboot Robbie spaekin to you?'

'Neil's getting the key for the annex,' I say. 'He's waiting for us.'

'You're gaen up those stairs noo,' says Marion. 'Tessa's come once, it'll no be so long afore next time.'

This time Alfred obeys.

'Don't mind on aboot him,' says Marion. 'Half the time he doesna ken what he's spaekin aboot. The rest of the time it's no wirth listening.'

Alfred and Marion disappear into the hallway. The listless atmosphere in the small shelter is soporific. Tessa looks around. On a fold out chair there's an old kitchen drawer filled with bunches of keys. It's a place things stay without being left deliberately, a space that no one ever designed or wanted, full of things that are waiting but are more likely never to be used again.

'Smells of dead moose in here,' says Tessa then adds, 'Maybe the annex isna such a good idea.'

A withered geranium surrounded by dead flies decorates the windowsill. She pulls a petal from the flowers scattering others onto the sill then glances up at me.

Her face is solemn.

'You make any sense of Dad?'

'I'm not sure he knows what he's saying.'

'What did he mean about having everything oot in the open?'

'No idea,' I say. 'We'd better go over. Neil's there.'

I step forward, bowing my head slightly into the wind. Tessa follows behind and then goes ahead with Tommy.

'Canna bring the kitten?'

Jenna's voice is high, thin and light, dragged away by the wind.

Tessa doesn't hear. She keeps walking, her arm interlocked with Tommy's.

The wind is hard in our faces, drying my lips. Neil glances at the quad bike blocking the doors to the garage where the farm vehicles are kept and frowns.

'Best get in afore the shooer comes over,' he says.

Dead ahead, over the roof of the annex, a belly of swollen cloud is swinging towards the farm. I search the sky for rainbows in the trails of windswept rain, but there's nothing except deeper darker grey. My gaze drops to the window of the room where Robbie and I were the night of the party.

Jenna calls again, 'Mum, I want to stay with the kitten. Ple-e-ase'

'No. It's too cold.'

'I'll stay with Jenna if you want,' I say.

She shakes her head and carries on, tightly tucked into Tommy's side.

I double back to the flowerbed, the hand of the breeze pushing on my back. Jenna is crouched in a spot where the wind is cut away. The quiet is sudden, shocking. My body relaxes and it comes back to me in a sudden flash – the tenderness on Marion's face when she looked at Alfred – it was the last thing I expected.

'Come on, Jenna. I'll hold your hand.'

'I don't want to go,' she says.

'You can't stay here on your own. Put the kitten down.'

'I'm calling her "Smudge".'

'Bring a flower instead,' I say.

I don't hear Ronald approach. I don't even sense there's another person out in the yard.

His mouth is only an inch away from my ear when he speaks.

'Poor day th'day, Christine.'

The hairs on the back of my neck stand up on end.

Chapter 34

There's no movement in the farmyard, a slight scuffle of hooves in the barn, the discontented lowing of confined animals. Large, cold drops of rain begin to fall.

I step forward, but Ronald shadows my movements and blocks my path. He stands very close.

'Mind on, the night of the party it was worse. Remember?'

Moving closer to Jenna is the only thing I can think of to make him back off.

'Not really. Too many cocktails,' I say.

The lie is wishful thinking.

'I wis serious,' says Ronald.

'Come on, Jenna. Let's go catch up with your mum.'

Ronald grabs my arm. He holds tight, preventing me from leaving. His breath is hard and low as if he's trying to control some great excitement.

'I knew you'd come back. You couldna leave Robbie alone and noo…noo you've set Neil against me as weel. Holy hell, Christine. What kind o woman are you?'

The sickly green light of the advancing storm reflects in his eyes.

'Aren't I guid enough?' he says.

'Not in a million years,' I say. 'Not if you were the last man left on the island.'

It sounds ridiculous – something I would've said a decade ago, but I say it anyway. Ronald lets go. He steps towards Jenna and crouches down.

'Whit's that you've fund?'

'It's a kitten. I've called her Smudge.'

'It must have been hiding from me when I did the rest.'

'What do you mean?' says Jenna, looking up.

'What? Has nobody told you what we do at the farm to kittens afore they open their eyes…?'

'Don't Ronald,' I say.

'…maybe Christine'll explain when you get home. Tell you

what, let's get away from these boring grown ups. Take you for a peedie ride in the fresh air.'

He takes the kitten and drops it down behind the flowerpots then takes hold of Jenna around the waist and hoists her up. She squirms briefly then settles, squashed against his body.

'Where are we going, Uncle Ronald? Canna have the kitten when we get back?'

'It's no good to me,' he says.

'Ronald, let her go.'

He carries her across the yard towards the quad bike. I take after them, the wind whipping my hair across my face, stinging my cheeks.

'Been on this one afore, Jenna?' he says. 'Fair zips along.'

He sets her down on the seat. She swings her leg round then leans forward to hold the handlebars.

'Can you look efter the kitten for when I get back, Christine?'

'Ronald, she's not been well. Listen to me.'

'Bairns don't feel the cold, woman. Any teacher kens that. You want to come, don't you Jenna?'

She nods.

'You ever seen the brough? You ken there's all sorts of guid stuff up there, bones an skeletons, might even be treasure.'

'Can't Christine come?'

'No enough room,' says Ronald, climbing up behind her.

'Please Ronald,' I say. 'She's not even got a coat... it'll be freezing up there.'

'She needs to see the place before there's nothing left.' Ronald turns the key and rolls the throttle. He winks at me then says in a loud whisper, 'Tessa won't have you back this time.'

He turns the machine and pulls away.

I'm too slow to block its path, still jelly-kneed after being unwell. I jog after them, hoping he's joking, hoping it's just a ruse. But he casts me a look over his shoulder and his smile turns to a sneer. I know he won't stop.

The quad bike see-saws from side to side as it lurches up the farm track. Apart from the white tips of her trainers Jenna is completely hidden behind Ronald's body. A few seconds later they're at the edge of the farm's willow plantation and heading up to the top of the brae.

Icy prickles spread over my skin, the air whips past without being drawn into my lungs. I search the farmyard for a way to make chase.

The steel doors of the old threshing barn are partly open. Inside there's a tall green tractor, its bucket loaded with tubs of magnesium supplement – nothing useful I could take up to the brough.

I look back to the car sitting in the weeds next to the barn wall. The maroon saloon is scarred with rust, the back bumper secured with plastic ties. It has no numberplate, no tax disk and one wiper. Despite all these obvious faults the windscreen is clean and fresh tyre marks lead across the grass.

The dangling side mirror knocks against the driver's door as I pull it open. The key is in the ignition, there's even a tree air freshener tied to the rearview mirror. The engine starts with a functional grunt.

As I flatten the accelerator the wheels spin and the car judders forward. The tyres search for grip in the greasy grass then all of a sudden the car flies forward as its front wheels reach the concrete and gain traction.

The air freshener flies sideways as I bounce over potholes, bottoming out on the centre ridge of the track up the brae. At the top the track dips, passes the wind turbines then follows a shallow slope towards the cliffs. The quad bike is briefly visible ahead, careering away from me over the uneven ground, mud and water thrown up by its tyres. Ahead, the track divides. Ronald turns the quad bike towards the narrow isthmus that leads to the brough.

The dead window buttons and reek of stale water in the car now explains the air freshener. I breathe through my mouth and swallow to prevent myself gagging at the combined smells.

Despite my efforts to keep control the car drifts sideways. It skids over the soaked ground towards a drainage ditch then veers towards a wire fence that prevents animals straying over the cliffs. My stomach tucks high and hard under my ribs. The back wheels find purchase just as the wire makes contact with the front wing and screeches over the metal. The car straightens out and flies along inches from the cliff edge.

I turn the wheel sharply to cut across to the other track.

There's no sign of Ronald. The horizon is a grey blur, rain blotting out the view over the sea. The single wiper sweeps upwards cleaning the mud splattered windscreen. For a second I see Ronald's head and shoulders before he disappears down the cliff path.

The car lurches and dunks into a hidden hole. I shift gear and force the vehicle forward, crunching its exhaust against the rocks. The land levels out unexpectedly and the car shoots forward then is caught in a fissure. It dives and tilts sideways, throwing me forward and comes to a complete stop. The door swings open and I shoot my arm out to prevent myself falling into the mud. I scramble out, limbs trembling, overtaken by waves of weakness and panic.

Jenna and Ronald are nowhere to be seen.

Chapter 35

The surface is treacherous to walk upon, but I run. The soil is only a thin film over the stone beneath, an oily residue from the oxygen-starved rotting grass floats on top of crevices filled with acidic water. I run towards the cliffs.

The quad bike is abandoned where track descends and narrows. A path dips below the lines of giant cow parsley skeletons. It hugs the cliff for a few metres then becomes exposed on both sides across a narrow saddle of land that then twists around the opposite cliff face and rises to the brough. Metal rods have been driven into the clay and a tattered rope is strung through their hoops. The flaking slivers of compressed clay scrape my knuckles as I guide myself along; here and there sea pinks grow out of the crumbling blue clay. In places the trodden path is no more than the width of my foot bordered by a scruffy line of grass that marks where the flagstone cliffs drop diagonally into the sea.

Above, four oystercatchers fly in tight formation, their wingtips nearly touching. The birds call shrilly, their bellies shine smooth and white. They soar, chasing the lead bird, then swoop and disappear over the cliff edge.

Beyond the steep drop is a protected cove, only a dozen meters wide with a crescent of pebble beech. The swell swirls inside the stone crevices, glubbing up against their sides and spouting flecks of bright froth. Waves collide and echo with chaotic abandon like some ancient brew pot, withdrawing to expose the fox-red stones at the base of the cliff.

The noise fills my head, its crashing rhythms swell monstrously. All at once the sea draws back and I become acutely aware of how high I am. Weakness sweeps through me, paralysing my limbs.

Tessa, please forgive me.

Something catches my eye in the cove, a movement, there's something alive down there. A seal is lying on its side, head crooked and scampering over its mauled belly is a sleek brown rat. It turns its head towards me and stops for a moment on the slack body then turns away to feed.

The animal's sudden movement releases me.

'Ronald!'

Rough steps cut out hundreds of years ago lead up the cliff face. More recently, yet still decades ago, metal hoops have been hammered into the stone further up. Unlike where I am now they hold nothing except tattered remains of rope.

Climbing up to the brough had always been exhilarating when we were children. The mound itself has sheer sides and is only thirty meters at its widest; a safe, sacred place reached by a single winding route.

Once we were up there it was secluded. We dozed in the heather or watched the seals with the pups in the cove, spying on the farm until it was clear and we could sneak back. Our transgressions were never discovered.

The climb is gruelling. Trembling with cold and effort, my hands fumble from handhold to handhold. Reaching towards the next hoop I catch my shin and feel a hot tear across my skin. Near the top, rock gives way to clay embedded with stones and there is nothing to grip except vegetation. Clawing at the seagrass I scramble over the edge. High with adrenaline, soaked and exhausted, I pull myself up away from the cliff and roll onto my stomach.

The tussocks are dented with the same boggy puddles as the cliff top. I lift my chin. Ronald is sitting on a stone bench set into the inner wall of the ruined chapel. It is where monks would have sat for their devotions, each assigned their own position beneath the dull liverish stone arches. At first the monks had scavenged ancient stones from the brough to build their chapel, then they'd doggedly hauled up their own. No roof remains on the chapel and the walls are fragments on all but one side that is closest to the cliff edge. There is a decorative band of pale stones about two feet from the ground.

Beyond the chapel there is nothing but pock marked grass and the spoil piles from the last archaeological dig. There is no structure left of the ancient Brough.

I reach forwards to steady myself and come to my knees. I shout against the wind.

'Where is she?'

'I let her go.'

I glance backwards. Grit spins off the cliff top blown into the boiling waves beneath.

'I don't believe you.'

'Tak a luk yoursel,' he calls, gesturing towards the chapel.

'Where is she? I can't see her.'

It's impossible to tell whether Jenna is hidden somewhere in the ruin. I get to my feet and stumble over the tussocks, land on my knees then rise again. All the time I keep my eyes on Ronald. When I reach the open end of the chapel there is nothing to see inside but worn clumps of grass and patches of reddish brown clay. Only the space behind the front altar is still concealed from view. If Jenna were hidden she would have to be crouching or lying down.

I step forward. In the shelter of the old walls there is a change in atmosphere. I notice the trefoils are carved into the red sandstone, softened by wind and rain. They are identical in colour to the walls of the Cathedral. Here and there, hand smoothed stones have been preserved from the elements, coarse blue-grey tufts of lichen points of contrast against the ochre stones.

After pilgrimage it must have felt a lonely place of supplication.

Ronald stands and comes beside me.

'Why won't you have me, Christine?'

A shiver sweeps down my spine.

'Where's Jenna? Please, that's all I want.'

I move further down the nave to try and get a better view behind the front altar.

'Am I no guid enough?'

'Always the joker, aren't you Ronald?'

'I wasna joking at the party.'

'Always fooling about…please, where's Jenna?'

'You had a guid laugh…'

'I was eighteen. None of it was serious.'

'You, Tess and Robbie … never room for anyone else. I fuckin saw you with him' - his voice rises - 'and now you're pretending nothin wis gaen on.'

'What're you talking about?'

'I saw you at The Blackhoose the night of Brian's wedding – I saw both of you. Standing in that muckle window. You couldna keep your hands off each other. I promised mesel if you ever came back again Ah'd tell Tessa.'

'Tessa?'

'And you couldna keep away, could you? I saw you aal together stopped on the street in toon… Tessa holding the peedie lass's hand, Robbie with his hands in his pockets standin between you, all smilin an spaekin. Cosy, cosy, like fuckin nothin had happened. All in broad daylight so nobody walkin past kent what you'd been doing. Then Robbie started acting all pally with Neil and agreeing to speak with Uncle Alfred aboot patchin things up with Tessa. It was seeknin…I wasna going to put up wae that. It's wasna right.'

'You were jealous.'

'I cheust can't stand anyone sayin one thing an daen another.'

There is a sharp hard glint in his eye, like a corpulent minister preaching about abstinence in lent.

'It was none of your business.'

'I made up my mind. I telt Robbie everything, had it out wae him. Telt him the bit even you don't ken, the one fact Robbie never found oot fae the night o the party… I was angry with you and pissin Dora, so I came oot here wae a few cans, watched the storm come home. Tessa didna see me, didno look aboot at all – too busy wae her man to mind on anyone else.'

'Who? What are you talking about?'

'Tessa and Tommy.'

'It's not true. Not at the party. I was with her, we were dancing. Tommy was inside.'

'You weren't with her all night. All those cocktails slipping doon, easy to loose track of where people are.'

He laughs and slaps his thigh.

'Holy hell, you were in a stinkin mood when your mum came, stomping awey through the farmyard back to the car…poor bloody Neil trying to close the barn doors.'

The truth sweeps around and under me like starlings leaving a wire. I didn't ask. I didn't know the right question – a sin of omission. There was never any suspicion in my mind that Robbie wasn't the father.

Tessa what have you done?

'Efter he wis seek in the toilet Tommy's night was over and

done…done early compared to other folks,' says Ronald. 'Neil cleared up like some fuckin wife and then let him sleep it off in the farmhoose. The sky was whitenin when things got interesting. Brian was still fuckin aroond with the music and Tatty flopped on the sofa. Most folk had pissed-off, but Tessa and Robbie were still drinking and spaekin, drinking and spaekin. They must have thowt I wis passed oot or something.'

He leans on the altar, a stone box filled with rubble.

'They kept bletheinging. Tessa said she wis sorry you'd gone early and that Robbie'd be disappointed. She kent it must be weird efter all this time to go fae being friends to being more. Put you in a dilemma.'

'I never said that.'

'Robbo didn't say too much at first. Then he'd started saying hoo much he liked you, but hoo it'd been hard to choose – made my fuckin heart bleed. Tessa chipped in noo and then saying how nice you were. Then it went quiet…really quiet. Like they'd stopped breathing. I ken what's gaen on.'

'Stop. I don't want to hear.'

'The wind was fair making a racket so I don't ken exactly what *he* whispered, but I heard her reply. She'd said he didn't have to choose. Then they slipped oot o the room, your twa best friends in the world – they must have done something fur Robbie believed he was Jenna's father. No, Robbie didn't ken aboot Tommy. Don't think he kent until I telt him the morning afore he went for the dive…never seen him so shook up. White as a ghost. Couldna speak. But Alfred called him in afore he could get away. Fair nearly knocked Neil over when he finally took off, must have had a dram too many. A demned pity.'

'It was you.'

'He'd gone oot before sobering up fully the morning afore. But drinking straight afore a dive. Weel….what do you think happened? Do you believe Tommy? Robbie didna make many mistakes.'

'It was your fault.'

'No. *You* should've stayed away, Christine.'

'I don't believe you. Tess wouldn't have lied. She wasn't even seeing Tommy.'

'She's my cousin Christine…and I want to think better of her.'

He leans forward, lowers his voice, 'But I ken whit I saw.'

He grabs hold of my arm. The wind skirts around the chapel, blustery and fierce, flattening the coarse humps of grass.

'Let go of me.'

'There's only one way up….and nobody's coming.'

He flashes a lopsided grin.

'Where's Jenna?'

'I wouldn't hurt her, whoever her father is. But you…you get away with everything, Christine. Too fuckin good fur anyone.'

He moves and blocks my way.

'They'll be looking for Jenna.'

'I don't think so. We've plenty time'

He catches my wrist, the skin burns where his fingers tighten. There's no way I can match his strength. The warmth of his breath reaches me in slow sickening pulses through the cold rain that dashes against my face. He slowly forces me towards him.

My heart hammers in my chest. Panic rises in my throat.

'Don't you ken? Ah'm done waiting. Neil'll get the farm, but Ah'll have you.'

His fingers dig deeper.

'Please, you're hurting…Ronald, we can be friends.'

My voice sounds frightened, unable to coax.

'I dinna want to be your friend.'

The rumble of a tractor echoes through the open end of the chapel caught on the breeze, but there's no sign of the vehicle on the brae, only the tilted body of the abandoned farm car.

Ronald glances around. In the second that he's distracted I twist myself free and move to put the altar between us. The sea pounds and breaks, muffled by the back wall. There's nowhere to go.

Ronald swings around, his face white, twisted with anger.

'If it wasna for you Robbie would be alive,' he says. 'If you hadna come back none of this would've happened.'

'It's your fault. Can't you see? Why did you tell him? He was your friend.'

'He wis too cool to be pals with Ronald. He never had time for me…neither did Tommy. Mind on you've done most the work yourselves, fuckin up yur lives. All I had to do wis tell him what I saw… cheust think all those years…then the first night back and you're in The Blackhoose together. Neil had no right to give it awey.'

This time he catches me around the waist. His skin is greasy with sweat. The wind catches his hair making it stand up then flatten against his skull. I step back onto the slab that once marked the position of the tabernacle. It is smooth and black like whale skin poking through the red earth.

'We can start again,' I say. 'Just tell me, where's Jenna?'

'I let her away,' he says.

'Is she safe?'

He doesn't answer.

'For God's sake, Ronald. It was all so long ago. We've all changed.'

He presses his lips against my cheek, his fingers force their way inside my coat, his wiry muscles intent.

Behind me is the nook where the Holy Sacrament would have been kept. My fingers search for a loose stone, but find nothing. Ronald's hand grips the back of my neck and he kisses me hard on the lips.

He pulls away, a look of menacing relish on his face, then the ground jerks and I'm thrown backwards. A crack opens beneath my feet. The clay topsoil shifts, shimmers for a split second and then transforms into a river of clay. I start to slide beneath the back wall of the chapel. It's as if the earth beneath my feet is evaporating.

I squirm to free myself – I would rather fall, but he won't let go. He crouches, keeping his footing and stops me sliding, then his fingers abruptly release and I'm falling.

There is nothing beneath me. I'm sliding, swallowed by the massive throat that has opened up under the collapsing chapel wall. There is nothing to dig my fingers into, nothing to slow my accelerating momentum.

Shadows grow above me, blocking out the sky. Rocks pass too quickly for me to grasp a handhold. My ribs scrape the outcrops, my kneecap crunches against a ledge sending me twisting sideways. A fist of stone strikes the centre of my back knocking the air out of my lungs. I flail and grab. The wind, with all its force and fury, provides no resistance to my fall.

Tessa, please forgive me.

Chapter 36

Once we paddled here in our wellington boots and made a secret mermaid cove. You wore seaweed in your hair and covered me with shells.

Tessa, please forgive me.

Once we rescued a jellyfish lying on the beach and it floated away in the waves, quite dead.

Tessa forgive me.

Once we stayed in bed until noon and pretended we were dying.

Tessa...

'Oh, oh...you're hurt. Stay still. Can you hear me? Don't fade on me.' There is a strangled laugh. 'Don't move, but if you can blink or twitch a finger that would be good so I know, so I don't think that you're...Please, Christine...Hey, come on now. Remember, you're my rock, my sounding stone, my shore....whatever that means... I never told you that did I? So how can you remember?

'Do you hear me? What were you doing up there? You knew it was unsafe. Christine...anything, a movement, so I know you can hear. Listen, there's some help. It's Neil...he's waving now, he's climbing down.

'I don't want to move your head because you're not meant to, but surely there'd be no harm to put something underneath? That's better, you're off the sand now. Oh, you're cold... but I know you can hear me...I believe you can hear me. I need to tell you something. I had the strangest phone call from the hospital...must have been some mix-up with contact details. The nurse told me they had my blood test results.

'She said I was pregnant. I told her it would have to be miraculous with the medication I'm on, and I can't remember the last time I had sex...anyway, she said she'd double-check. Then I realized...she wasn't talking about me. She was talking about *you*...it was *you* they were meaning. Then she said something about needing to check for antibodies...said you'd had slapped cheek…and they wanted to do another blood test.'

Her voice ceases. The wind growls around the cove. Flecks of water land on my face. Close by, water sluices and retreats. Further out, the kelp beds will be dancing in the murky blue. I drift away with the whistling cries of birds.

Then footsteps on the stones and Neil's voice.

'Ah've called the coastguard. How is she?'

'She's not moved. I'm trying to keep her warm.'

'Here's me jacket. Whit are you doin here?'

'Mum wanted photographs of the cliff where the graves are washing out. I heard shouting…then this crack and then…it opened up… a huge section under the chapel just slumped… just fell off the side of the cliff…nothing to hold it underneath. Then I saw someone falling…I didn't know who it was…or, I mean, what was she doing up there? She knows it's unsafe…and where's Ronald? Is he coming? I thought I saw Ronald.'

'He's no goin anywhere for a peedie minute.'

'Is he okay?'

'He'll live.'

Someone's fingers are held softly against my neck, coarse but warm.

Neil calls my name.

'Christine?'

There's a warm pressure on my forehead, a hand moves and he touches my cheek. I hear him release a long sigh.

'Ronald's always had a mean spirit, turned it into a joke sometimes. But… I won't have any more to do wae him.'

'She's bleeding,' says Lindsay.

'Wrap this roond. Those coastguard boys should be fairly quick to come by here.'

'The tide's coming…do you think we should move her? Christine, can you hear me? I never said thank you. She came back, despite everything….when I asked her to, she came back. What if she doesn't know how much I love her?'

'She came back for you?'

'I persuaded her to take the job at St Olaf's.'

'I thought it was for someone else.'

'Isn't there anything we can do? She's shivering so much, and…'

'Tak another layer fae me.'

'Christine, come on. Don't you think about going anywhere… I'm going to be a good sister from now on… I'm going to be the best auntie.'

'Whit's that? A bairn? I didn't ken.'

'I got a call, they thought I was her. They told me… and then I didn't get chance to tell her in the car. I wanted to tell her in private…I didn't even know she had a boyfriend, not a real one.'

Soft lips touch my cheek. Lindsay…

'Christine, please don't die.' Warm drops roll onto my cheek, mixing with the rain. 'Why were you up there, Neil?'

'Alfred was shouting oot the window, waving his arms, hollering like a madman that Ronald had stolen the bairn. We all thought he wis seeing things – he'd niver let us play at the brough, telt us it was a kirkyard not a playgroond. Tessa and Tommy went to help Marion with uncle…I couldn't work oot why there wis no sign of Jenna or Christine then I saw the quad bike and field car'd gone and there was no guid reason fur it.'

'Why would Ronald take Jenna?'

'He was….I don't ken how his mind works, but he wis always spoiled, could niver stand being telt no. Always thought the world owed him something. Christine coming back set something off in his mind, he couldn't let the past rest.

'Christine didna ken that he'd put Jenna off as soon as he'd gaen over the brae, peedie lass had wandered roond other side of the willows and taken the long road back to the farm. Ronald couldna stop being angry, couldna stop wanting her.'

He pauses. A whirring, thudding noise is moving closer.

'God, she's so pale. It's me…it's Lindsay. Please…I'm here for you…I always have been…Christine, can you hear me?'

Her sob is stolen by the breeze.

'I don't think I can manage without her.'

'Right enough, I was thinkin the same,' says Neil.

The wind, rain and swell fade. His voice is soft and lilting.

'Since we were bairns she's been the only one…mind that night we played cards… all comfy together, and I ken nothing'd change my mind. But she wis always Tessa's freend, no mine. I saw her all the while and still…every time I see her, whether she's sad or happy then that's me, my whole day scunnered or fine. Even if it wasna with me…I wanted to see her happy. I ken she mustn't think o me much, but Ah'm all day in the cab thinkin on her. I ken that I can't change anything…but I always wish I'd never let Tessa have that party.'

There's a pause. The roughness of his skin catches like a cat's tongue, gently brushing the strands of my hair as he strokes my cheek.

'Ronald said he was rescuing her, but that's not what I saw… not what I saw at aal… and I didna ken before I pulled him away that she was falling, that the cliff had given way…why've I always waited too long?'

His hand lies quiet and still.

'Was it at The Blackhoose?' he says suddenly. 'Was it Robbie?'

There's another pause, the world turns, throwing the water from its sides. I start to slide, rolling with pebbles, sucked underneath a rolling wave.

'Do y' think she'll ever be happy here?'

Chapter 37

There's whirring and coldness and noise. Capillaries squeeze, emptying themselves. The body shutting down to preserve the heartbeat.

Lines, circles and spheres of pain. Jagged arches of pain. An underwater forest of faces.

Light and voices and pain.

And a voice, slow and sleepy. And someone crying. White strips rolling, rattling, flying along an antiseptic chute.

Faces and people and pain. The kind faces are frightening me.

The warm hand is gone.

Captive, hauled, skimming a sea of pain. Breathless, sweating …hollering. Pushing and pushing.

Please…help me.

Is it me?

Am I shouting?

Swallowed in deep red pain.

How long was it before the pain stopped?

How deep?

How cold?

Chapter 38

Ligaments spread electric-white pain at the smallest movement. Everything stiffens rapidly and it's unwise to stay still for long. Tessa visits the hospital.

'I'm sorry,' I say.

'What are you sorry aboot?' says Tessa. 'You're a hero goin after Jenna. I don't ken what Ronald was playing at – Neil's chucked him oot completely noo. Never been much use on the farm, always earning a pound rather than lending a hand. He'll end up on Westray. There's still second cousins oot there with a farm. I can't understand him. Neil says it's best no to try.'

She gives a half smile.

Without make-up she looks older and younger at the same time. Her skin is moonish, offsetting the deep-blue of her eyes. I find her beautiful. She takes my hand.

'Feels like I've been in a fight,' I say.

'Can you get some painkillers?'

'I want to sleep.'

'Shall I turn off the light?'

I nod. She clicks the switch then pushes away the jointed hospital lamp.

'I'll wait a peedie while,' she says.

I close my eyes, but do not sleep and she does not leave. When I open my eyes she's looking at me.

'I didn't think about how alone you would be,' I say.

'Ssh. I thowt you were goin to sleep,' she says.

'It wasn't as if *we* had an agreement.'

'Aboot Robbie?' says Tessa.

'About anything…'

'I always thowt we'd love each other's bairns,' she says quietly. 'When you went…so much went with you. I wasn't ready to have a baby, sure as hell Tommy wasna ready to be a father.'

'It was Tommy?'

Her lip trembles.

'You know me – regular as clockwork. I'd worked it oot

straight away. I knew Robbie. I knew he'd be a good Dad. At the party when I saw him come oot of that room with you I saw part of him was just like the other boys as weel. No one knew aboot Tommy, it was a huge joke for us to keep something secret from you all. After the party I broke it off with him, he moved on. I didn't want to lie to you or lose you, but there was no going back.

'Then you came back for Anne and Brian's wedding, you looked so different to everyone else. No one thowt you'd actually come and then I caught a glimpse of you and... I couldn't wait for everyone else to buzz off so I could speak to you alone. I'd hoped that one day we'd see each other and like each other again and we did. I was so cross with Jenna when we had to leave the reception early at the hall.'

'Tessa...'

'I've played that afternoon in the car when I told you over and over agaen in my head, wondering if I'd said something differently, if I'd used better words you might no have been so hurt. I tried to think o the best way to say it, but I didn't ken what to say. It would've been easier if it'd been the truth. I'm fair rubbish at lying, you ken it's true. I'll never forget the way you drove away, that look on your face.'

'It was... I was in shock. I'd lost everything.'

'But you came back, and I'm glad. And now you ken my peedie girl. You should've seen her as a baby, Christine. She was so bonny and...I didn't know half the time what I was doing, but I love being her mum. I love...Oh, I'm sorry, what a stupid thing to say.'

Tears slide over my cheeks down to the pillow. She pats my hand. Silence falls. Gradually they cease and, finally, I speak.

'You know I felt the same seeing you...you looked amazing...dazzling in that red. I was so nervous... seeing everybody. It felt like my first day at school, being an incomer again, until you came and talked to me.'

'Poor Jenna, aal that chocolate cake,' says Tessa. 'God, what a mess it was to clear up. But she did look cute in that dress. Mind she'll have grown oot of it now. Sssh, don't cry. You'll be all right. You'll get another chance.'

The blurry hospital room floats around me. There is another

wave of pain. The tiny lights of the alarms and machines remind me of the ghosts in the lights. A green light winks at me, regular as a lighthouse.

Finally, the muscle constriction loosens, a sob escapes my lips.

'I wanted to make things up with Robbie as well at the wedding,' I say. 'We listened to the band after you'd gone, had a few more drinks. Everybody was having a good time, kids running around like it was school disco. We laughed a lot. And we had so much to catch up on, he wanted to hear all about the south, everything I'd been doing. The music was too loud and it was roasting in there, so we walked over to The Blackhouse.'

'The Blackhoose?'

'There was that stillness you get on summer nights sometimes – when you don't know if you're waiting for dark or light…it was almost by accident that we kissed. Not really anything at all…except, it was so quiet, so still and it had been so long since we'd seen each other.'

'You and Robbie?'

I smile even as the tears flow.

'In the morning I went straight to the airport without going home…'

'He was with you?'

'…switched off my phone and sat watching the planes take off and land, bags being loaded and unloaded, gulls being chased off the runway.'

'Were you going to tell me?' she says.

Her voice sounds loudly around the ward.

'Did Rob…were you going to do it agaen? '

'I wasn't going to come back again. It was a mistake. We didn't contact each other.'

'You expect me to believe you?'

'I hope you do.'

'Why did really you come back, Christine?'

'I'd promised Lindsay I'd come home. The wedding was just a side reason. She'd been low for weeks and I'd promised to come. I was always finding a reason why I couldn't come back, that I was too busy with studying. Then I never showed up. I was sure anyone who saw me would know straightaway what I'd done, where I'd been the night before. She'd been waiting for me…when I didn't come, she tried to commit suicide.'

'I didn't know.'

'Dad says people talk about you less, not more, when something like that happens. She huffed aerosol cans in the workshop, Dad found her in the morning after the wedding. Really, it was my fault.'

'She survived.'

'Dad did mouth to mouth until the ambulance arrived. She couldn't breathe at all by herself to start with, even with oxygen. She's lucky not to have brain damage. When she told me about the advert for a position at St Olaf's and asked if I'd apply I couldn't refuse. I swear I didn't see Robbie except in your company when I came back again…'

I'm taken off guard by a cramp radiating around my back and have to pause.

'Ronald told Robbie he'd seen us together at The Blackhouse. It was just before he went out on the boat, after he'd gone to see your dad. Don't you see, everything's my fault.'

My head is leaden with fatigue, swamped with hormones and medication.

I've lost the baby I never knew I carried.

Why didn't I realise? How can my body be so unfaithful?

A body that sobs and shakes, and doesn't deserve rescue.

'You need to rest,' says Tessa.

Her voice catches with rising tears.

She lies beside me on the hospital bed, the light weight of her arm over the top of the blanket. I sleep, briefly, deeply. When I wake she is still there, her eyes staring at the ceiling.

'Was Robbie the father?' she says when she sees my eyes open.

'He has to be.'

My tears run freely, welling up as if they run in my veins.

'Did we always have so many secrets?' she says. 'We did everything together. We knew each other so weel.'

'I don't know…Tessa, can you forgive me?'

'Ssh.'

'I don't expect anything. I know…I don't deserve anything.'

Chapter 39

In the morning Tessa is gone. The nurse brings tea and codeine. Half an hour later I limp the short journey to the bathroom. I stick a fresh sanitary towel into my underpants and go back to bed. I curl up as tightly as my other injuries allow.

The even grey tone of the sky stretches away above the roof of the hospital. The crevices and crannies of the hospital walls are wet through from the soundless rain.

I exhale deeply, methodically pushing out the stale air inside my lungs and try to control the pain. I picture the oystercatchers playing catch-me-if-you-can with the waves, skittering backwards and forwards in the shiny bed of pebbles.

'Do you want anything, Christine?' the nurse asks, then leaves.

The hours pass, the pain eases. Later in the afternoon, I hear two pairs of footsteps, one dainty, the other with clipping heels.

Tessa stands by the bed. She takes a tissue from the box by my bedside and wipes my cheeks. There's a gentle pat on my shoulder, a child's hand.

'Christine's got a poorly puggy,' says Tessa.

'Mum's gettin me a apple turnover if I'm guid,' says Jenna.

She withdraws her hand then does a strange straight-legged march over to the window and plants a kiss on the glass, leaving a misty mark.

Tessa sits at the side of the bed. She rests a hand on the blanket around my shoulders.

I uncoil a little. I press on my tummy to cushion the cramps, pain shoots from my knee and ribs. It's hard to keep my breathing regular, to remain calm.

'I'll call the nurse,' says Tessa.

'No. It's passing.'

'What aboot the doctor?'

'There's nothing they can do.'

'I'm going to call Lindsay.'

'I'm fine,' I say.

A contraction spreads around my abdomen. The band of

muscle squeezes inwards, gathering and tightening, forcing me to into a foetal position.

'I'll call her,' says Tessa. 'She wanted to ken if you were awake.'

She steps into the corridor, the room is hollow without her. Outside, the gutter drips. Everything in view is slick with water, from the plants wedged in the stonework to the flat ivy leaves that flap in the breeze.

Lindsay arrives twenty minutes later. She carries dampness and cold on her clothes.

'I'd no idea what to bring,' she says. 'Dad put in a dressing gown, I picked up a few magazines, chocolate, crisps, popcorn – I thought you must be peckish…and Lucozade I thought…but you don't really like it so I went with apple and mango juice.'

'You sound like you're throwing a party,' I say.

Her eyes glisten. Her cheeks are flushed from coming inside.

'Sorry…I didn't know what to get…I don't know what to do. I can take it all away again if you like.'

'It's okay,' I say. 'Thanks.'

'I should have told you in the car. I should have given the hospital your mobile number but…I was so excited…I wanted to break the news…I didn't even know you had a proper boyfriend. Everything would have been different, you'd never have gone up on the brough if you'd known…'

Tessa tries to interrupt, but Lindsay continues.

'…but I didn't. And you're right to be angry. Christine. If I'd told you…'

'It wasn't your fault. The doctor said that…it could have been the virus not the fall.'

'Ssh,' says Tessa.

She steps closer to the bed.

'It's none of my business. But I never thought it'd happen to you…God knows, I should have got pregnant by now. Maybe my body knows better. But I think about it… and maybe if I did have a baby, it'd be good for me. I may not cope so well to begin with, but then…well we didn't know how sick Mum was, we were just kids, but Dad says she was better once she went back to work and as we got older…'

'Mum?'

'When we were born, she was up and down all the time. She'd

217

spend days hardly eating or drinking, reading all night and sketching, then suddenly shooting off to some hole in the ground forgetting we existed, but she changed, she's worked hard. She's an amazing person.'

'Dad said something like that about you.'

Lindsay looks at Tessa then back at me. It is new to see her like this, neither high or low, yet with strong emotion.

She smiles sheepishly.

'Do you think I'll ever level out? God, I've wrecked your room. I wanted to make it nice, so you'd come and stay. I wanted it to be a thank you.'

'For what?'

'Coming back.'

The conversation falters. Lindsay sits on the chair by the bed holding my hand. Tessa stays standing. Jenna breathes on the windowpane and draws stick figures with her finger.

Then Lindsay eventually breaks the silence.

'I said thank you to Neil by the way.'

'He won't expect anything,' says Tessa.

'What for?' I say.

'Don't you remember?' says Lindsay. 'Practically pulled the launch out of the water when it arrived, waving and shouting like a lunatic. He'd have come in the helicopter if there'd been room.'

'I didn't know.'

I try and sit up. The movement causes the muscles over my abdomen to contract. I brace myself against Lindsay and wait for the pain to pass.

'What else happened?' I say.

'He broke Ronald's nose,' says Lindsay. 'Sent him packing.'

'Tessa told me.'

'He said something to me on the beach,' says Lindsay.

'He's always had a crush on you,' I say.

She shakes her head.

'On me? Christine. It's never been on me.'

'What do you mean?' I say.

'Can't you see? It's always been you.'

I imagine Neil's face, his hair wet, bending over me with the cliffs behind him.

'Think about it,' says Tessa. 'I've seen for years.'

218

Chapter 40

The barley stubble reflects the sun like golden needles in endless rows. A careful eye finds the first sage-green blades of daffodils in the banks along the road. A line of posts strung with wire separates the field from ditch and road. Their silver edges are coarsened by another winter, their forebears shrinking into the ground. Perched on top of the posts are the hooded crows, their claws in tight communion with the faded wood. Each bird belongs to their post; they are exactly where they are meant to be. Winter is passing.

Whatever Robbie was to us, he's gone. Life continues. My grief has no more or less importance than anyone else's. His mother, father and brother will never see him again. There will be no letters or birthday cards, no more smiles or tears, no more sharing a glass with a friend.

Sometimes a deep feeling of utter unimportance strikes me so hard I feel I will buckle and never rise. I carry the hollow cross of life.

Humility, grief at the loss of a child. Sometimes there's nothing to hold on to – and I fall. And I am gathered up.

We turn off the road from Kirkwall to Orphir. We leave behind the sharp cliffs that tilt towards Scapa Flow.

A gentle hill bisected by mottled stone rises away from the single track road. Mustard-yellow lichen have spread in slow methodical blotches over the barren stones scored with names – minuscule victories of life.

Further on, there's a turning circle in front of high wrought iron gates with thick diagonal spurs. They are topped with ornate pikes and flanked by two smaller entrances. At the dead end there is a flatbed trailer loaded with a small yellow excavator. Its metal arm is bent over double, the narrow scoop curled upwards.

We park some distance from the gates. I walk alone over the tarmac and my gaze returns to the bright yellow of the digger. It becomes a dark silhouette against the paling sky as I move past.

The side gate yields easily to my touch.

This is my first visit to the grave. Strangely, the headstones give no clue to their age, some are uncannily pristine even though they are a hundred years old. I work methodically from the oldest to the newest. The headstones become intermittent, there are gaps until the grass spreads out uninterrupted to the far wall.

The ground must settle. A year can pass before a new stone is erected, until then simple wooden pegs with a name mark the disturbances in the turf.

Here is the one for Robert Muir. My limbs feel weightless, as if I could lift in the air and float like a dandelion seed.

Who did you love, Robbie? What was it you wanted?

The words of a prayer my dad taught me years ago rises to my lips. I become a pillar, balancing, breathing – a living vertical line amongst the horizontal rows.

The cold pinches at my fingers. I wipe away the strands of hair blown across my lips and smooth my tears.

Robbie lies alone, no descendants. I'm sad and sorry. Yet I can't keep hold of this grief. It's not the same as love. It erodes. The swells retreat and the empty space is recolonised. Even when the hope has to be sown by other people, it grows.

The sky is peach and copper blue, the sun dipping to the northwest. The intense beauty is balanced by the chill of the advancing shadows. I turn and leave.

Neil has left the car and is waiting for me at the gates.

His affection, loyalty and patience were always there. I see that now.

I'm no good at belief – that bit of faith that makes up the last ounce of certainty, but I can have faith in someone else. I'm inspired by others when I cannot find it within – by my sister who saved me, by Tessa who loves me. There are no more secrets – there is forgiveness. If I want to, I find I can pray.

Neil drives us down the hill away from the cemetery and around the edge of town. He parks the car by the sea wall. We walk together on Scapa beach. The oystercatchers dance over the sand chasing the tide.

He takes my hand and my heart beats a shade faster. In the very last of the evening light, in the final catch of the day, I see the relief in his eyes. I smile and together we move on.

Bookclub Questions

General Questions

1. Is The Oystercatcher Girl a romance?
2. Is there a hero or heroine in The Oystercatcher Girl?
3. Whose life changes most because of what happened on the night of the party?
4. What role does the landscape have in shaping the narrative of The Oystercatcher Girl?
5. Are there any of the main characters who would have told the story more honestly?
6. The title of the book references an ancient Christian myth where the oystercatcher saves the child Jesus by concealing him in seaweed. Who is the oystercatcher girl in the novel?

Specific Questions

1. Who does Christine love most?
2. Does Christine forgive anyone?
3. Lindsay is the stronger sister. Discuss.
4. Alfred's weakness is that he loves Tessa too much. Is Marion's weakness that she loves Alfred too much?
5. Gill and Catherine are perfect parents. Discuss.
6. Is there any logic to the choices that Robbie makes?
7. Ronald gets what he deserves. How is the theme of justice explored in The Oystercatcher Girl?
8. Does Tessa deserve a friend like Christine?
9. Can Christine ever be happy on the island?

About the Author
Gabrielle Barnby

Gabrielle Barnby works in a variety of genres including short stories, poetry and children's fiction. She lives with her husband and four children in Orkney, Scotland. Gabrielle's short stories and book reviews have been published in *Northwords Now* and *The Stinging Fly*. Various pieces of her poetry and prose are available in local anthologies including *Waiting for The Tide*, *Come Sit at Our Table* and *Kirkwall Visions, Kirkwall Voices*.

Gabrielle also edits monthly writing pages in *Living Orkney* magazine and runs local writing workshops. She has been commissioned to compose and perform poems at local anniversaries and events and last year performed in the Orkney Storytelling festival.

In 2015 her first collection of short stories *The House With The Lilac Shutters* was published by ThunderPoint. In the same year she won The George Mackay Brown Short Story competition.

More information about her work and occasional pieces of flash fiction can be found at www.gabriellebarnby.com. She is also on facebook and twitter @GabrielleBarnby.

More Books From ThunderPoint Publishing Ltd.

The House with the Lilac Shutters:
by Gabrielle Barnby
ISBN: 978-1-910946-02-2 (eBook)
ISBN: 978-0-9929768-8-0 (Paperback)

Irma Lagrasse has taught piano to three generations of villagers, whilst slowly twisting the knife of vengeance; Nico knows a secret; and M. Lenoir has discovered a suppressed and dangerous passion.

Revolving around the Café Rose, opposite The House with the Lilac Shutters, this collection of contemporary short stories links a small town in France with a small town in England, traces the unexpected connections between the people of both places and explores the unpredictable influences that the past can have on the present.

Characters weave in and out of each other's stories, secrets are concealed and new connections are made.

With a keenly observant eye, Barnby illustrates the everyday tragedies, sorrows, hopes and joys of ordinary people in this vividly understated and unsentimental collection.

'The more I read, and the more descriptions I encountered, the more I was put in mind of one of my all time favourite texts – Dylan Thomas' Under Milk Wood' – lindasbookbag.com

The Bogeyman Chronicles
Craig Watson
ISBN: 978-1-910946-11-4 (eBook)
ISBN: 978-1-910946-10-7 (Paperback)

In 14th Century Scotland, amidst the wars of independence, hatred, murder and betrayal are commonplace. People are driven to extraordinary lengths to survive, whilst those with power exercise it with cruel pleasure.

Royal Prince Alexander Stewart, son of King Robert II and plagued by rumours of his illegitimacy, becomes infamous as the Wolf of Badenoch, while young Andrew Christie commits an unforgivable sin and lay Brother Brodie Affleck in the Restenneth Priory pieces together the mystery that links them all together.

From the horror of the times and the changing fortunes of the characters, the legend of the Bogeyman is born and Craig Watson cleverly weaves together the disparate lives of the characters into a compelling historical mystery that will keep you gripped throughout.

Over 80 years the lives of three men are inextricably entwined, and through their hatreds, murders and betrayals the legend of Christie Cleek, the bogeyman, is born.

The Wrong Box
By Andrew C Ferguson
ISBN: 978-1-910946-14-5 (Paperback)
ISBN: 978-1-910946-16-9 (eBook)

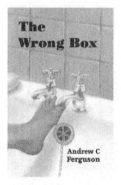

All I know is, I'm in exile in Scotland, and there's a dead Scouser businessman in my bath. With his toe up the tap.

Meet Simon English, corporate lawyer, heavy drinker and Scotophobe, banished from London after being caught misbehaving with one of the young associates on the corporate desk. As if that wasn't bad enough, English finds himself acting for a spiralling money laundering racket that could put not just his career, but his life, on the line.

Enter Karen Clamp, an 18 stone, well-read schemie from the Auchendrossan sink estate, with an encyclopedic knowledge of Council misdeeds and 19th century Scottish fiction. With no one to trust but each other, this mismatched pair must work together to investigate a series of apparently unrelated frauds and discover how everything connects to the mysterious Wrong Box.

Manically funny, *The Wrong Box* is a chaotic story of lust, money, power and greed, and the importance of being able to sew a really good hem.

Mule Train
by Huw Francis
ISBN: 978-0-9575689-0-7 (eBook)
ISBN: 978-0-9575689-1-4 (Paperback)

Four lives come together in the remote and spectacular mountains bordering Afghanistan and explode in a deadly cocktail of treachery, betrayal and violence.

Written with a deep love of Pakistan and the Pakistani people, Mule Train will sweep you from Karachi in the south to the Shandur Pass in the north, through the dangerous borderland alongside Afghanistan, in an adventure that will keep you gripped throughout.

'Stunningly captures the feel of Pakistan, from Karachi to the hills' – tripfiction.com

QueerBashing
By Tim Morriosn
ISBN: 978-1-910946-06-0 (eBook)
ISBN: 978-0-9929768-9-7 (Paperback)

The first queerbasher McGillivray ever met was in the mirror.

From the revivalist churches of Orkney in the 1970s, to the gay bars of London and Northern England in the 90s, via the divinity school at Aberdeen, this is the story of McGillivray, a self-centred, promiscuous hypocrite, failed Church of Scotland minister, and his own worst enemy.

Determined to live life on his own terms, McGillivray's grasp on reality slides into psychosis and a sense of his own invulnerability, resulting in a brutal attack ending life as he knows it.

Raw and uncompromising, this is a viciously funny but ultimately moving account of one man's desire to come to terms with himself and live his life as he sees fit.

**'...an arresting novel of pain and self-discovery' –
Alastair Mabbott (The Herald)**

Changed Times
By Ethyl Smith
ISBN: 978-1-910946-09-1 (eBook)
ISBN: 978-1-910946-08-4 (Paperback)

1679 – The Killing Times: Charles II is on the throne, the Episcopacy has been restored, and southern Scotland is in ferment.

The King is demanding superiority over all things spiritual and temporal and rebellious Ministers are being ousted from their parishes for refusing to bend the knee.

When John Steel steps in to help one such Minister in his home village of Lesmahagow he finds himself caught up in events that reverberate not just through the parish, but throughout the whole of southern Scotland.

From the Battle of Drumclog to the Battle of Bothwell Bridge, John's platoon of farmers and villagers find themselves in the heart of the action over that fateful summer where the people fight the King for their religion, their freedom, and their lives.

Set amid the tumult and intrigue of Scotland's Killing Times, John Steele's story powerfully reflects the changes that took place across 17th century Scotland, and stunningly brings this period of history to life.

**'Smith writes with a fine ear for Scots speech, and with a sensitive awareness to the different ways in which history intrudes upon the lives of men and women, soldiers and civilians, adults and children'
- James Robertson**

A Good Death
by Helen Davis
ISBN: 978-0-9575689-7-6 (eBook)
ISBN: 978-0-9575689-6-9 (Paperback)

'A good death is better than a bad conscience,' said Sophie.

1983 – Georgie, Theo, Sophie and Helena, four disparate young Cambridge undergraduates, set out to scale Ausangate, one of the highest and most sacred peaks in the Andes.

Seduced into employing the handsome and enigmatic Wamani as a guide, the four women are initiated into the mystically dangerous side of Peru, Wamani and themselves as they travel from Cuzco to the mountain, a journey that will shape their lives forever.

2013 – though the women are still close, the secrets and betrayals of Ausangate chafe at the friendship.

A girls' weekend at a lonely Fenland farmhouse descends into conflict with the insensitive inclusion of an overbearing young academic toyboy brought along by Theo. Sparked by his unexpected presence, pent up petty jealousies, recriminations and bitterness finally explode the truth of Ausangate, setting the women on a new and dangerous path.

Sharply observant and darkly comic, Helen Davis's début novel is an elegant tale of murder, seduction, vengeance, and the value of a good friendship.

'The prose is crisp, adept, and emotionally evocative' – Lesbrary.com

The Birds That Never Flew
by Margot McCuaig
Shortlisted for the Dundee International Book Prize
2012
Longlisted for the Polari First Book Prize 2014
ISBN: 978-0-9929768-5-9 (eBook)
ISBN: 978-0-9929768-4-2 (Paperback)

'Have you got a light hen? I'm totally gaspin.'

Battered and bruised, Elizabeth has taken her daughter and left her abusive husband Patrick. Again. In the bleak and impersonal Glasgow housing office Elizabeth meets the provocatively intriguing drug addict Sadie, who is desperate to get her own life back on track.

The two women forge a fierce and interdependent relationship as they try to rebuild their shattered lives, but despite their bold, and sometimes illegal attempts it seems impossible to escape from the abuse they have always known, and tragedy strikes.

More than a decade later Elizabeth has started to implement her perfect revenge – until a surreal Glaswegian Virgin Mary steps in with imperfect timing and a less than divine attitude to stick a spoke in the wheel of retribution.

Tragic, darkly funny and irreverent, *The Birds That Never Flew* ushers in a new and vibrant voice in Scottish literature.

'...dark, beautiful and moving, I wholeheartedly recommend' scanoir.co.uk

Toxic
by Jackie McLean
Shortlisted for the Yeovil Book Prize 2011

ISBN: 978-0-9575689-8-3 (eBook)
ISBN: 978-0-9575689-9-0 (Paperback)

The recklessly brilliant DI Donna Davenport, struggling to hide a secret from police colleagues and get over the break-up with her partner, has been suspended from duty for a fiery and inappropriate outburst to the press.

DI Evanton, an old-fashioned, hard-living misogynistic copper has been newly demoted for thumping a suspect, and transferred to Dundee with a final warning ringing in his ears and a reputation that precedes him.

And in the peaceful, rolling Tayside farmland a deadly store of MIC, the toxin that devastated Bhopal, is being illegally stored by a criminal gang smuggling the valuable substance necessary for making cheap pesticides.

An anonymous tip-off starts a desperate search for the MIC that is complicated by the uneasy partnership between Davenport and Evanton and their growing mistrust of each others actions.

Compelling and authentic, Toxic is a tense and fast paced crime thriller.

'...a humdinger of a plot that is as realistic as it is frightening' – crimefictionlover.com

In The Shadow Of The Hill
by Helen Forbes
ISBN: 978-0-9929768-1-1 (eBook)
ISBN: 978-0-9929768-0-4 (Paperback)

An elderly woman is found battered to death in the common stairwell of an Inverness block of flats.

Detective Sergeant Joe Galbraith starts what seems like one more depressing investigation of the untimely death of a poor unfortunate who was in the wrong place, at the wrong time.

As the investigation spreads across Scotland it reaches into a past that Joe has tried to forget, and takes him back to the Hebridean island of Harris, where he spent his childhood.

Among the mountains and the stunning landscape of religiously conservative Harris, in the shadow of Ceapabhal, long buried events and a tragic story are slowly uncovered, and the investigation takes on an altogether more sinister aspect.

In The Shadow Of The Hill skilfully captures the intricacies and malevolence of the underbelly of Highland and Island life, bringing tragedy and vengeance to the magical beauty of the Outer Hebrides.

'…our first real home-grown sample of modern Highland noir' – Roger Hutchison; West Highland Free Press

Over Here
by Jane Taylor
ISBN: 978-0-9929768-3-5 (eBook)
ISBN: 978-0-9929768-2-8 (Paperback)

It's coming up to twenty-four hours since the boy stepped down from the big passenger liner – it must be, he reckons foggily – because morning has come around once more with the awful irrevocability of time destined to lead nowhere in this worrying new situation. His temporary minder on board – last spotted heading for the bar some while before the lumbering process of docking got underway – seems to have vanished for good. Where does that leave him now? All on his own in a new country: that's where it leaves him. He is just nine years old.

An eloquently written novel tracing the social transformations of a century where possibilities were opened up by two world wars that saw millions of men move around the world to fight, and mass migration to the new worlds of Canada and Australia by tens of thousands of people looking for a better life.

Through the eyes of three generations of women, the tragic story of the nine year old boy on Liverpool docks is brought to life in saddeningly evocative prose.

'...a sweeping haunting first novel that spans four generations and two continents...' – Cristina Odone/Catholic Herald

The Bonnie Road
by Suzanne d'Corsey
ISBN: 978-1-910946-01-5 (eBook)
ISBN: 978-0-9929768-6-6 (Paperback)

My grandmother passed me in transit. She was leaving, I was coming into this world, our spirits meeting at the door to my mother's womb, as she bent over the bed to close the thin crinkled lids of her own mother's eyes.

The women of Morag's family have been the keepers of tradition for generations, their skills and knowledge passed down from woman to woman, kept close and hidden from public view, official condemnation and religious suppression.

In late 1970s St. Andrews, demand for Morag's services are still there, but requested as stealthily as ever, for even in 20th century Scotland witchcraft is a dangerous Art to practise.

When newly widowed Rosalind arrives from California to tend her ailing uncle, she is drawn unsuspecting into a new world she never knew existed, one in which everyone seems to have a secret, but that offers greater opportunities than she dreamt of – if she only has the courage to open her heart to it.

Richly detailed, dark and compelling, d'Corsey magically transposes the old ways of Scotland into the 20th Century and brings to life the ancient traditions and beliefs that still dance just below the surface of the modern world.

'…successfully portrays rich characters in compelling plots, interwoven with atmospheric Scottish settings & history and coloured with witchcraft & romance' – poppypeacockpens.com

Talk of the Toun
by Helen MacKinven
ISBN: 978-1-910946-00-8 (eBook)
ISBN: 978-0-9929768-7-3 (Paperback)

She was greetin' again. But there's no need for Lorraine to be feart, since the first day of primary school, Angela has always been there to mop up her tears and snotters.

An uplifting black comedy of love, family life and friendship, Talk of the Toun is a bittersweet coming-of-age tale set in the summer of 1985, in working class, central belt Scotland.

Lifelong friends Angela and Lorraine are two very different girls, with a growing divide in their aspirations and ambitions putting their friendship under increasing strain.

Artistically gifted Angela has her sights set on art school, but lassies like Angela, from a small town council scheme, are expected to settle for a nice wee secretarial job at the local factory. Her only ally is her gallus gran, Senga, the pet psychic, who firmly believes that her granddaughter can be whatever she wants.

Though Lorraine's ambitions are focused closer to home Angela has plans for her too, and a caravan holiday to Filey with Angela's family tests the dynamics of their relationship and has lifelong consequences for them both.

Effortlessly capturing the religious and social intricacies of 1980s Scotland, Talk of the Toun is the perfect mix of pathos and humour as the two girls wrestle with the complications of growing up and exploring who they really are.

'Fresh, fierce and funny…a sharp and poignant study of growing up in 1980s Scotland. You'll laugh, you'll cry…you'll cringe' – KAREN CAMPBELL